HUIZACHE WOMEN

Estella Gonzalez

Arte Público Press
Houston, Texas

Huizache Women is funded in part by a grant from the National Endowment for the Arts. We are thankful for its support.

Recovering the past, creating the future

Arte Público Press
University of Houston
4902 Gulf Fwy, Bldg 19, Rm 100
Houston, Texas 77204-2004

Cover design by Ryan Hoston
Cover art, "Mujer árbol" by Camila Zaccarelli

Library of Congress Control Number: 2023943424

♾ The paper used in this publication meets the requirements of the American National Standard for Information Sciences—Permanence of Paper for Printed Library Materials, ANSI Z39.48-1984.

22 23 24   4 3 2 1

For all the *madres, tías, hermanas y abuelas tercas*, keep your thorns sharp and your roots deep. Stay forever *chingona*s!

Contents

Gracias and Acknowledgements

Mucho, mucho amor to my beautiful husband who continues to support me in my writing journey. I'd also like to thank my mother and my tía Ramona for that memorable research trip to El Chuco and Chihuahua in the early days of my manuscript. Without them, this novel may never have been "birthed."

My immense gratitude to Dr. Nicolás Kanellos, Gabi Ventura, Marina Tristán and the rest of the wondrous staff at Arte Públco Press for their care and faith in my first novel.

Mil gracias to the Escritorx writing group for their patience, feedback and friendship: Cindy, Wanda, Monique, Charmaine, Karen and Charlie. Your enthusiasm and interest buoyed me through this arduous process.

Many, many thanks to the writers, readers and faculty at Cornell University, including Helena María Viramontes and Maureen McCoy, who reviewed and fine-tuned my very first draft.

Abrazos for the tireless Laura Pegram, Editor-in-Chief at *Kweli Journal* who published and nominated the first stand-alone chapter, "Angry Blood," for a *Pushcart Prize*. In my toughest moment, you lit a fire under me!

I'd also like to express my gratitude to editor extraordinaire Sandra Gúzman for including an early version of "La Llorona and La Malinche" in her groundbreaking anthology, *Daughters of Latin America: An International Anthology of Writing by Latine Women* and to the editors and publishers of the *Pasadena Weekly* who published "Amor Eterno" and "I Hate My Name."

I would like to recognize the following authors for their invaluable books: *Tristan and Iseult* by Rosemary Sutcliff; *Santa* by Federico Gamboa; *From Coveralls to Zoot Suits: The Lives of Mexican American Women on the World War II Home Front* by Elizabeth R. Escobedo; *Ringside Seat to a Revolution: An Underground Cultural History of El Paso and Juárez* by David Dorado Romo; and *Cine Mexicano: Carteleles de la Época de Oro 1936-1956* by Rogelio Agrasánchez Jr.

I'm grateful to Chilean artist Camila Zaccarelli for her sublime woodcut and for her permission to use it. It's perfect!

And to all the *chingonx* who love and bloom on both sides of the *frontera*. Stay strong *y afilen los colmillos*!

CHAPTER 1
Santa

When Merced saw the framed movie poster for *Santa* on
the wall of the *tiendita* she stopped so hard, she almost fell.
Lupita Tovar, the most beautiful movie star in all of Mexico,
in the world, blazed before her, an angel with her eyes tilted
up toward the heavens, her hands posed in prayer. A rumble,
then a roar surged through Merced's body until her mouth
opened.

"*Un ángel*," Merced sang softly as her finger touched the
cold glass protecting the poster, protecting Lupita. Slowly she
traced over Lupita's thin black eyebrows before touching her
own.

The number 5 was prominent at the bottom of the poster.
Although she could not read most of the words, she knew it
would cost *cinco centavos* to see it projected in the movie tent.

She knew she'd have to lie to her aunt Pina to keep some
of the money she earned selling the *ancho chiles* at the *mercado* in Villa Ahumada. But her aunt could sniff out a lie
quicker than a dog could smell out the chorizo hidden in the
dovecote. No, she'd have to start setting aside a penny a day
if she could. One penny would not make a difference to her
aunt, not right away, anyway.

Every evening from then on, instead of paying the penny to return on the train, she offered some of the remaining *chiles* to those farmers heading back to El Sueco instead of those heading back to her little town. Instead of dropping her off at the *placita* in El Sauz, she would make them drop her off a mile down the main highway. Tía Pina would have overheard the gossip about her niece taking rides from men.

"Pina will catch you for sure," her oldest sister Cleófilas told her as they rode the train down to Villa Ahumada.

"Don't you tell her Cleo" Merced answered as she held her basket of *chiles* carefully. The glossy skins of the *chiles* looked liquid in the dim morning light.

"You're not supposed to be watching those kinds of movies, anyway," Cleófilas said.

Merced rolled her eyes at her older sister, who was always preaching instead of helping.

Merced placed every penny she saved in a tin box she kept buried near the *huizache*, a tree so stubborn, it kept growing back every year, even after her father, Plutarco, burned it down to its roots. The next year, ten saplings would grow in its place.

"Something so stubborn deserves to live," he said one warm spring day after trying to dig up its roots.

From then on, the *huizache* tree became her preferred place to rest and to hide her secret possessions from her sisters and aunt. Now it was a place to hide her money.

Every morning, Merced would be sure to get up earlier than her aunt and sister and head out to the fields with her hand-woven basket. Night would be cracking with a filmy glow revealing rows of dark green leaves, some bulging with swollen ancho *chiles*. As harvest time neared, the cool fall air filled with woodsmoke from the fires stoked by field hands working the cattle ranch on the other side of the field. Cowboy coffee, Merced thought. She had tasted it once before when she had snuck up on the field hands sitting around the fire. One of them had given her a taste in exchange for a kiss.

Sometimes, she would kiss the farmers who brought her back to El Sauz, dropping her off, just before they continued on to the capital. Sometimes she'd hitch a ride with Mennonite farmers who would just nod and look straight ahead. Merced preferred those pale silent men who left her alone. She would sit in the back of their wagon and watch the Sierra mountains shadowed by fiery sunsets. Sometimes, she would break off a piece of the Mennonite cheese the farmer would offer. Its salty firmness comforted her.

"Your feet are dirtier now," Pina told her on the fifth night she arrived by Mennonite. "Don't they clean that train?"

Merced rubbed the back of one leg over the front of the other. She looked down at her cracked dusty toenails, the *centavos* in her pocket steadying her weary body. When she handed them over, Tía Pina looked her in the eye.

"Hmm, you're making less money this week," she said.

"*Mentira*," Merced snapped back. "I'm making more than Cleo."

❀❀❀

"Maybe I should send you all to Ahumada," Pina said as she stored the money in her apron pocket.

When she would sit at the table to eat her share of beans and tortillas, her father would say nothing. He'd just continue to eat the tortillas Cleófilas tucked in between the quilted tea cloths.

Sometimes, while Cleo, Plutarco and Pina were on the far ends of the rows tending to the *chiles*, Merced would lay out her *rebozo* between rows and lie down to contemplate the blue sky. Sometimes, she would close her eyes and let the aroma of the fresh, green *anchos* roll around inside of her. Sometimes, if she was still hungry after eating her lunch, she would roast *chiles* over a makeshift fire under the *huizache* and enjoy them folded into a tortilla.

"That stained the earth, didn't it?" Pina remarked when she saw the remains of an earlier fire. Luckily, she didn't see the stems and seeds littering the back of the tree.

❀❀❀

Now that she had enough money to attend the tent theater, Merced had to figure out a way to slip out that evening. Everyone usually went to bed at sundown, but Merced had deliberately chosen this *Santa* evening to clear and wash the dishes and tend the fire in the wood-burning stove. Cleo had eyed her sister, aware that Merced planned on escaping to the plaza but kept her sister's secret. When the candlelight was snuffed out in Plutarco's room, Merced breathed easily. Quickly, she went over to the corner behind the stove to pull the recently unearthed tin box she had hidden under the logs. It was gone!

Merced crouched and ran her hands down under the logs where she knew she had placed it. Nothing. Her heart nearly cracked until she heard Plutarco's door open. Lately, her father had started waking up from his deep sleeps to visit the room she shared with Cleófilas. This time, instead of going to their room, he went straight to the kitchen. Merced's heartbeat faster. Plutarco stood between her and the door.

"*¿Buscas esto?*"

His hard, calloused hands gripped the rusted, dirty box. The coins clinked inside the box as if they were trying to break out. Plutarco must've found the box when she was busy grinding corn. As he walked toward her, she knew she would have to either let him keep the money or let him see her breasts. That's what he had been demanding now when he found her alone. She knew he demanded the same of Cleófilas.

She eyed her father and lifted her blouse. His hands trembled as he handed the box to her. Beyond her father, she saw the door to Pina's room open slightly, then close. Before she could snatch the box away, he grazed her nipples. Merced's body froze. The clattering of the tin box against the stove broke her trance as she pulled down her blouse and pushed Plutarco down with all the strength she used for pushing cattle away from the barbed-wire fencing.

As she crashed into the night, her breath could be seen in the moonlight. Behind her the door slammed. She stopped. The song of the crickets was all she heard. Tears ran down her cheeks. An aching pain throbbed in the back of her throat, but she pressed it back until it settled around her heart. Plutarco had let her get away in exchange for more favors, favors owed to a father by his daughter, he would tell her before she closed her eyes.

When Merced got to the plaza, a larger tent had been erected around the smaller one she had seen earlier. At the entrance she gave the man in the straw hat her five *centavos*. Men and women from El Sauz and Villa Ahumada were there. Some she recognized, and others were new and strange, including some women with dyed blonde hair. They looked like actresses from the movie posters she sometimes saw in Juárez when she and Cleo traveled there for the farmer's market. The movie projector had been set in the center aisle, its power cord snaking out under the tent. As the crowd waited for the movie to start, a *conjunto* played a *norteño* song. Rufina, a tall girl she knew who sometimes invited her to sit by the fires on cold fall mornings, waved her over. Rufina's brother Moti stood up the moment he saw her.

"Are you here to see the movie?" he asked, tipping his hat back to see her better.

Merced tilted her head, her voice still caught in her throat.

"We're going to see it, too," Rufina whispered, looking furtively at her brother. "Can I sit with you? *Estos pendejos* always talk during the movie."

"I can't find a chair." Merced shrugged and tightened her blouse around her waist.

Rufina instinctively wrapped her *rebozo* around them both. Most of the benches in the back were filled up, but there were blankets on the floor in front, where the two girls ended up sitting. The tent was full of people from the area. Ranchers, *señoras* who only left the house to go to church, farmhands, daughters, mothers, some fathers and sons, all looking up at the wall, waiting for the movie to begin. Before it started, a man with a hulking camera began taking pictures of the audience, his flash tray exploding. He caught one of Merced and Rufina wrapped in the *rebozo*. Rufina smiled straight into the camera, while Merced looked straight at the wall.

Suddenly, the lights dimmed, and the whirring of the film projector started. Everyone quieted down. The moment Lupita's name appeared on the wall, the audience clapped.

❀❀❀

Merced hated harvest time. It meant earlier mornings and longer nights. It meant cold lunches in the field and heavy baskets. As she tracked the field, she would crouch down to feel the girth of the *chiles*. If they were firm with a deep green, she pulled them from the plant. If there was a remnant of the blossom, she left them.

"They're still babies," her aunt Pina would tell her. "They need more time."

As the sun rose and the soil warmed, Merced could feel the sweat forming over her lips and under her blouse. Her arms and back ached when she got home. Quickly, before her father returned home, Merced would fill a bucket with water and sponge the sweat off her body before her father tried to touch her. Afterwards, she'd rush out to the woodpile and stoke the fire in the stove. Cleófilas would come in and begin kneading the dough for the tortillas, while Pina busily chopped onions, tomatoes and garlic cloves for the salsa.

Harvest season meant fresh roasted *chiles*, salsa, *rellenos*, and it also meant traveling to Juárez as well as Villa Ahumada. The first time Merced traveled to the big city, Ciudad Juárez, she and Cleófilas had hitched a ride on the back of a neighbor's wagon. Now, they drove the wagon their father had bought a while back.

On the driver's seat, Rufina and Hernán, her oldest brother, sat chatting, sometimes looking back at the sisters sitting behind the open boxes of tomatoes, onions and *chiles*, discussing what to do about her father.

Cleo's mouth flattened. "He needs a wife."

Merced rolled her eyes. "Who? Nobody will marry him. He's too . . . *cabrón*," Merced offered.

Cleo burst out laughing so hard she nearly fell off the wagon. Suddenly, she heard laughter in front of them.

"Your mother married him," Rufina said after she wiped tears from her face. "I heard he was handsome when he was young."

"Handsome men are the worst," Hernán said, even though he was handsome enough.

Merced loved Hernán, who was never crude like his younger brother Moti. Some cool, fall mornings he would offer her his thin cotton jacket as warmth. No kisses, no touching necessary. This made Merced want to touch him all the more.

"How would you know?" Rufina asked her brother.

"Look at Dad," Hernán said, slapping down the reins on the horses' haunches.

Rufina nodded, recognizing that their own father had another family in Chihuahua. At least, he was rich, Merced thought. At least, Hernán and Rufina's father had bought a wagon and two horses to haul their harvest. They didn't have to lug heavy baskets to the market every week. And they had a servant too, an *indita* from Creel.

Merced looked up at the dawn peering over the sierras. She had heard that Pancho Villa and his men had buried gold up in the caves, that it had never been found. One day she would hike up there and find it.

"It's probably buried deep in a cave," Plutarco told them one night while they cleaned up the kitchen.

"Puro pedo," Tía Pina said. "That's an old legend."

"Who says?" Plutarco said, facing his sister. "Donaciano?"

Pina turned red, pressed her mouth shut. Merced knew that her aunt was in love with the owner of the *tiendita*. Donaciano was not handsome at all but he was rich. His mother, Doña Margarita, owned a big store in Chihuahua that served some of the city's politicians. Rumored to have been Pancho Villa's favorite lover, she inherited a crate filled with his gold bars. Too bad Doña Margarita and Plutarco would not let Pina marry Donaciano.

Merced had heard Plutarco tell his sister that she was supposed to take care of him until he found another wife.

"That was Mamá's dying wish," Plutarco would remind Pina.

"When's that gonna happen?" Pina would cry out in desperation.

Once, she called him a *pinche culero*, insulting his masculinity, and Plutarco punched her right in the nose.

Merced had never seen Plutarco punch anybody. She had only seen bloody fights in the movies. Sometimes, the field hands would tussle but none had thrown a punch, none had bled. Since Tía Pina's nose would not stop bleeding the next day, Merced had to take her to the doctor in Villa Ahumada. Throughout the train ride, Pina kept her eyes closed. Sometimes a few tears slid down her cheeks. Her breath stank of a miserable night because it had been too painful to rinse out her mouth. The doctor set her nose and did not ask any questions.

"How much?" Merced asked.

"Your bill's been paid," the receptionist said, barely looking up from behind the counter.

The fragrance of rose water reached out to Merced. It was a miracle. She looked up at the picture of the Virgin of Guadalupe that hovered behind the receptionist.

When they returned home, Cleo ran over to them before they got to the door.

"Donaciano was here," she said. "He beat Plutarco bad."

Pina smiled slightly from under the gauze bandage.

"Where are they?" Pina asked as she lowered herself onto her bed.

"Behind the dovecote," Cleófilas said. "The last I remember, Donaciano was punching him in the face."

By the time Merced and Cleo reached the dovecote, Donaciano was gone, but Plutarco sat in his favorite spot on the log that served as a bench. His eye was swollen, and blood had dried around his lip.

"*¿Qué chingados ven?*" Plutarco snarled, daring them to stare at him. "Bring me the bottle of *pulque*."

Cleo quickly returned with a bottle full of the cloudy liquor. Without a word, Plutarco pulled the cork out and drank down half of it. His daughters watched, fascinated by the cuts and the swollen swelling eye closing into a slit. After they had dragged Plutarco back to his bed, the sisters sat at the table eating what was left of the beans and tortillas.

"Now what?" Merced asked.

Cleófilas ate in silence.

Merced knew that all of El Sauz would be talking about the fight. That night would be the last showing of *Santa*. Next week, it would be *Candelaria* with her favorite actress, María Félix. Next week, she would be free to go wherever she wanted, and she could leave messes like these behind her.

CHAPTER 2
The Coffee Cure

Alma, my mom, has stuffed fresh, used coffee grounds into tube socks and then shoved my feet into them. I have to keep these socks on for the rest of the day until either Grandma Merced or my mom come home from their cleaning gigs in the suburbs of Alhambra and Pasadena. It means I have to keep them on all night. My aunts, Suki and Norma, don't dare touch these socks until my mother and grandmother say so.

By the next morning, the once white socks have turned a deep orange, as if I had stepped into a bucket of Fanta.

"What's the coffee supposed to do?" my mom asks her mother.

"It's supposed to bring down the swelling in Lucha's tonsils. That's what Moti told me."

No matter, my tonsils get so infected, they nearly choke me in my sleep. After the sock treatment fails, Grandma Merced decides to take me to Tijuana. One of her clients at El Yuma bar told her about a hospital run by a doctor in TJ who charges less than the hospitals in California.

"Is it a real hospital?" my mom asks.

Grandma rolls her eyes.

The next day, Moti comes early in his boat of a green station wagon, *un garganchón*. He works at the Farmer John slaughterhouse in Vernon and always smells like stale blood. But that morning, all I can smell is the coffee.

"Maybe she's too American," Moti says when Grandma Merced tells him his coffee-grounds remedy didn't work.

"It worked on me."

"Her feet aren't as tough as yours," my mom whispers to Moti so that my grandmother won't hear. "You have horse hooves."

My mom walks me over to the back of the pickup and tells me to lie down on the thin blankets laid out over the car's bed. The soggy grounds push up against the soles of my feet, squishing their brown liquid through thick tube cotton. The moment I lie down, I knock out. The cigarette smoke, Grandma Merced's laughter, the *ranchera* music coming from the radio, they all fade away as I sleep in the warm sunlight. By the time I wake up, a big blue sign welcomes us to Tijuana.

"*Ya llegamos*," Grandma Merced announces as she opens the backdoor.

Moti lifts and carries me through the glass doors of a two-story building. A nurse in her white, starched hat and white polyester dress rushes over and puts her hands on me. She doesn't look like the stern nurses I usually see at the Kendall clinic, where my mom usually takes me. Those nurses walk around in blue smocks and white pants looking more like the school-cafeteria workers than nurses.

"Over here," the nurse in her stiff white cap yells at some orderlies, who lay me down on a gurney and roll me down a hall lit up by fluorescent lights.

"Where are they taking Lucha?" My grandmother's voice grows fainter.

As we wait for the elevator, the orderly asks me what I have in my socks.

"*Café*," I answer before I knock out again.

Later, I wake up surrounded by masked doctors and nurses. I want to scream but can barely breathe. One doctor holds down my hand and sticks me with a needle. A thin little hose connects me to a plastic bag. Clear liquid drips slowly down into the hose.

"Count back from 100," the doctor says in English.

I do and the next time I wake up I'm on my stomach, mouth open, drooling bloody saliva. My throat burns so bad I can barely swallow. But I can breathe. When the doctor comes in to check on me—he's so beautiful—I can barely look at him.

"*¿Y cómo se siente la señorita?*"

I nod my head and try to smile to show I feel better. I'm embarrassed that such a handsome doctor has to see me looking like a stinky baby, but he nods and promises some *gelatina*, which I immediately translate to Jell-O. I hate Jell-O. Still, I'll gladly eat it if the cute doctor says I should. He has dark hair, hazel eyes and one of those thin little moustaches that reminds me of the Pedro Infante movies that my grandmother and mother love to watch. Now I see what they see, and I think I'm falling in love.

CHAPTER 3
Women Like Her

"Where have you been?" Alma asked her sister Norma, who was pushing herself through their bedroom window. "You're going to wake up Suki."

"Dancing," Norma huffed as she struggled to get up and push down the tight cotton skirt that had hiked up around her thighs.

"¿Con quién?"

Norma put a finger up to her lips, then walked into the tiny bathroom they shared with their mother, Merced, and her boyfriend, Leandro. Suki slept soundly on the top bunk, her rhythmic snoring steady. Alma followed Norma.

"You were with those *pachucas* weren't you?" Alma whispered. "I saw you."

Norma smirked and pulled her long black hair into a bun on the crown of her head.

"It's so fuckin hot in here," Norma said. "Let's sit outside on the fire escape."

"But you just . . ." Alma trailed off when she saw Norma's pencil-thin eyebrows arch like María Félix's.

Alma knew better than to antagonize her older sister, so she quickly followed her. Maybe if they spoke outside, Merced wouldn't hear them. Maybe she wouldn't slap them around, for a change. Now that Leandro was back in El Paso from his trip to Tucson, maybe there would be some peace at home. Alma winced as Norma slammed the window open wide so she wouldn't ruin the cotton skirt she had bought at Woolworth's, her first purchase after they had moved from Juárez to El Paso.

As the two sisters settled on the metal ladder, Norma pulled out a box of Faros and a book of matches from her bra. She shook one out for herself and one for Alma. Those smoking times were the only quiet times for the sisters. Alma jumped a little at the hiss and glow of the match lighting up Norma's calm face. Alma knew Merced wouldn't hear them, but there was always that chance that their mother would check on them. She was so nervous, she almost dropped the matchbook. Before opening it, Alma looked closely at the cover: The Kentucky Club.

"Where'd you get these?" Alma whispered.

"Where do you think?" Norma shouted.

"But you have to be twenty-one."

"Ha, no you don't," Norma said and inhaled deeply, then tilted her head up.

Smoke blew up into her nostrils as it poured from her mouth into the night air. In the soft glow of the streetlamps and stars, Norma looked older than her eighteen years. In the smoke cloud, her older sister reminded Alma of the dragons she had seen on the placemats of the Chinese restaurants she'd visit with Merced and Leandro.

❀❀❀

Mermaids always haunted Norma. She remembered Merced telling her that if she ever bathed on Good Friday or Holy Saturday, she would transform into a mermaid. Even if she was on her period, Norma would have to wait until early Easter Sunday morning to bathe.

Years ago, before she worked the cabarets, she and her sisters Alma and Suki would play *Lotería*. She would always carefully study the mermaid image on the *lotería* card as well as on the label on the can of lard. *La sirena* leaned back, half submerged in the blue-green ocean, her black wavy hair touching the top of the water. One arm shot straight into the sky, while the other bent back, as if she were pulling on a bow, ready to shoot her arrow. What amazed Norma were *la sirena*'s bare breasts with their little pink rosebud nipples. *La sirena* looked up at the sky, searching for something to shoot.

"I want to be a mermaid," Suki said while they played in the shade of the pecan tree in their patio.

"*La pera*," Norma called out the next card.

"But you wouldn't be able to dance or go to the movies," Alma said, placing a pinto bean on the pear image of her cardboard sheet.

"I could explore the ocean," Suki said. "And play with whales and dolphins."

"*El catrín*," Norma called out the card showing a dandy. "What about a husband?"

Suki looked up, past the tree branches, into the sky. Then she placed a bean on the fancily dressed young man with an ascot and pince-nez.

"I'd marry a *sirena*," Suki announced.

"*No seas mensa*," Norma chided, throwing a bean at her little sister. "You'd have to marry a merman."

"I hate men," Suki said. "Look at the way Papá treats Mom."

"She's mean," Norma said. "If you treat men nice, they treat you nice."

Suki wouldn't budge.

Instead of finishing the game, the girls threw beans at each other until their father shouted at them to get into the house.

❀❀❀

Now that Norma was known as "*La Sirena de Juárez*," Norma felt as if her sister Suki had cursed her. Norma had to work every night of the week except Sundays. Saturday nights were the worst because the soldiers from Fort Bliss came in. By Saturday morning, she'd be drowning in whisky and coffee, gearing herself up, pulling on her trumpet-style dress shimmering with aqua-green sequins. Her hair, freshly dyed by one of her fellow dancers, gleamed gold under the spotlights. Norma could barely sing her songs, but the soldiers and other *juarenses* didn't mind.

"I die for your love," one of the soldiers told her after her show.

Through the roar of the whisky and band music, Norma could barely hear him. She'd let this young soldier light her cigarettes and buy her shots until her next number. On her last night at the Tivoli Cabaret, she drank so much, she fell on the stage floor. She tried to get up, but her tight-fitting dress left no room to maneuver her knees.

"*A nadar, sirena*," one of the *cabareteras* called out. "Start swimming."

Finally, Norma just tore her skirt open, freeing her legs. As the audience laughed and clapped, she walked backstage. The soldier who had lit her cigarettes waited for her with another shot. That night, she followed him back to a hotel room. On Easter Sunday, she woke up alone in the room that glowed blue with the rising sun. As she showered, she thought of Suki and whispered, "*La sirena de Juárez*."

※※※

When the soldier with the scar over his left eye knocked on her dressing room door at the Tivoli Club, she was pleased. She had noticed his thick black hair shining in the cabaret's dim lighting.

"*Buenas noches, señorita*," he said as he walked in. He had taken off his garrison cap, unlike other soldiers Norma had met. And unlike the others, he spoke with a nice Spanish, not broken, not mixed with English.

"*¿Me haces el honor de salir conmigo?*" he said, asking her out.

"*Señor soldado*," Norma said, smiling as she smoothed her hair. "*Ni sé su nombre.*"

"*Eduardo Velásquez, a sus órdenes*," the soldier answered playfully saluting her.

That did it. Not only was he willing to take orders from her, but he looked trim and muscular in his khaki uniform. His sharply creased pants and shiny shoes were too neat to resist. Although he stood above her, Norma knew he was her height without her high-heeled shoes.

"Another guy?" Ceci, one of the chorus line dancers, chirped across the smoky room. "You're such a slut."

Norma and the soldier did not hear her as they were already out the door and heading into the sharp Juárez night. Eduardo led her to the Kentucky Club, which was teeming with his fellow soldiers from Fort Bliss. Once inside, Eduardo led her around the dance floor like a Mexican Apollo. When she stooped over to adjust the strap on her shoe, she noticed a watch on the dance floor, scooped it up and slipped it into her purse.

"*Ahorita vengo*," Norma whispered into Eduardo's ear.

"*¿Adónde vas?*"

"*Al baño*," she said.

Inside the toilet stall, she carefully pulled the watch out. The watch band was thin, but she could tell it was silver. The crystal was scratched and its clasp broken. Norma looked at the back of the watch: "Zacatecas 1950." That was thirteen years ago. She put it close to her ear. The watch tick-ticked above the murmuring women and the muffled music. The band fit perfectly around her wrist, shining like a strip of moonlight against her dark skin. She'd have to hide it from Merced, otherwise it would be pawned before the week was out.

Outside, Eduardo waited for her. Instead of finding him annoyed like the other soldiers were when she took too long in the bathroom, he smiled and held out his arm.

❀❀❀

When Norma stumbled in, her younger sisters and niece, Lucha, held their hands up to their noses and tried not to vomit. Norma hadn't bathed in days but knew she couldn't have smelled worse than when her mother, Merced, hadn't washed for a week after Leandro dumped her for Gertrudis.

All her life, men and even some women had paid tribute to her beauty. *Ay qué bella* this. *Qué belleza* that. But Norma always lived somewhere far, far away, with a husband or boyfriend, like a fairytale princess who would never return home. Now, here she was, live and in person, after having left her third husband in Delano.

Instead of silk pumps, Norma wore Reeboks—too big, too torn up and too sweaty—on her clown-sized feet. Her pink cotton shirt looked clean but it was hard to tell with the stretched-out cotton sweater she wore over it.

Merced did all the talking, as always. All Norma did was listen. The basic rule when it came to Merced was to just listen. Alma, Suki and Lucha listened, keeping their mouths shut, because Merced had a long reach and didn't care if you were fourteen or forty.

"Now what?" Merced asked. "Do you need money? Why did you come here?"

Before she knew it, Norma was talking about her life as a wife to a soldier, a Tejano who was a dream but wouldn't let her leave Brownsville to visit her own mother when she asked. He also refused to let her have babies because he wanted her to get an education first. But she had two babies, anyway: a boy and a girl. The Tejano had kept them.

"I'm no white woman," Norma said over and over. "How was I supposed to go back to school at my age?"

Merced nodded in agreement.

Norma felt like a little girl again, even though she was forty. Still, it was hard to tell because of her smooth brown skin. After the Tejano, she confessed, there was Gabriel, who took care of another wife back in Coahuila. He, too, refused to let Merced visit her. He moved her to Delano, almost a hundred miles away. But she would still sneak out to visit her mother.

"I remember that one time when I came out for Nochebuena," Norma started, "Leandro and Gertrudis had just moved into the yellow bungalow and were celebrating their first Christmas together."

Merced stared dry-eyed at the floor as Norma remembered the steaming blue ceramic pot filled with tamales. Through the sheer curtains, Norma could see the Serbian cemetery across the street, with its oak trees that the neighborhood children would climb and sit in for hours. Leandro, just back from his shift at the Long Beach steel plant, brought out a bottle of Hornitos tequila, a bottle he reserved for special times, as Norma remembered. Gertrudis carried a tray with coffee and *buñuelos*. Their little Christmas tree blinked with its heavy lights, lights that belonged on the porch not on the skinny little tree.

"It was very cozy," Norma said, her eyes closed, a slight curve to her mouth, relishing the memory.

Suddenly, she heard Merced stand up and stomp back to her room. Norma's eyes popped open.

"You are such a *cabrona*!" Alma yelled at Merced and turned to Norma. "She's going to torture us after you leave."

Norma puffed on her nearly burnt-out cigarette, sucking on it until the ash crumbled and fell in her lap. Her hand swept gently over her lap, brushing the ash down to the scuffed floor.

"*Mira*," she said, "it doesn't matter what I say or do. *La cabrona* will never be happy until Leandro comes back to her, and that he is never going to do that."

For a few hours, Suki, Alma and Norma sat at the kitchen table whispering about El Paso del Norte Hotel and Leandro. Merced could hear everything because they talked as if everybody but them was deaf. She popped wide awake the moment she heard Norma say *"Todavía lo quiere*, she still loves him." It was the first time Norma ever said it out loud.

"¿Por qué?" Alma asked. "He treated her like garbage."

The door to Merced's bedroom opened so quickly, it sucked the air out of the kitchen. Merced walked out, her head bowed down, its crown silver-gray. Her eyes squeezed tight, then relaxed.

"He made me laugh," she whispered, her eyes still closed. *"Era tan lindo."*

Norma's hand rose to stroke her mother's head but suddenly pulled back.

"I'm sorry, Mami, *pero* . . . Leandro's dead."

Merced finally looked up, expressionless. Norma looked straight into Merced's eyes, unafraid of her mother's clenched fists, her sudden reach for Norma's hand.

Merced's mouth formed the question *"¿Cómo?"*

Through the kitchen window, the summer wind blew the voice of Jaime Jarrín announcing a Dodger game on someone's transistor radio.

Alma sniffed a little bit, and Lucha wanted to go back to her room and listen to her new Missing Person's cassette tape in her fake Walkman.

"¿Cómo?" Alma echoed.

Slowly, Norma's right hand transformed into a gun, its barrel aimed at Merced, whose eyes grew until she finally said, "Gertrudis!"

Norma shook her head. Over Jaime Jarrín's voice, she told her mother and sisters that Leandro died at the Casa Blanca bar when he was celebrating Mexican Independence with Gertrudis. Some *desgraciado* wearing a fedora gunned him down like a dog.

"Went through the top of his head," Norma said.

Merced looked at her hands and closed her eyes tight as if she was wishing for something.

"Where did you hear this?"

"Where else? El Yuma."

All this time, Norma never took her eyes off of Merced. Suddenly, her eyes lit up. "Gertrudis wants your house."

Merced fisted her palm as Norma went on with her story. She said Gertrudis never left her little yellow house on Rowan Avenue, right on Whittier Boulevard where all the *cholos* used to cruise.

"Did you hear that Gertrudis wants the house?" Norma asked.

Norma told them about the first house they lived in when they moved to East LA. from El Paso. Yellow with a red-shingled roof.

"It was a nice house, like a castle. Good furniture, too."

"Did you visit them?" Alma asked.

"Yes," Norma acknowledged. "One time. Eduardo was stationed here, and we went to visit them. I think, they had just married."

Merced's mouth winced but she stayed still. When Norma finished her cigarette, she suddenly got up.

"*Tengo que mear*," Norma announced.

Alma jutted her chin toward the green-tiled bathroom. Once the door shut, Norma heard Merced whimper. After washing her hands, she opened the medicine cabinet. Bright orange pill containers glowed against the white metal. Norma grabbed one, read the word "heart" on the label and knew. She returned, anxious to continue her story.

"All this time, Leandro was just a bus ride away, and now he's dead," Norma said as she sat back down on the couch.

Merced didn't even blink during the telling of how Leandro died on the operating table from a heart attack while the doctor tried to remove the bullet.

"The bullet was almost out," Norma said, lighting up another cigarette. "But his heart was too weak."

Merced also had a weak heart and high blood pressure. Norma had seen the bottle of beta blockers in the medicine cabinet. She had studied them, wondering how many and how long it would take for them to kill her and finally free her from this family. That was another rule that was beaten into her as a Catholic: "*La Virgencita* does not accept suicides . . . she'll throw your ass in Hell."

Norma noticed Lucha paying close attention to her words. Her eyes were lowered but her ears were wide open. *Yes, listen to me*, thought Norma. *I'm telling you something.*

"Gertrudis was the kind of woman who liked to have nice things and the one nice thing she really wanted he couldn't give her. He wanted his house back," Norma said.

At that mention of the house, Merced slammed her palm down on the kitchen table. She knew she was in for a long and bloody war with Gertrudis and Leandro's ghost. It had started years before, when Gertrudis danced with Leandro at El Yuma.

"Why would Leandro want our house?" Lucha asked, but no one answered her.

It was too hard for Norma and Merced to explain without getting enraged.

"Leandro married Gertrudis because she was going to have his baby," Merced managed before holding her breath and closing her eyes.

Her granddaughter and daughters waited, wondering if she would explode or die on the spot.

Merced took a deep breath and said, "He loved her more than he loved me."

Norma had suspected but now she knew the truth. Merced had rooted herself to this yellow house in Boyle Heights like the *huizache* tree in the front yard because she was still in love with Leandro.

"He bought Gertrudis a little house in Montebello, where all the *italianos* used to live," Norma said.

"I gave up everything for that man," Merced confessed solemnly. "He took everything from me except for this house."

"He was good at taking things. Very smart," Norma said, stroking Lucha's hair. She hoped her niece was listening.

"*Ingrato descarado*," Merced whispered.

"He even took . . . our childhood," Norma added.

Merced's hands knotted in her pockets. "I'm thirsty," she said, stood up and slid her hands up and down against her throat. "Let's go to El Yuma."

Norma turned to Lucha. "*M'ija*, this woman wants to take away our house and all your *abuela* can think of is her next drink."

Merced slammed her hand on the table again, but by this time Norma was too old to care if Merced punched her in the face for not shutting up. Before Merced could say anything else, Alma stood up and told them she'd drive them.

CHAPTER 4
Merced Knows

Yeah, Merced knows. She's a *puta*. She's a *cabrona*. Not a decent woman. She likes to drink. Hell, Merced likes to get drunk. And she loves fucking men, big *chingón* men with smooth, beautiful bodies. And sometimes she's a fool, especially for Leandro. For him, *es un amor eterno*, always an eternal love. Her first love, so how can she forget him?

Leandro had loved Merced because she wasn't a decent woman. Because she voiced her opinions, her *críticas*. He wanted to hear her. Leandro was the first man who didn't tell her to shut up or slap her for saying the truth. It all started that first day they met forty years ago at the Mercado Cuauhtémoc on Calle Obregón, in Juárez. Under the bright stone-blue sky, stuck way in the back of Calle Obregón, Merced was sitting against the *mercado*'s golden wall behind her piles of *chiles*, waiting with the other vendors from little Chihuahua towns and *ranchos*. She had such a variety: *anchos*, *típicos*, *negros*, *de la tierra*. She and her two daughters had picked them early in the morning in the cool shadows of the San José hills.

Enveloped by the heat of that hot August day and the exhaust fumes of aging cars and trucks, Merced sat on her thin woolen blanket, competing with the other vendors for the *juarenses*, American soldiers and tourists. Merced had never gone to Juárez to sell *chiles* on her own until that day. For fifteen years, her husband Donaciano had insisted on coming with her, but on that hot, sticky day, he was too sick with the flu to accompany her.

"And the girls?" Merced had asked Donaciano while she was getting ready in the dark of early morning.

"Pina will take care of them," he told her.

Merced's Tía Pina would make Suki and Alma milk the cows, kill a chicken for dinner and clean out the cow stalls — they were chores Pina had always made Merced do ever since she could remember.

Merced did not argue when Donaciano told her to just go. Merced went out and boarded her friend Rufina's pickup, its bed piled high with so many fat, red sweet potatoes, Merced could barely fit her own load in. Rufina drove quickly all the way down to Juárez, past Ahumada, Casas Grandes and El Ojo del Lucero. Merced ignored Rufina's yammering and watched the mountains and hills flow by in shadowed silence.

At the market, as the sun burned across the turquoise sky, the hours went by without one customer. Merced scratched the sweat under her breast through the stickiness of her rough-cotton blouse. The cigarette smoke from passing men and the exhaust fumes from cars choked her and made her eyes water and sting so badly she had to close them every few minutes. The few women who stopped to look at her *chiles* didn't buy a damn thing.

Donaciano had told her to find a spot on the ground next to Rufina's stall, because customers would want to buy *chiles* before buying the *camotes*. Next time, she would tell Donaciano to rent one of the wooden stalls, as her *comadre* Rufina had advised.

"That one thinks she looks like María Félix," Rufina called over from her stall.

Merced looked at the woman Rufina pointed out at the bakery across the street from the *mercado*. She looked beautiful with her black eyebrows arching like flying birds. But her hair looked nothing like the gold hairdos of movie actresses Blanca de Castejón and Marlene Dietrich. This gold was a burned orange or an over-ripened *chile*. Her shiny dress glowed purple then black and matched her shoes with her toes painted red poking out the peek-a-boo front.

"That's a quality dress," Rufina said squinting her eyes. "I wonder if it's silk."

"Where would a *pinche juareña* whore get that much money?" the woman in the next produce stall asked.

"From up North," Rufina said.

"*Imposible*," the other vendor said. "They're still fighting *los japoneses*."

"*Ay, mensa*. Don't you know it's the soldiers who can get all that stuff?" Rufina said rearranging her sweet potatoes.

Merced fingered her long thick braid held together by a ragged ribbon. The fancy woman's hair fell down in thick waves. *I'm more like a sweet potato*, Merced thought as she pulled at some loose strands, all brown and sun-baked.

It was worse when men stood over her, staring down while they smoked their skinny brown cigarettes, like she was one of the *chiles* laying out there just for them. They threw kisses, whistles or words like "*qué sabrosa*." At times, Merced wanted to look up at them and see how they liked being stared at, and one time she did. Instead of looking down and away as usual, she looked straight into the black eyes of a tall man who walked up to her smiling under his fedora.

"*Hola, preciosa*," he said.

"*¿Qué se le ofrece, señor?*"

"Call me Leandro."

His eyes smiled at her and scanned her body. When he offered to buy three dozen *chiles anchos*, she smiled at him. It was her first sale of the day after three hours of sitting in the suffocating heat of the Cuauhtémoc market. As she handed him the change, Leandro caressed her hand. Under his warm fingers her skin pimpled and cooled. She quickly pulled it back.

"You think you're Pedro Infante or what?" Merced cracked, then quickly shut her mouth.

She stared at Leandro, waiting for him to do something, because she knew Donaciano would have smacked her the instant she said it. Instead, Leandro smiled, just like Jorge Negrete did in all his movies, with that little arch in his black eyebrows. Then he laughed and told Merced he'd come back for her later.

"*¿Pa' que?*" Merced asked.

"I'm going to steal you," he said, grabbing a *camote* from Rufina's pile while she waited on a customer.

As Merced watched him walk away, she saw his shoulders and back ripple under his white cotton shirt. His hat was nothing like the cheap, thick hats worn by her husband back in their *pueblito*. No. Leandro's hat reminded her of the gold coins she imagined Pancho Villa had supposedly buried in the rocky hills nearby. His hands had felt soft and thin, too. No blisters or callouses like hers or Donaciano's or anyone else's she knew.

"That guy thinks he's *muy chingón*," Rufina said, looking down, rubbing her forehead. "He's cute but tricky." She turned to Merced and said, "Stick to your man. These *juarenses* are pigs."

Donaciano with his balding head and hard hands was an honest man, Merced thought. He got up at dawn, loaded sacks of flour into his storeroom, lifted bolts of cloth onto his store shelves and made money. But Donaciano was nothing like Leandro. On their wedding night, Donaciano had told Merced to climb on top of him because he was too tired. As always, she had to do the work.

❀❀❀

The next time Merced was at the market, Leandro took her to Fanfaro's department store and bought her a dress and shoes. She liked the way the blue fabric made her dark eyes shine.

"*Se llama lino,*" Leandro explained.

She mouthed the words in front of the full-length mirror. The blue velvet pumps pinched her toes, but her ashy legs looked shiny and wet under the silk nylons he also bought her. When she walked out of the dressing room, she still felt like an *india* straight out of El Sauz.

"It's the hair," the sales lady said. "Untie the braid."

The moment the sales lady loosened the ribbon holding her braid, Merced's hair seemed to burst out, flowing straight down, past her butt. The saleslady informed them that there was a salon in the store's basement.

"Betsabé can help you with this girl," the clerk told Leandro, looking doubtfully at Merced's mop of hair.

I don't want to cut my hair, Merced thought, but her lips refused to move.

Leandro escorted Merced to the salon, kissed her and said he would come back for her in an hour. For the first time, she noticed a little black mole dancing just above his upper lip.

By the time Leandro returned, Merced's black hair was pulled back and held by a little net the stylist called a snood. Merced's face felt heavy with powder, blush and mascara. Her raspberry lips looked swollen.

"Men like that look," the stylist had assured her.

Merced didn't believe it until Leandro took her to El Colón movie theater to see "*Doña Bárbara*" with María Félix.

"That's her," Leandro said, never taking his eyes off the screen the moment she appeared.

María Félix was half Yaqui, *an india just like me*, she realized. *How can a woman like that exist*, she thought, touching the netting holding her hair. Suddenly she realized what she had done. What would she say to Donaciano about her eyebrows when she went back home? She pictured Donaciano's face. He would whip her. And what about Rufina? She would figure it out.

"I have to get back to El Sauz," Merced told Leandro, who had plans to take her to El Paso for dinner before she headed back.

The couple walked over the bridge and down El Paso Street until they reached the alley behind the Hilton Hotel.

"Let's get a little Presidente," Leandro said, referring to the brandy he preferred.

When he pushed open the door to a bar, a dark coolness reached out to them. Leandro's arm pressed her to the round counter. Under a circle of orange-gold light, two bartenders, one Mexican, one Anglo, shook out drinks from something that looked like a giant bullet.

Leandro called out to one of the bartenders and asked for two Presidentes. Merced wanted to show him she could drink like María Félix. She wasn't afraid of his love or his passion.

"*Tranquila*," he said. "Take it slow. You still have to get back to your little husband."

"I know."

By the time they left the bar, Merced felt warm and light floating over the sidewalk as she and Leandro walked back over the bridge. Once back in Juárez, Leandro lit a cigarette.

"Can I try it?" Merced asked.

Leandro smiled and pulled one out of a little red box with a drawing of two lions wearing little crowns. He lit it in his mouth, then gently placed the thin cigarette in her mouth.

"*Como la* Bette Davis," he chuckled.

"*¿Quién?*" Merced asked, inhaling and exhaling the smoke with a cough.

"Another actress," he said, his black eyes growing darker.

❀❀❀

After Merced had packed up all her unsold *chiles* and loaded them into Rufina's pickup, Leandro came by and told her she was beautiful.

Merced narrowed her eyes and turned to a smiling Rufina, who was ready to drive back home.

"Look at me," Leandro said.

Merced turned and looked up into his black eyes.

"What do you want?" she said. "I have to leave."

"Come with me."

Merced thought she heard a train in the distance, chugging toward her. She shook her head, her thick black braid, shorter now, banging hard against her back.

"*Estás loco*," Merced told him.

"Crazy for you," he said smiling.

Rufina said something, but all Merced heard was blood pounding through her ears like the train that sped through El Sauz, through the heart of Chihuahua.

Leandro held out the crook of his arm to her. Without even thinking about it, Merced looped her arm into his and squeezed into him.

Rufina's honking barely cut through the thumping blood in her ears. Merced never looked back as she walked away, keeping up with Leandro's long-legged strides. Barely breathing, Merced almost fainted right there in middle of a crowd of local pedestrians, soldiers, beggars and American tourists. Leandro easily supported her weight on his arm as they ambled through the streets of Juárez, down Calle 16 de Septiembre, past the Nuestra Señora de Guadalupe Mission, the domed Customs House and the cabarets where her oldest daughter would someday work. After crossing the wooden Santa Fe Bridge leading to El Paso, the border guards nodded to Leandro.

"Why don't you take the trolley?" one of the guards asked.

"*Es más romántico*," Leandro said, hugging Merced tighter, squeezing her until she almost fainted again.

"*Ay, sí*," Merced whispered, "so romantic."

Just then, a streetcar clanged behind them.

"Hurry up, *mi amor*," Leandro whispered back, pulling her across the trolley tracks along the bridge, away from the guards who looked at Merced like she was a sweet tender *camote*.

As soon as they crossed over into El Paso, the train rumbling in her ears quieted down little by little and faded. By the time they got to the El Paso del Norte Hotel, the Dome Bar was crowded and most of the tables were taken, but the bartender made a space for them at the circular wooden bar. Merced pulled her black *rebozo* tight around her arms and chest, noticing the well-dressed customers.

"*Siéntate*," Leandro told her. "You look beautiful."

Merced looked up at the dome built high up over the circular bar. The sunset's light glowed through the blue and green glass.

"Look," she said, pointing up just as the bartender set a cocktail in front of her.

Leandro said nothing, just squeezed her into his body.

Merced laughed a little, thinking of her husband back in El Sauz. Cleo and Merced's daughters would have to take care of him now.

❁❁❁

The next morning, Merced felt like she had feasted all night long. It was like she had eaten every *chile*, *asadero* and tortilla in Chihuahua. It had been all Leandro, with his creamy skin, delicate mole and thick, shiny black hair. She was exhausted. She had done everything to please Leandro, twisting her legs, waist and arms around him, squeezing then loosening her grip.

The El Paso sun blazed down on her breasts and stomach and on Leandro's back and butt, which she stroked and patted like a ball of tortilla dough. Then she climbed on top of him.

"Again?" Leandro asked into the sheets.

"You smell like bread."

Leandro mumbled but didn't turn over. On one side of the bed, the thin green curtains lay on the floor. Merced remembered pulling on them so hard, the metal rod hit her on its way down. The blankets were bunched into a far corner of the room. When had they thrown them over there? She barely remembered it all, there were only flashes of memory. There had been a knocking or pounding on the wall when they were at the height of passion.

"You're too loud," Leandro had whispered, but in the light from the streetlamps, she could tell he was smiling. She continued to moan as she had never done with Donaciano.

❀❀❀

As the priest began reading from one of the Gospels about Jesus Christ's agony in the Garden of Gethsemane, Merced bowed her head, her white lace mantilla clinging to her black hair like a spider's web. But Jesus' suffering couldn't compare to her own that morning. Instead of Jesus' misery all she could think about was her lover Leandro and María Félix in the movie *Doña Diabla.*

"You look like her," Leandro had whispered, then kissed her in the cool darkness of the theater.

Merced had felt like the dangerous actress, sitting there in the dark with Leandro's arm around her, the velvet seat cushioning her against the reality of traveling back to El Sauz for the Easter Sunday ceremonies.

Black lace hanging over other women's heads reminded her of María Félix's strapless dress, with its lace bodice and her matching opera-length gloves. As Merced lowered herself down on the wooden kneeler, the priest began describing Judas Iscariot leading a crowd of armed men to arrest Jesus in the garden. The two-hundred-year-old cathedral soared above her with its carved stone arches and gilded domes. Donaciano kneeled next to her, his profile like the rocky mountains she had seen on their way to Creel, to their honeymoon hotel fifteen years earlier. They had been an hour on the road, passing beef ranches spotted with cows and bulls. Steam-engine trains rolled by them heading into the Copper Canyon.

"*El Rostro de Cristo*," Donaciano had called out, pointing to the jagged stones protruding like the nose and chin of Christ under the midday sun.

"Pancho Villa buried gold up there," Donaciano had said.

When she asked him why he hadn't gone up there to look for it, he laughed and tousled her hair as if she was a little girl. She pulled away, her hands curled into fists.

"I'm not your little girl," she said, her eyebrows arching.

Donaciano quieted, stared at her, then slapped her twice before stopping the car by the side of the road and forcing himself on her. Cars screamed by their shaking DeSoto. When Donaciano started the car up again, Merced breathed deep to stop herself from sobbing, from feeling the burn between her legs.

"*Ya cállate,*" he snarled.

Her tears kept sliding down her face, the bright blue sky scorching her eyes. When she closed them, a glowing green square seared her eyelids. She thought she saw Christ's face.

When they reached the hotel, Donaciano left her at the door with the luggage. "I'll be back later."

When he came back, he smelled of smoke and perfume. He lay down next to her, not bothering to change out of his clothes. As soon as he started snoring, Merced crawled out of bed to sit in the room's lone chair next to the window. Outside, drunken men serenaded, then shouted at their women.

Merced jerked her head up to dispel that memory and focus on the cathedral altar. Donaciano leaned his head against his cupped right hand. Her daughters Norma, Alma and Suki sat to his other side, their eyes wandering. When Merced caught their eye, she raised her eyebrows, her mouth a straight line. The girls quickly bowed their heads.

Merced closed her eyes and inhaled the wax and incense. Her stomach growled. She tried imagining Jesus' face, but María Félix's kept popping up, black lace breaking her face into fragments. Merced's mouth dried. When the priest led the congregation in reciting the "Our Father," Suki told her mother she needed to pee.

"Hold it," Merced said without opening her eyes.

Suki could not, and soon Alma was tapping her mother's shoulder and pointing to the puddle underneath the pew. Merced closed her eyes again.

"Take her outside," she told Norma. "Clean her up."

"You clean her up," Donaciano whispered sharply. "You're her mother."

Merced rose and led a wide-eyed Suki to the restroom, where she pulled off Suki's socks and panties and threw them into the sink. As she rubbed her daughters' thighs and ankles clean, Merced began sobbing. Suki stared at her mother, then wrapped her arms around her neck, knocking off the mantilla. Merced held onto Suki until the sobbing and shaking of her body subsided.

❀❀❀

Merced periodically visited Rutilio, the new bartender, at the El Paso del Norte Hotel's Dome Bar. In between her shifts, he drank with her and made her laugh as the nights without Leandro flowed into months. One day, he made a special drink for her.

"It's a Mai Tai," Rutilio said, sliding it to her. He knew Merced preferred her brandy but was always trying to make her try something different.

After downing her drinks, Merced would always look up at the multicolored skylight that gave the bar its name. The bar's tall marble columns and round stained-glass window to the sky made her feel as if she were in church. She was no longer as nervous as the first time she sat at the circular bar, when all the customers had seemed like movie stars. In her beige housekeeping uniform, however, Merced felt more like the comedienne India María than María Félix among the women who wore furs and styled their hair like Veronica Lake.

Out of the blue one evening, Rutilio invited her, "Let's go dancing."

"Where?"

"El Popo."

"*Ay, sí.*"

Rutilio laughed and poured her another drink. After his shift and a few more drinks, he escorted her from the hotel to El Popo, not letting her change out of her uniform.

"If I let you go change, I know you won't come back," he said as they moved through the Chihuahuita neighborhood, past the Fat Boy Hamburger, Sacred Heart Church and up El Paso Street.

Leandro's friends would see them, she knew, but so what. In fact, she smiled at the cab driver parked on the street, who sometimes drank with Leandro. Her heels clicked harder and louder on the cracked sidewalk as she was accompanied by their blurred reflection on Newberry's store window. Rutilio and she looked like they were escaping from someone.

Merced wished she could escape from her job at the Plaza Hotel, from her daughters, from everything for a week. Just a week to rest her body from all the cleaning, cooking and whoring. Just a week. They finally reached El Popo, a *norteño* bar where couples pressed up against each other, dancing to *conjunto* bands that wandered in and out of bars until they were paid to stay. The heat made the bar feel like the inside of someone's mouth.

"They're good," Rutilio said as he pulled her onto the dance floor.

She hadn't danced in years, not since her own wedding, and then it had been a stiff, clumsy waltz. Before that, as a young girl, she loved learning the latest *norteño* hits like "*La Barranca.*" And now, here she was wearing her hotel uniform and dancing on the floor with other, younger couples, fighting for space as she kicked and bounced to "*La Vaquerita.*"

Her shoes almost flew off, but for the first time since she was fifteen, she didn't care. She felt like she was flying, even though at first she stepped more on Rutilio's toes than on the wooden dance floor. Back and forth, back and forth, bounce, bounce, twirl, twirl, and then the close embrace. Sweat ran down her back and from under her arms, staining her smock.

"I can't breathe," she said.

Rutilio wouldn't stop. With his arm tight around her waist, he'd spin her around, then kick and stomp like some horse as she tried to keep up. When she finally got him to listen, he laughed and led her to the bar for a beer and a cigarette. Her legs and feet were already tired from her hotel work, especially the fucking, but Rutilio kept smiling that crooked grin of his, so how could she resist.

On the dance floor, the other couples kept bouncing and bumping into each other to the rhythm of the accordion and guitar. When another band came in, Rutilio dragged her out again.

Someone whistled and shouted *"¡Aviéntala, Rutilio! ¡Aviéntala!"*

"I have to work tomorrow," Merced insisted.

"It's already tomorrow."

"Do you live near here?"

Rutilio nodded and quickly led her off the dance floor, pushing a path through the other couples. Merced nearly fainted from the heat and sweat. Finally, they made it to the rickety door that led to a back alley. Rutilio led her to a wooden stairway behind El Popo and climbed to his studio apartment on the second floor. The music pounded through the floor of his tiny room, sparse except for a bed and a chest of drawers.

"Jesusita en Chihuahua" vibrated through her body as he climbed on top of her. *"Jesusita"* was still with her three hours later as she walked back to work at the Plaza Hotel. She tried to remember Leandro's lips to compare them with Rutilio's. There was no comparison. Nothing could compare with Leandro's love-making.

Leandro had turned out to be as thin as his mustache when it came to earning money or loving her. What an idiot she'd been. She'd thought their passion would last forever, but, of course, that was before Leandro started up with some cabaret girl, a real-life *cabaretera* just like in the movies. He later left for a ship-building job in Los Angeles. Now, the only thing that kept her going was the thought of finding him, being with him in their very own house without the threat of Donaciano, her daughters or anyone intruding on her happiness. Nowadays, working and hooking as a hotel maid in La Plaza, she felt like an open wound, throbbing every time she walked the hotel's hallways and entered a room to clean or please a john. When the john threatened to turn her in or left without paying her, she hated Leandro even more.

CHAPTER 5
Catch One

Bodies undulated under flashing, colored lights as the music pumped through the speakers. Suki knew the moment she stepped onto the dance floor with Lily that she would never want to leave.

The DJ glowed red, perched above the dance floor, spinning, listening through his headphones. Odyssey's "Native New Yorker" echoed off the neon-lined walls. In the dim light, Suki and Lily sung the words to each other. Suddenly, Lily grabbed Suki's hands and spun her around in a practiced dance twirl, just like those dancers they watched on *Fiebre* and *Dance Fever*. When Lily came in to kiss her, Suki froze.

"It's okay," Lily said, nodding her head to the couples closest to her.

Under the gleaming disco ball, men danced with men, hugging and kissing. Other women sat close to each other in the booths surrounding the dance floor. For a moment, Suki almost forgot that she was at Jewel's Catch One. And Suki had caught one, the one and only Lily, her *preciosa*.

She wasn't used to dancing freely, lovingly in a disco without keeping her distance. At the straight clubs, women usually danced with each other without being bothered by some wanna-be Tony Manero lotharios. It's when they sat down that the men would surround them, demanding their time to dance. A polite "no" usually didn't work.

"Are you lesbos or what?"

One time, Suki danced with a guy who kept pushing up against her so she could feel his erection. When she tried to push him away, he'd hold her tighter. As soon as the dance number was done, she and Lily left.

But here was a new world, a world of men and women who could dance alone or in pairs or in groups. And there were many black and brown dancers. At Jewel's Catch One, onlookers watched, drank and chatted. But once France Joli's "Come to Me" blasted through the speakers, everyone quickly moved onto the dance floor and began swaying to the song's slow start.

"Come to me," Lily sang, "because I will comfort you."

As the sound of the synthesized violins washed over them, Lily spun her around, Suki's long black hair whipping around, whipping the couple next to them. Suki now understood why Lily had asked her to wear her fringy blouse and low-heeled platform shoes. Lily herself didn't like to be twirled: "I'll throw up."

At a break from dancing, they sipped tequila from shot glasses. Lily took Suki's hand, squeezed it and let it rest on her thigh. Lily's fingernails shined under the strobing lights. Just two weeks ago, Suki had only known Lily as her mother's lawyer, the one who would help Merced win back ownership of her house. Now, Lily was her girlfriend. At least, she hoped she was. Suki had never dated a lawyer before, especially one who loved to dance. Before that, she had dated Gloria in high school, but she eventually dumped Suki for a boy. The next one, a history major in college, was a white girl who left her to travel Japan. She had asked Suki to go with her, and Suki had been tempted but couldn't leave her young niece. Over the next couple of years, she dated a few other girlfriends she'd met at school or at her receptionist job. Lily seemed too good to be true.

"Heaven knows, I never wanna leave you," Donna Summer crooned to "Brooklyn Dreams."

Back on the dance floor, Lily and Suki twirled around the concrete pulsing with rainbow hues.

CHAPTER 6
Conjunto

Every night in Boyle Heights, men, married or single, went to El Yuma for drinks, music, a kiss, a squeeze. *Thank God, Alma didn't cry anymore*, Merced thought. *She knew better*. Alma now pulled her weight at El Yuma, chatting up the men, collecting the big tips as if these men worked in offices, not in downtown warehouses or Long Beach shipyards. The men were decent enough, mostly neighborhood men, although sometimes they hovered too close, especially that old *sinvergüenza* Don Pedro.

The first time Alma started wearing lipstick to the bar, Merced knew Don Pedro had something to do with it. Merced didn't recognize her face. Her mouth looked like it wanted to say something, something Merced didn't want to hear. But Alma told her nothing. When Merced saw Don Pedro hovering near the bar but unwilling to share the best brandy in El Yuma with her, well, she knew then he wanted Alma.

Don Pedro showed up like a weed in an empty field. *Mala yerba*, Merced called him. *Mala yerba* never dies. Don Pedro had a taste for young women, especially women from troubled families. He knew about Merced and her past lives in El Paso and Juárez. And he knew about her daughter Norma's past in the hotels of Juárez. He was aware she was eager to escape Merced. Don Pedro could tell by the way Merced narrowed her eyes every time he bought Alma a shot, that he would have to rip Alma away from Merced.

One evening after buying her one more shot, Merced leaned over the bar into Alma's face.

"Don't be stupid," Merced told her, grabbing the shot glass from her hand.

Don Pedro quickly slid to Alma's side. Merced leaned back and walked to the other side of the bar. She knew better. Don Pedro owned El Yuma and also a couple of bars on Sunset Boulevard. Why he drank at El Yuma instead of his nicer bars in Hollywood, no one knew.

"He likes the *mexicanas*," one patron told Merced.

"It pisses off his wife," another told her.

Don Pedro never wore a wedding ring. Merced knew plenty of married men without wedding rings.

One night, when a conjunto band showed up at El Yuma, Merced filled herself up with brandy, was floating above the men, Alma and all the other women. The accordions, guitars and *norteño* music filled her with nostalgia for the nights when she and Leandro used to go out in Juárez.

"He likes bar women," Moti told her as they watched Don Pedro dance with Alma on the small, crowded dance floor. Like Leandro and Merced, he had also found a refuge in El Yuma.

"Why doesn't he hang out with the white bitches in Hollywood?" Merced asked. "He's got the money."

Shrugging his shoulders, Moti answered, "Maybe he's in love."

Merced almost spit out her shot of brandy. How could a rich important man like Don Pedro love a woman like her daughter? Alma was pretty but looked more Indian than the truly beautiful women he could find at high-class night clubs, she supposed.

Merced watched Don Pedro's white cowboy hat and crisp white shirt glow in the smokey darkness. When the *conjunto* started playing "*Jesusita en Chihuahua*," Don Pedro and Alma crossed the floor smoothly as if gliding over ice. Except for his bouncing pot belly and graying hair, his sixty years melted away. In the darkness, his face lost its wrinkles. Alma smiled throughout the dance, her golden hair, freshly dyed that day at Cesar's salon, burned like a candle in the reddish lights of the bar. When she caught Merced's eye, she didn't look away.

"Like mother, like daughter," Moti laughed and offered Merced a cigarette.

La cabrona is soused, Merced thought. She knew she had lost Alma that night.

Just then, Alma ran over to her. "Don Pedro would like to take me out to eat after we finish tonight."

Merced looked at Don Pedro, who was talking to one of the singers. And then, before she knew it, the guy was singing "*Sabor a Mí.*" That old *sinvergüenza*. Merced knew what he was up to.

"There's a diner on First Street . . ." Alma started.

"*Bien*. But I'm going with you."

Alma bit her upper lip.

"Don't make a face, or I swear I'll slap you right here in front of that *pinche* good-for-nothing."

Alma, flushed, walked back to Don Pedro.

Babosa, Merced thought. *Always crying for nothing. Wait until she has kids and a husband, then she'll know about crying.*

When Don Pedro started crossing the room toward Merced, she almost threw the bottle of brandy at him. It took all her strength not to crack him in the nose when he sat his ass down in front of her and leaned over the bar, close to her face.

"Doña Merced," he said in a low voice, "I would like to ask your permission to take your daughter out to eat tonight. As a gentleman, I will treat her with all the respect she deserves."

Merced narrowed her eyes. What made him think he was different from all these other men in the bar?

"Bien," Merced whispered, "but I'm going with you, *y ya estuvo."* She started serving drinks to the band members, who had just finished their last set. Don Pedro looked her over, and for a minute she thought he was going to reach over and grab her by the neck. But he just sat there, twisting on the stool for a good five minutes before going to the men's room.

Merced walked around the bar and followed him through the paint-chipped green door. Quickly, she locked the door behind her, and before he could zip up, grabbed his *pito* and started rubbing it like a rosary.

"So," she said, "is this what you want from my daughter?"

He grew hard and heavy like a gun. Don Pedro didn't move, just kept looking at her. When he grabbed her right breast, she knew he was like the others. Merced squeezed his balls, and he came. After wiping her hands on his shirt, she washed them. He was still standing by the sink when she left. Merced didn't see him leave, but the rest of the night, Alma kept looking for him.

"What did you say to him?"

"Nothing," Merced said. "I just showed him something."

Alma twisted her mouth. That's when Merced lost it and slapped her across the face.

As they walked home, Alma blubbered over Don Pedro. Merced kept mumbling that she was ungrateful. Alma cried all night, while Merced slept so well she didn't wake up until ten the next morning. Merced had slept so hard, she didn't hear Alma leave during the night with Don Pedro. Alma didn't come home for a week. When she did, instead of being properly ashamed, she came waltzing in, singing *"Ojos de Juventud"* so loud, she woke Merced up.

Qué bonito, Merced thought. Spending the week with a strange man who's not her husband. Already, the other men at the bar would snicker at Merced whenever she served them, looking at her like she was a fool.

"Oye, Merced," one patron had said. "When will I get a week with Alma?"

Merced threw a pitcher of water at him that smashed into the post right behind him. Moti quickly took the man outside before he could jump over the bar.

Merced burned at the memory. Through the partially opened door, she could see Alma turning on the burners in the kitchen to warm up the clay pot of beans. The smell of charred corn tortillas soon floated throughout the house.

"Is that you, Alma?" Suki called out from her bedroom.

Alma quickly stepped over to the door of their small bedroom and half whispered, "Don't wake up *la bruja*."

Merced shot up from her bed and grabbed the thick belt Leandro had left behind. Before Alma could run back to the kitchen, Merced swung at her back. Before she could swing again, Alma grabbed the belt and yanked it out of Merced's hand. Suki rushed to the door to see her sister whipping their mother. At first, Suki thought she was dreaming, because it should have been Merced beating Alma, not the other way around.

"*¡Agárrala, Suki!*" Merced yelled.

Suki froze, stunned by the sight of her mother on the floor, cowering, her arms covered in welts.

Finally, Alma tired and threw the belt at Suki before running out the back door, leaving behind her half-eaten bowl of beans and a tortilla burning on the stove. Suki grabbed it and threw it in the sink.

❀❀❀

Alma has always hated thunder, ever since she lived in El Sauz. Thunder meant lightning, lightning meant electrocution, fire, destruction. But this time, she had Don Pedro by her side. He would protect her from the lightning, from Merced.

"You excited?" Don Pedro asked, gripping her hand during her time on a plane.

Alma looked up the aisle at the stewardess dressed in her brown and orange uniform as she pushed the beverage cart forward. As they flew above the thunderheads, Alma tried to calm herself, tried not to look out the window.

"It will only be an hour," Don Pedro assured her. "Only an hour."

Alma closed her eyes and whispered, "*Ave María, madre de Dios.*"

"Look how pretty the lightning looks," Pedro said, pulling her close to him and pointing out the window.

Alma shook her head and scrunched her eyes. Why was she running off with this man? They were going to get married. In Las Vegas. Why?

Because I love him, Alma thought, although she knew she was escaping Merced. She had to. She felt bad about leaving Norma and Suki alone with her, but she just had to leave. And why not Don Pedro? He was kind, *un hombre decente.* Rich, too. That's what he told her, anyway. When she opened her eyes, the stewardess was looking down at her. "What would you like to drink?" she asked smiling.

"A Coke," Alma said.

"No, no," Don Pedro said. "We have to celebrate. Two brandies."

The stewardess smiled as she pulled out two little bottles. The beverage cart became the housekeeping cart Alma used to push down the halls of the El Paso del Norte Hotel. Suddenly, Don Pedro reminded her of the johns Merced forced on her.

Alma breathed heavily as Don Pedro unscrewed the little bottle and emptied it into the plastic cup filled with ice cubes.

"*Salud*," he said, raising his cup. "To my beautiful bride."

Alma blinked. A tear ran down her cheek as she gripped her cup, but she brushed it away with her palm. Johnny Walker splattered onto her tray, on her new dress. When she started to cry, Don Pedro held her gently, comforting her.

❀❀❀

By the time Alma had dumped Don Pedro, her marriage had been on the skids for a while. It started right from their honeymoon.

"You're my wife now," he told her, holding Alma's hand gently. "It's okay."

Alma flashed back to the first time a white man at the hotel had raped her. "Pretend you're my wife," the john had told her.

Mercifully, he had been quick. While Alma lay in bed stunned and bleeding, the john covered her with the linen sheet. He put on his white underwear, black pants and slipped on his white shirt. The hiss of the belt sliding quickly through the loops made her wince. Once he slipped on his black tasseled loafers, he picked up his suitcase. Without looking at her, he slipped out the door. Then it flew open. Merced walked up to the bed and ripped the sheet off her shivering body.

"What are you waiting for?" Merced asked. "We got to get back to cleaning."

Her mother went straight for Alma's smock, crumpled beside the bed. The bills flapped limply in Merced's hand.

"Not bad," she nodded and slipped the money into her pocket. "Get up."

As Don Pedro unzipped her dress and pulled down the straps of her bra that night, she pushed the memory away. But the moment Don Pedro inserted himself into her without looking at her face, the john's face kept appearing. Don Pedro was now her husband, and Alma couldn't even scream like she did that first time. When Pedro was done, he cradled her like a baby as tears and mucous streamed from her face.

"It's okay," her husband assured her. "You'll get used to it."

Alma never got used to it. They had moved to Las Vegas, where Don Pedro was trying to set up another bar like El Yuma in a barrio. The high-rise hotels reminded her too much of El Paso del Norte. The young housekeepers looked like she and her mother did when they sold themselves to male guests.

Merced had always seemed untouched by their time "house-keeping" and kept it a secret from Norma and Suki. Now, whenever Alma passed by a hotel with a "housekeeper wanted" sign, she would shiver and her heart would pump fast.

For weeks after they were married, Alma avoided Pedro's amorous overtures. She'd go to bed right after dinner or use her period as an excuse. When the weeks turned into months, Pedro finally lost his temper.

"You're my wife," he said pushing her back into the bed so hard that Alma popped up onto her feet like an acrobat.

"I'm pregnant," she screamed as she ran out the door of their house into the neon-lit night.

That night, Alma bought a Greyhound ticket for East Los Angeles.

❁❁❁

Alma first learned about labor pain when she got her first period at thirteen. They were living in a tenement in Segundo Barrio, El Paso, and as in most barrio tenements they had to share a bathroom. At first, Alma thought she had bad diarrhea and was feeling sorry for the next person who had to use the toilet. Then she saw that blood had soaked through the panel of her underwear and through to her skirt.

It's cancer, Alma had thought as she ran to wake Norma up from a sound sleep.

"*No seas mensa*," Norma grumbled as she sat up. "It's your period."

Norma showed her the clean rags she kept in the closet and how to fold them in between her legs. Later, Alma would be able to afford the manufactured pads she saw in drugstores. But for now, she had to make do with the rags and the pain. Alma changed into a clean pair of panties but made the mistake of forgetting her bloody panty on the bathroom floor.

"Norma!" Merced screamed down the hallway. "What are those *calzones* doing on the floor?"

"*¡Son de Alma!*" Norma yelled from the door.

Alma knew she had to get her ass over to the bathroom before Merced grew even angrier.

The ice-cold water ran from the bathroom faucet over the stained panties, filling the sink with pink water. Merced showed her daughter how to rub the soap over the panty panel, then scrub the panel against itself.

"Never show your blood," Merced lectured. "Nobody wants to see or smell it."

For the cramps, Merced had Suki pluck fresh leaves from the spearmint that grew in clay pots on their little balcony. Without Merced's approval, Suki also brewed the mint with some chamomile flowers, since they were known to soothe fear. Norma also warmed some washcloths to put on Alma's stomach. Alma was about to ask for another washcloth when Merced came into the room to check on her.

"Better get used to the pain," Merced warned. "Women have to suffer in this world, thanks to Eve."

Alma closed her eyes as the cramp squeezed and then let go of her stomach muscles.

"When you have a baby its worse," Merced went on. "The labor pain is punishment for eating that apple and lying to God."

❁❁❁

The night seemed like it lasted forever. Every time the Greyhound made a stop, Alma's seat jerked forward, waking her up to the yellow glow of a bus depot. Passengers stirred, some jumped up and grabbed their bags and suitcases. Alma closed her eyes and tried to sleep, but the thought of Don Pedro chasing her through the night kept her awake.

"What time is it?" someone asked.

Alma looked at her watch, but the second hand was not moving. She shook it and held it to her ear. It couldn't be 11. The night felt deeper. More like morning.

"Two o'clock," someone answered.

Suddenly the bus driver climbed down and out of the bus.

Let's go, let's go, Alma thought, clutching her sweater close to her stomach. She felt hungry.

The bus driver climbed back up and walked the aisle. "Sorry, folks. You're all going to have to get off the bus. We got a flat."

Alma lost her breath.

"Fuck," someone said.

"Language! There's ladies on board!" the driver yelled as he walked up to the young man dressed in a T-shirt and cotton jacket. "You apologize!"

The man mumbled an apology.

"Next bus will come out in an hour."

The passengers around her all stood up and grabbed their belongings. Alma waited until the bus emptied, then stood up. The driver smiled and tipped his hat as he handed her a transfer. Alma smiled a little and stepped down. In the depot, the smoke and sweat overwhelmed Alma. She ran to the bathroom, unbuttoned her sweater and vomited into the sink. She ran the water but threw up again.

"*¿Qué pasa, m'ija?*" she heard behind her. "*¿'Stás bien?*"

Someone was rubbing her back. Alma gulped down the cold water from the faucet, then let the water run down her scalp. The hand moved around and around, rubbing out the nausea and fear. When Alma finally looked up at herself in the stained mirror, she looked like she was twelve years old again. Behind her, a woman about Merced's age, in a red leather jacket and bright orange hair, blinked through thickly mascaraed eyes.

"*Ay, m'ija,* I hope you feel better soon."

Alma took a deep breath and shook her head. "The cigarettes," she said. "I don't like the smoke."

"*¿Quieres un café?*"

Alma nodded.

The woman led her through the crowded and smoky waiting room. Alma barely resisted the urge to vomit again. She leaned into the woman, her perfumed hair blocking out the cigarettes and coffee. When she closed her eyes, Alma thought she was by the sea. The mermaid from the *Lotería* playing card popped into her head.

"You smell like a mermaid," Alma said before she could stop herself.

The woman stopped, then smiled at her. Alma waited for the blow.

"Just call me Sirena," the woman said, then held her closer.

Once outside, the cool night air filled Alma's lungs. Her sweater warmed her as she clutched Sirena's leathered arm. When Sirena opened the glass door to the diner next to the waiting room, the aroma of coffee and stench of cigarettes blew over them. The chatter in the room and the clamor of dishes energized Alma to quickly run past a couple ahead of them and claim two red leatherette stools at the counter.

"*¡Aquí!*" she said to Sirena.

"Two coffees, please," Alma said to a pale waitress with copper beehive hair.

The waitress barely nodded as she handed them a couple of menus. That was when Alma remembered she had left her purse on the bus. She turned to see the bus being towed away. The nausea started rising into her throat.

"I'll pay you back," Alma promised Sirena, putting her hand over hers.

"It's okay."

Alma smiled a little and then felt a jabbing at her shoulder. She turned to see the bus driver, hat in hand.

"You forgot this," he said, handing her the purse she'd left behind on her seat.

Alma fought back the nausea long enough to hug the driver, who patted her back. Sirena smiled and rubbed slow circles, then eased Alma back onto her stool.

"We now leave in a half hour," the bus driver announced before he headed out the door.

The red-headed waitress set down a coffee cup and a glass of milk in front of them.

Alma had ordered coffee but she drank the milk, anyway. Then, offered to pay the tab.

"The bus driver already paid for it," Sirena said, pointing her chin at the depot.

When they boarded the replacement bus, the driver waved the women over to the front seats. Half of the window had been slid open, and the seats behind them were loaded with boxes.

"You sit by the window, Mama," Sirena said as she settled herself into the seat next to Alma.

Before Alma knew it, the bus had pulled into downtown Los Angeles, and Sirena was gone.

"Don't forget your purse," the driver said, tipping his hat to Alma.

She clutched the purse tightly to her stomach and stepped into the bright Los Angeles sunlight.

CHAPTER 7
Alma's Regret

Alma hated yearning. What was the use? After her first pregnancy, she used to yearn for her slim waist, her virginity, her freedom. What for? Now all she missed was her mother, but Merced only saw her as an ungrateful daughter who had abandoned her for some old man. She still loved her but what could she do? And even when she gave birth to Lucha, Merced still thought she was useless.

"Too bad she's not a boy," Merced said, cradling Lucha in her arms. "Why didn't you name her after me?"

Alma didn't know what to say. She remembered thinking that she just wanted to be a little girl again, back in El Sauz, eating *biscochos*, not worrying about Merced, Papá, men or money. She just wanted to sleep without fear, without waking up to Merced yelling, banging pots or slapping her. She just wanted to wake up to the smell of mesquite burning in the cast-iron oven in the kitchen, the *comal* warming tortillas *de maíz* or the aroma of *menudo* simmering. She missed hearing the rooster crow, the *comadres* chattering and the horses clip-clopping on the cobblestone streets.

Every morning, now, Alma wakes up to that awful, loud gibberish Lucha plays on the radio when she blow-dries her hair in the tiny blue bathroom that creates echoes like a canyon. The burros from her girlhood sounded better than those singers. Her head starts to hurt if she doesn't get up quickly and go the kitchen, where she can hear the latest soap opera heroine either crying or begging on the TV. Alma can't get enough of them. She'll sit at the table for hours, her ashtray by her side, sucking on cigarettes. In between the smokes, she'll pull a *chicharrón* from its greasy white bag and crunch on it loudly. The TV has cast a spell on her, her face softening when the heroine finally unites with her handsome hero or tearing up when they face tragedy.

"*Pobrecita*," she'll say. "Crying's no good unless there's a man around."

Crying's not good in this house. All it ever gets you is a slap or, if you're lucky, just an eye roll. Alma is proud that Lucha has never cried in front of Merced. Lucha doesn't even cry in front of Alma, her own mother. Whenever Alma cries, Lucha just pats her on the back.

CHAPTER 8
Tristan and Iseult

"THERE WAS ONCE a King of Cornwall, whose name was Marc, which in the ancient Cornish tongue means a horse—for which reason there was a story told of him that he had horse's ears. This was not true. He was a man like other men, and a warrior more than most." *Tristan and Iseult* by Rosemary Sutcliff

None of these words make sense to me when I first read *Tristan and Iseult* for Mr. Hanrahan's class. Where the fuck is Cornwall? It has to be somewhere in England or Great Britain because it seems like all these tragedies take place either in England or Greece, but at least the Greeks have cool goddesses like Athena and women like Medea who can actually take revenge.

"It's a romance, Lucha," Mr. Hanrahan says. "Girls like romances."

On the book's cover, there's a drawing of a red-haired woman and a black-haired man with a page-boy haircut. It looks like the haircut I had when I was about four years old. Both touch each other with open hands. Both characters look softly into each other's eyes. The cover doesn't look like those on Harlequin romances I see on the book racks at Thrifty's. Usually, the woman is looking up at a half-naked man with her mouth open and eyes closed. I'm a girl who likes boys. I guess I like romances. I did like the story of Cupid and Psyche because she actually completes her labors, just like Hercules. Of course, she always manages to get some help from Greek goddesses or some of the animals.

I start reading *Tristan and Iseult*, thinking maybe I can put myself in Iseult's shoes and Jorge in Tristan's. But after the first pages, I'm already done with the book. First of all, why would I be okay with being married off to some *viejo* twenty years older than me when the handsome Tristan is young, like me.

"That's how they did it back then, Lucha," Suki says. "Younger women were married off to older men."

"But why?"

"So, they could have like thirteen kids by the time the woman's thirty."

Gross! First of all, I wouldn't want that many kids. Actually, I don't want one. And second of all, gross! And this Tristan dude . . . Yeah, he's a babe and he can take on big opponents like that Irish knight Morholt but he let his true love marry his uncle. Double gross.

"Your *abuelo* was thirty when he married Merced, and she was fifteen," Tía Suki comments casually while dusting one of the big plaster *santos* on the shelf behind her.

I almost fall out of my chair. Grandma Merced's always flirting with younger men at El Yuma, the market or at Thrifty's, and her big love, Leandro, was five years younger.

"Don't act so shocked, Lucha," Tía Suki says. "That's how they do it in a lot of countries today, not just in medieval times."

"Why?" I finally ask.

Suki shrugs her shoulders. "I think it's because her family was poor."

In *Tristan and Iseult*, everybody is either a knight, a queen, a king or in Iseult's case, a princess. Nobody's poor, but the woman still can't choose, and even when she does, she still can't get the man she wants.

"That sucks the wad," I say. "Is that why Grandma left him? Because *abuelo* was old?"

Suki stoops to adjust the San Judas statue.

"She left him because she fell in love with Leandro."

❊❊❊

The first time, I feel like a fire burns me out, just the way a flame burns a candle wick. Or maybe I feel more like a match. Yes, it's more like a match, sizzling, hissing with heat and fire. And after it's over, I feel like a walking blister. Is this love?

"Sounds more like lust," Tía Suki says, smiling at me like I've discovered something.

"But I can't stop thinking about him."

"Oh, no," Tía Suki says, looking at me all sad. "Your first love."

Crap. Grandma Merced always says that love is just a crock of shit. *Pura mierda*, she says.

Tía Suki looks worried but all she says is, "Be careful."

Before I realize it, I say, "I'm so screwed."

Tía Suki tells me I'll be okay if I pay attention. That song by New Order starts playing in my head about being "Shot right through with a bolt of blue." It's about a love triangle, which is a terrible thing, if Tristan and Iseult are any clue. Maybe it's more "Out of the blue" because I never knew what love was or what it is. There are way too many confusing songs about it. I think about turning off my Walkman. The love songs now feel too real. Now, they seem to make sense.

The next day in algebra class, I try to see if I still feel the same. This time, it's not a bolt of blue but tiny bubbles popping in my chest when I see Jorge walking down the hallway. I open up my locker quickly and try to be all casual, pretend to dig through my books. Suddenly, my ponytail pulls back. It hurts.

"Pay attention," Tía Suki's words bounce around my head.

I really want to smile, but I don't want Jorge to get the wrong idea that it's okay to pull my hair, so I don't turn around. And he pulls again, a little harder.

"Hey," Jorge says. "Lucy."

I turn around and look him in the eye. Am I smiling? I think I am. Ugh. But I'm trying to pay attention.

"My name's not Lucy."

Jorge takes my hand. My fingers scrape against the dry scratchy part of his knuckles.

"I know," he says. "I just think you're too pretty for a name like Lucha."

What? I don't understand. I like "pretty," but what's wrong with my name? Is it ugly?

"If I call you Lucy, you can call me George."

The bell for the next class suddenly rings, and he can't hear me ask, "Why George?"

He pulls at my hand because he wants to go to class with me. With *me*. This time, I'm the match about to cause another blister.

❀❀❀

I fall in love with Jorge Ibarra when he makes me laugh over his stupid comments in algebra class and later when he asks me if he can copy my homework. He is a beauty, too, with thick, shiny brown hair, fair skin with a sprinkling of pimples. Like a chocolate cupcake so sweet and rich. He's not like the Mexican chocolate I find on my *abuela*'s shelves. Nah, he's white like milk and sugar mixed in together. He's like the "Golden Brown" song I heard on KROQ: Except I change the "she" into "he" when the lead singer croons about the girl running through his mind. I start doing that with all the love songs. My friend Gaby tells me the song is about heroin, not love, but I still love singing with it whenever I hear it on the radio. It's slow and sounds old and romantic, especially because of the harpsichords. Did Tristan and Iseult dance to harpsichords? My love makes me dizzy and nauseous some-times, especially when Jorge comes near me. I don't tell Grandma Merced or my mom about him because they're too excited about Norma and the yellow house to listen when I try to tell them I met a boy who doesn't make fun of my Coke-bottle glasses or big butt. Jorge pays attention. He likes me for my smarts, my sense of humor, my nice attitude. Not like my grandmother, who's always ordering me around, telling me, "Fix yourself up." I don't feel like it but I don't say it to her face. No, I'm still too wimpy for that. But as soon as my grandmother, my mom and Norma leave for El Yuma, I call up Jorge and tell him he better come over now if he wants to copy my algebra homework. My stomach flips when I see him on the white, hot sidewalk, walking his funny little jumpy walk, his brown feathered hair lifting up in the air. I wait for him to knock because I don't want to look all desperate.

"Hey," he says, smiling his wide smile like that cartoon shark I used to watch when I was a kid.

"Hey."

Like a *mensa*, I just stand there staring at him up close so I can see every hair on his upper lip. Instead of leaning down to kiss me like I'd hoped, he walks past me to the kitchen table, where I've set up my algebra books and homework.

"Is this it?" he asks, looking down at my notebook filled with equations I copied down from the blackboard in Mrs. Spadaro's class.

Then, while we both sit at the kitchen table, all alone, he pulls out a cigarette and lights it on the gas stove, just like my grandmother does.

On the radio, "Suddenly" by Olivia Newton-John and Cliff Richard, the most romantic love song ever, starts play-ing. Jorge's cigarette smells like the smoke that sometimes comes from behind the neighbor's garage and breaks the mood. Grandma Merced's angry face pulses through my haze. I know the risk: beating by water hose in the front yard. The pain doesn't scare me as much as the public humiliation,

but Jorge's worth every whack. When Jorge offers me the
joint, I think, "Jorge, I love you," and take a deep, smoky
drag.

Suddenly, the world feels soft, mushy like the inside of
sweet bread. I think about the magic love potion Tristan and
Iseult drank. Iseult felt her soul melting into Tristan's, and
vice versa. I melt into Jorge and suddenly we're kissing and
kissing, his beautiful lips opening mine, his warm smoky
tongue gliding over my teeth. I back away, giggling. He pulls
me in for more, but I can't stop giggling. Then I feel his hand
on my leg, and I stop and look deep into his light brown eyes.

"You got something to eat?" he asks.

I remember the *burritos de papa y chorizo* wrapped in
foil in the fridge. My grandmother bought them from the Al
and Bea's luncheonette on Beverly. I know she's been saving
them for her dinner, but Jorge needs to eat something. So, I
unwrap the foil, stick a burrito in the micro for a minute and
then give it to him. His lips and teeth sink into the soft, greasy
tortilla. I wish I was that chunk of burrito.

"Aren't you gonna eat with me."

Of course, I eat with him. He even feeds me like those
lovers in movies do. At least that's what I remember. I'm sure
Tristan fed Iseult too.

After he leaves with my homework, I open the window.
How quickly the day turns into night. Grandma Merced and
Mom will be back late from El Yuma to smell the love. I finally know passion and go to bed without even finishing up
my US History homework.

It's a deep sleep, until, through my dreams I hear yelling,
then slapping and "*¿Qué chingados?*" and "It's those neighbors, isn't it?"

I am fully awake when my grandmother starts pounding
on me.

"*Mira esos ojos.*"

Yes, Jorge had mentioned my bloodshot-eyes, and I had
seen "Up in Smoke" too many times to forget about the eyes.

Maybe the pot and love get to me, because before I know it, I open my big mouth and say, "*Es pasión.*"

My eyeballs crack red-looking straight into Grandma Merced's eyes. Of course, she slaps me so hard my molars cut into the side of my mouth. But tonight, even blood tastes like love. I'm not even pissed this time. Nobody can call Lucha Carrasco a wimp now. Not even my tough-ass grandmother, the *chingona* of the *chingonas*, who knows about love and how I have to bleed for it. Thanks to Aunt Norma, I know about Mom's homemade abortion. I know about "the recipe" my grandmother brewed over the stove one early morning for some neighbor girl, who was supposed to get married in a month. But of course, I keep my mouth shut. No choice.

"You wear me out," my grandmother says.

On the way to her bedroom, she calls my mother a *sinvergüenza* for having a worthless marijuana daughter who shows no respect.

Nothing and no one's gonna stop me. No way. No mothers, no grandmothers, no Coke-bottle glasses. Nothing and nobody. I have not only tasted love, I've smoked it down to a little *cucaracha*. I'm ready for the world. So, get out of the way. I put on the headphones and press play. Stevie Nicks sings "Edge of Seventeen" as the door slowly opens and my mom comes into my room and sits down at the edge of the bed. Blood fills my throat and mouth, but I keep singing.

❈❈❈

"Hey, TJ," I hear a girl yell from across the mall as Jorge and I sit near the fountain.

I pick her out from the crowd, her blonde hair gleaming under the sunlight that pours through the skylights running down the center of the mall's white ceiling. At first, I think she's just another white girl from Pasadena who took the wrong freeway. But no, she's actually Patty Landa, Yoli's best friend and a blonde Mexican from school who's trying to pass herself off as a *gabacha*.

"Nice pants, TJ," she says, jutting her chin at my red corduroys.

I hate these pants, and that's why I am searching through the sales rack at Wet Seal, the "it" place for jeans. Meanwhile, she wiggles the Guess label on her butt pocket.

"How did you know?" I say, smiling.

"Know what?" Patty asks, looking past me at Jorge.

"That I'm from TJ."

"You're not from TJ," Jorge says, laughing.

"She thinks I am," I say, like those *cholos* at schools do. "She thinks I'm from Tijuana."

"She looks like a *mayate*," Patty says. "All TJs look like *mayates*."

Jorge stops laughing the moment she says that terrible word the first time. Little does Patty know that Jorge is from TJ. Even though he's light-skinned like Patty, his brothers are dark like their father. He told me that when he goes back to visit, he always has to fight off, not only boys, but men who are bigger than him who make fun of his family. Even his own cousins and uncles are assholes about calling his brothers names because they are so dark they can be mistaken for Blacks.

"I'll show you a TJ, Patty," I say grabbing Patty's back pocket with its dumb Guess logo. The harder she pulls away, the stronger my grip. Finally, the pocket rips off, leaving a dark blue stain on her ass. I run out of the store and throw the raggedy piece of denim over the balcony.

Patty runs over to the balcony and looks down. I knew those were her only pair. And of course, I knew she paid about $50 for those jeans because I've seen them at the fancy jean store at the Pasadena mall. I wanted to push Patty over the railing. "TJ" means being poor. It means being dark like an *india*. Luckily, Jorge grips my arm and guides me to the "down" escalator. We head into the noisy darkness of Electric Planet.

"You are a TJ," Jorge whispers, brushing his lips along my ear until my skin is goose-bumped.

Yes, I really am a TJ. Patty did know.

❀❀❀

"Men never marry *putas*," Grandma Merced once told me. "They just fuck them, then leave. Sometimes, they pay."

All my life, I've been warned about being a *puta* by not only my grandmother but also by my mom. For them, *putas* are the epitome of a pitiful woman, a disgusting woman who not only lets men use her but does not have the sense to stop being a whore.

"And you better not dress like one either," Tía Norma chimes in. "Because those clothes will make you believe you're a *puta*."

I never meet a *puta* in real life until Grandma Merced points her out. I'm helping my grandmother close up El Yuma when she jerks her head at one of the women sitting at the end of the bar.

"*Esa vieja*," Merced whispers under her breath, "*es puta*."

I try not to stare, but in the big bar mirror behind Grandma, I see the woman in between the multicolored bottles that line the mirror. Her lined eyes remind me of Elizabeth Taylor's. For a moment, I think it's *the* movie star with her sprayed-up hair, dangly fake diamond earrings and dark eyebrows. A little streak of gray lines the part in her black hair. In the dull light of the bar, a little gold chain glows around her neck.

"How do you know?" I ask as quietly as possible.

"The owner told me," Grandma Merced answers without looking up from the glass she's drying.

The woman doesn't look like a *puta*, at least not the kind I see on TV or in the movies. They're always young, thin and stupid. This woman looks smart and more like someone's mother or aunt. She looks as old as my mom. It's now 2 a.m., and the bar is closing, but Elizabeth isn't budging. She just sits smoking, spinning her highball glass in between her palms. It glitters like a little star under the lightbulbs. Suddenly, the Donna Summer song "Sunset People" pops into my head.

That disco song is about *putas*. The song buzzes in my head as I sweep the floor around the bar. Outside, Boyle Heights is quiet. I'm so glad it's Sunday morning. No school today and, since Suki has moved in with her girlfriend, I can sleep in until I get up to make lunch for my grandmother and mother. I sweep around Elizabeth, who doesn't look up from her glass. A couple of guys from the *tortillería* across the street play their last pool game in the green glow of the lamp shade.

"Who are you waiting for?" Merced asks Elizabeth. "We're closing now."

Elizabeth looks up, her green eyes a little watery, her smooth skin flushed with alcohol. She lifts a finger, asking for one more moment to finish the last of her brandy.

"*Gracias*," she says, lifting herself off the torn vinyl stool. From her black handbag, she pulls out a bill and leaves it on the bar counter.

"Keep the change," she says, wobbling a little.

Merced sweeps up the bill, holds it close to her face.

"*Mira nomás*," she says. "She left a fifty."

"She must be doing pretty good," one of the pool players remarks.

"*Es la Reina de la Primera*," the other one says.

I always think of Grandma Merced as the queen of First Street. But she's really the queen of the bars. Elizabeth is the queen of the men.

"She's the favorite of the owner of the *tortillería*," Merced reveals with a smile.

I've seen the *tortillería* owner around with his wife and two kids. He never steps into the bar but does work late at the tortilla factory. Sometimes, I've seen the lights in his office when my grandmother and I walk back home.

"He's a hard worker," Grandma Merced scoffs. "He spends half his nights with *esa vieja*."

I notice the office lights again as we cross First and head down Indiana. According to my grandmother, Elizabeth lives close by in a house once owned by her own mother.

"It's a nice little house, but she has too many cats."

Maybe she was more a queen of the cats, because my mother later tells me that the owner threw her over for a younger woman, one of his own factory workers. Later that afternoon, as I lay in bed, half asleep, I hear my mother and grandmother talking after coffee.

"The wife's gonna find out," my mother says.

"She should blackmail him," my grandmother replies. "It's only fair. She spent the best years of her life with this guy."

A shattering crash makes me jump. I run into the kitchen to find my mother crying, her hand bleeding from a gash. She's cut herself on one of the clay cup shards.

"Are you still crying over that?" Grandma Merced huffs. "It's been over ten years."

"Ten years since what?" I ask, but they say nothing.

My mom stifles her sobs, shakes her head and puts a rag over hand.

CHAPTER 9
Backfire

Donaciano remembered well that last morning before Merced left him for good. She had gotten up early to fill the tin tub with hot water. Still in bed, he heard her walking back and forth between the stove and bathroom, hot water sloshing and dripping. Then he heard her splashing, washing herself with a bar of Ivory soap form his store. Merced was humming a melody from the radio, "*¿Cómo Fue?*" by Beny Moré. Usually, Merced just coughed and snorted while she washed herself. Donaciano's eyes opened. Now all the other little gestures made sense. Months before, searching for a clue to her coldness, Donaciano had found a tube of lipstick the color of blood in one of her drawers. Under a couple of *rebozos* in the armoire, he found a pair of red leather shoes with a "Made in the U.S.A." stamp just inside the heel.

"You know we can't afford these," Donaciano had told her, dangling the shoes just out of reach. "Take them back."

Merced's face curled into a frown. When she saw Alma and Suki staring at them from their bedroom door, she froze.

"Rufina gave them to me," Merced told him, the lie coming easily.

Before he knew it, Merced flew at him and ripped the shoes from his hand. She gripped them against her chest until her knuckles turned white.

Donaciano froze. It was obvious: Merced loved someone else. He raised his hand, ready to slap that love out of her. But this time, instead of crying or looking away, Merced offered up her face to him, her eyes black diamonds.

"You'll pay for this, *cabrona*," Donaciano threatened.

Merced closed her eyes and waited for the blow.

Finally, her husband dropped his arm. "You'll never see the girls again," he said. Merced opened her eyes and laughed. "They're better off here," she snapped. "I don't have time for them or for you."

"What kind of . . ."

"A tired one," Merced told him.

Before Donaciano could say another word, Merced slipped out the door into the bright-hot morning, red shoes dangling from her hand. He ran out after her.

Just then, Rufina's red Chevy rumbled to a stop in front of the house, it's passenger door wide open like a hungry mouth. Merced jumped in, and dust and exhaust clouds hid the backs of Merced's and Rufina's heads as they drove away. Donaciano coughed and turned back to the house, thinking about how he would tell his daughters that they would no longer have a mother.

❀❀❀

Donaciano never knew about Merced's secret lover in El Paso. That day, when he heard Rufina's red Chevy truck returning from Juárez, backfiring and bumping over El Sauz's main street, Donaciano knew Merced was never coming back to him. Still, he rushed out from his store to wave down Rufina.

"*¿Dónde 'stá?*" he asked her, the empty front seat between them.

Rufina pressed her lips in between her teeth until her mouth was just a line. She turned off the engine.

"*En El Paso,*" Rufina said, jerking her head toward the main road. "With some *fulano* she met at the Cuauhtémoc."

Donaciano knew that Rufina wouldn't tell him anything about this new man, so he did not bother to ask her. Donaciano should have followed them to El Paso that day. Or he should have pushed Rufina out of that truck and driven down the highway for that ungrateful *puta*. But why should he have to beg his own wife to come back, especially after he had given her everything? Why would a husband have to plead like some pilgrim praying to the Virgen for a favor?

By eight o'clock that night, all of El Sauz knew about Merced's desertion. When Jorge Negrete began singing *"Amor con Amor se Paga"* on the radio, Donaciano closed the store, walked to his house in the back and told his daughter Norma that she would have to take over all the cooking and cleaning.

"Your mother isn't coming back. She's in El Paso."

"Why's she in El Paso?" Norma asked, holding her ten-year-old sister Suki.

Alma looked up from her sewing. They stared at him as if he had driven Merced away.

"Por puta," Donaciano said, then walked into his bedroom and shut the door.

He stretched out over the bed and lay there until Norma knocked when dinner was ready. Donaciano went to the kitchen and sat at the table, silent. Just then, he heard a dog barking. Then a knock. It was Rufina, yelling through the door.

"Donaciano? Norma??" she yelled.

Donaciano swung the door open, nearly hitting himself. Rufina had changed into a freshly ironed white dress that glowed in the moonlight.

"What do you want?"

"I'm sorry about Merced," Rufina said, looking into the kitchen. "Can I help with the girls?"

"No," Donaciano whispered. "You've done enough."

He locked the door, then finished his dinner. He could hear his daughters sniffling as they cleared the table and

washed the dishes. All night, he heard them but felt paralyzed. Memories of Merced in the blue velvet dress she wore
on their wedding day haunted him. Pina had made that dress
for her, knowing that Donaciano liked pretty things. That was
the problem—Merced had been a very pretty thing at fifteen,
a María Félix look-alike but shorter, browner. The first time
she put her small rough hands in his, his heart had cracked.
Plutarco, Merced's father, died soon after their wedding, and
Tía Pina left El Sauz without a word. Cleófilas stayed behind
and married one of the local ranch hands. After fifteen years
of marriage, Merced was cold as stone whenever he came
near her.

❀❀❀

The more time Merced spent in El Paso, the more time
Donaciano spent attending to his store, looking over at the
wares he'd been able to accumulate with his money and time.
The cabinets were packed with bolts of cotton, calico, linen and,
sometimes for special occasions like weddings, satin and Irish
lace. For most of his customers in El Sauz, cotton and muslin
were just fine. Donaciano had made little curtains for his
shelves. Few people in the town knew he could sew. His
mother, Doña Margarita, had taught him when he was little,
after his father had abandoned them for Donaciano's governess.

Alongside his mother, Donaciano made dresses, pants,
sometimes suits. Soon, their small dress shop in Chihuahua
was making a small profit that allowed him to go to second-
ary school. Doña Margarita wanted him to be an accountant
or a lawyer, but Donaciano wanted to design dresses.

"No, no," his mother said. "You need a more manly job.
How else will you find a wife?"

Many of the "nice" young women in Chihuahua liked
him. He was tall, like his father, and light-skinned, like his
mother. His suits looked expensive, thanks to his sewing
skills. Still, as soon as the girls' parents learned about his father and the governess, the girls dropped him. One time, he

started flirting with his mother's young assistant, Pina, a girl from the small nearby town of El Sauz, but Doña Margarita quickly put an end to their little affair.

"Oh, no," she said. "No son of mine is marrying some dirty *india*."

"But you hired her," an exasperated Donaciano countered.

"I know," Doña Margarita answered. "She's good enough for sewing but not good enough for my family."

Donaciano's mother had come from a family of Spaniards who'd lost everything during the Mexican Revolution. But his mother still held onto the memory of a multi-roomed hacienda and servants for every chore.

"We used to own all the land east of Chihuahua, as far as the eye could see."

By then, she would be into her third or fourth glass of sherry, her head nodding. While she dozed, Donaciano would pull out a small book, a copy of *Madame Bovary*. For a bookmark, he used a mini bouquet of thick black hair strands held together by a thin black velvet ribbon. If Doña Margarita had known to whom the hair belonged, she would have thrown it into the fireplace. Donaciano would brush it against his lips as he read about the French bourgeois wife who drove her doctor husband to bankruptcy. Doña Margarita didn't approve of the subject matter but liked the idea of her son reading French literature, even if it was in translation. Once Margarita fell into a deep sleep, Donaciano would whisper into the black strands, "*Je t'aime, Pina. Je t'aime*."

❀❀❀

At her goddaughter's birthday, Doña Margarita chatted with Elena, Angélica's mother, and the other mothers of Chihuahua's eligible daughters. Their favorite topic: their children's ingratitude. Their second favorite topic: the unending search for experienced and reliable help. From the corner of her eye, Elena watched her Angélica dance with Donaciano.

"You're so lucky you found Pina," Elena said. "She sews like an angel. Did you see the dress she made for Angélica?"

Doña Margarita smiled stiffly. Although Pina had proved herself a skillful seamstress, she'd also had the audacity to make her son Donaciano fall in love with her. For months now, she saw them exchange looks whenever they thought she was out of the room. Today, she caught them kissing in the backroom of the dress shop. "*¡¿Qué hacen?!*" she had screamed.

Donaciano and Pina parted, nearly knocking over the dress forms. Doña Margarita clicked her tongue at Pina who quickly rushed out of the room.

"What do you think you're doing?"

"Nothing, Ma," Donaciano said in a low voice.

He held his arms behind his back, reminding her of his stubborn boyhood. Although he was six feet tall, his bowed head put her in the mind of a schoolboy caught red-handed at a prank.

Now on the dance floor, those same arms were flailing around like a rag doll tossed in a windstorm as Donaciano desperately tried to keep up with Angélica in some new American dance.

"*¿Qué bailan?*" Elena asked.

"I think it's called the 'Charleston,'" Doña Margarita offered.

Previously, she had caught Donaciano dancing in front of the three-way mirror at his shop. He had just seen the Charleston performed in one of those godless reels he so enjoyed watching at the penny arcade.

"You look like a monkey," she told him after she stopped laughing.

Donaciano panted a little, trying to catch his breath before answering his mother.

"It's from New York," he said. "I have to learn it for Angélica's birthday party."

Doña Margarita's eyes softened and her heart leaped with the hope that her stubborn son would propose to her god-daughter. But when she caught him kissing her seamstress, she nearly lost all hope. Donaciano's father had been the same. He had fallen in love with Donaciano's teacher and had run off to the capital with her, and Doña Margarita hadn't heard from him in years.

"Angélica truly admires your son," Elena said.

"He admires her too," Doña Margarita lied.

When they started dancing the foxtrot, Doña Margarita decided that the only thing for her to do would be to fire Pina. Maybe if he couldn't see her . . . but then she remembered her husband Augustín's mulishness.

"I love my dress," Angélica whispered in Donaciano's ear. "The appliqués are exquisite."

"Exquisite," Donaciano repeated, thinking of Pina's nimble fingers sewing the tiny stitches around the sequined flowers. He looked down at the cascading flower patterns twinkling under the chandeliers that lit up the ballroom. He smiled at their brilliance, at the gown's beauty and at the memory of Pina's kiss.

For a moment, Doña Margarita regained hope that her son would come to his senses. She pulled Elena toward one of the alcoves with a window overlooking the cathedral.

"Don't tell anybody," Doña Margarita whispered as she spread open her gloved fingers to hide her mouth from the others. "I think Donaciano is ready to propose."

"Are you sure?" Elena said through a shaky smile. "Angélica would love that."

As Doña Margarita nodded her head, her fist tightened and pressed into her palpitating heart.

On the dance floor, Donaciano bounced lightly on his feet, keeping time with the rhythm of the music, bobbing along with Angélica. He looked above her, staring into a space Doña Margarita knew was filled with Pina Fierro. When Angélica looked up at Donaciano, her eyes fluttered like butterflies, but Donaciano's mouth curved down. When she said something, he blinked as if he was waking from a dream.

"*Qué bueno*," Elena sighed. "Angélica has been in love with Donaciano since she was a little girl."

"I remember when she told me that she wanted to marry him," Doña Margarita said, her fingers fanning over her mouth. If her son heard about her marriage plans, she was sure he would do something stupid like elope or, even worse, impregnate Pina.

I'll kill him, she thought, scaring herself with the violence of her thoughts. She was starting to sound more like her father than her refined mother. *Ay Dios*, what would her parents think if their grandson married a *campesina*? Doña Margarita knew they would blame her.

When the orchestra struck up "Blue Danube," Donaciano led Angélica back to Elena, bowed and walked over to his mother.

"How about a dance with me, *hijo*?" Doña Margarita asked her son. His eyes widened but he bowed, led his mother to the dance floor and began a slow swirl around the floor.

"What did you talk about?" she asked, trying to keep herself focused on his face, a slight dizziness taking over.

"We just talked about her dress. She thinks it's exquisite," Donaciano said, smiling.

Doña Margarita knew what that smile meant: Pina.

"She loved the delicate stitches on the appliqués and the color," Donaciano continued. "It reminds her of jade, her favorite stone."

The dizziness was overwhelming her. She leaned into his ear. "You need to propose to her," she whispered loudly. "Tonight."

Donaciano stopped dancing. The rest of the swirling couples narrowly avoided the mother and son. Doña Margarita fanned herself and loudly announced she needed some air. She gripped her son's arm, leading him through one of the

French doors facing the back garden. The cool night air brought her to life. Donaciano slouched against a plastered wall, his eyes closed.

"Did you hear me?" Doña Margarita said.

"I don't love her," Donaciano answered.

"That doesn't matter."

I don't matter, Donaciano thought. *Only money matters.*

"You propose to her tonight, or I get rid of Pina," Doña Margarita threatened.

"You can't . . ." Donaciano stuttered.

Doña Margarita's stony face blocked his protests. He gave her a slight nod. He knew that he would have to propose that night so that his mother would leave him alone. He also knew he would have to tell Pina so that they could elope.

The next morning, he found Pina already at her sewing machine, creating the new dress he had fashioned just for her without her knowing. She smiled down at the bobbing needle as if it were singing to her with its clatter. She looked up at him, still smiling.

"I'm enchanted with this dress," Pina said, sounding like one of those party girls from the previous evening.

Donaciano swallowed, stood her up and told her about his engagement.

"*Pero* . . ." Pina started. "I thought . . ."

Donaciano held on to her hands as if to steady himself and her.

"If I didn't, then Mamá said she'd have to let you go."

Pina's mouth went flat, her lips disappearing into her face. Her eyes dulled, then blinked rapidly.

"So what!" she said, punching Donaciano in his gut with those bitter words.

"We can run away," he said. "We can leave for Chile or Argentina, or maybe Spain?"

Pina's forehead scrunched. "I don't want to run away, Donaciano," she finally said.

"Then what?"

"You can open a shop in El Sauz," Pina said. "I can work for you there."

"Then why not just marry me?"

Pina stepped closer to him until they were nearly nose to nose. "You know why," she said.

Pina's brother had ruined everything with his drunken ways. Plutarco had not only squandered his life but also the life of his family, with his drinking and womanizing. Because of him, Pina, Cleófilas and Merced had been reduced to *campesinas*. Now, Pina had to take care of Plutarco because she had promised her mother on her death bed to take care of not only her motherless nieces but also her feckless brother.

Donaciano stopped short of calling that pure stupidity. He didn't want to insult her mother's memory. But if Donaciano was willing to disobey Doña Margarita, why couldn't Pina disobey her mother or her brother? It seemed so simple to him.

"Will you marry me if I can convince Plutarco to let you go?" Donaciano asked, squeezing Pina's hand. He knew his mother would soon be at the shop.

Pina almost wavered but she knew that Plutarco would destroy himself and the girls if she didn't stay with him. She had seen the way he looked at his own daughter, who had just turned thirteen. Pina feared the look in Plutarco's eyes every time he opened the door to the room she shared with her nieces. When he started seeing La Panocha, the owner and madam of one of the biggest saloons in Chihuahua, Pina was relieved. At least he would leave her, Merced and Cleófilas alone.

Pina squeezed her eyes tight as if she was making a wish and nodded, hoping she could free herself to marry Donaciano.

Donaciano looked up at the white plastered ceiling, at the unlit lamp with its glass shade, at the crack that snaked from the center of the ceiling to the wall opposite him. He remembered the money his grandmother had left him, the money his mother kept in a safe in the main house. It would be enough not only for a little store in El Sauz but also a house behind it.

❀❀❀

Angélica looked confused, even after Doña Margarita told her that Donaciano had fallen in love with a poor *india*.

"The seamstress?" Angélica asked. "But she's darker than the devil!"

"She must have cast a spell on him," Angélica's mother Elena declared. "She must be a witch."

Elena's maid, a Rarámuri girl dressed in a starched apron and a black dress, set a porcelain teapot and cups on the table. She was no more than ten years old. For a moment, Doña Margarita pitied the thin, small girl, then as soon as the girl left, she forgot her until she returned with the little cakes and sandwiches.

"She's very good," Elena whispered. "But she's too pretty. We may have to get rid of her soon."

"Get rid of her now," Angélica said, nearly hysterical. "I hate these *inditas*. All of them."

"Enough, *m'ija*," Elena said, bent over her sobbing daughter, smoothing her hair and wiping her tears with a linen handkerchief. "They're not all alike."

"Yes, yes, they are," Doña Margarita said. "Listen to your daughter. Hire one of those Mennonite girls instead."

"How could he?" Angélica kept repeating. "Donaciano is so respectable."

When the young maid came back to the parlor to retrieve the teacups, Angélica would not look at her. The girl smiled at the stony faces, as she had been taught, then quietly left.

"She mocks us," Angélica said, twisting the pearl necklace at her throat until it formed a tight knot.

Elena sat closer to Doña Margarita. "Can't you talk to Donaciano?" she whispered. "Maybe if you told him about Angélica."

Doña Margarita knew her stubborn son would never change his mind. He was besotted with Pina. Nothing could break her hold over him unless he fell in love with someone else. Angélica was not the one.

Tired of the tears and whispers, Doña Margarita rose from the sofa. Elena walked her to the door, held open by the little maid.

"I'll see what I can do," she told her *comadre*. "But Donaciano's stubborn."

Elena took her friend's hand. "*Mil gracias, comadre*," she said. "Do what you can."

❀❀❀

Three years after his mother died, Donaciano sold the dress shop in Chihuahua and tracked down Pina to El Sauz, where he decided to open up his own little store. By that time, she was no longer the fresh, young girl with whom he had fallen in love. Donaciano did not recognize the young woman who used to show up to his dress shop in Chihuahua with hair pulled neatly into a tight bun and wearing a clean, pressed dress. Now, the sunburned woman who stepped into his shop wore her hair in a disheveled braid and dressed in a clean but faded cotton dress.

"Pina?"

The woman looked up from the barrels of rice and beans that sat close to the store's doors. She looked up as if waking from a dream.

"Donaciano? What are you doing here? Is this your store?"

Donaciano's heart pounded. Her ring finger was bare, although he knew that many husbands in the town could not afford a ring.

"*El destino manda*," Pina said flatly, using Doña Margarita's favorite phrase to indicate irrevocable destiny.

Her widowed brother still refused to consent to her marriage, she later told him.

Donaciano was enraged but staid even after she proposed he marry her niece.

❁❁❁

Merced grew up in a section of El Sauz where there were no cafés, no theaters, nothing to do after church except walk around the metal gazebo that stood in the middle of the plaza. Girls clockwise, boys counterclockwise. From his little store, Donaciano would observe her. He had also seen her at the outdoor movie with all the other *sauzeños*. One time, when she had visited his store with Pina to buy a sack of flour, she had asked him what he was reading. Pina turned away, pained.

"The Sports section," he said looking from the newspaper to her brown, pimpled face.

At first, he thought she was blushing, but her face actually burned red from having harvested her father's *chiles* and yams that morning.

"What does this say?" she asked, pointing to the headline.

That's when Donaciano knew she had never been to school. Even Pina had learned to read a little at the local school.

That night at the makeshift, outdoor movie, Donaciano noticed Merced's passion for the protagonist of the film "*Santa*," who longed for her soldier Marcelino. Santa was bitter after having lost all of her lovers and friends, except for Hipólito, the faithful blind piano player at her brothel. Merced was captivated by Santa's desire, her hunger.

That kind of hunger was not there in Merced the day Donaciano told her he wanted to marry her, but he would eventually see her bitterness after a decade and half of marriage and children.

❁❁❁

Merced feared her father's hands with their jagged fingernails and hardened knuckles. When they gripped a little clay cup of *pulque*, she knew it would not be long before those hands would be on her. At night, when the house was dark and quiet, she would sometimes wake up to her aunt Pina's hands glowing in the gold candlelight, a gleaming sliver of a needle between slender fingers jabbing away at a soft, almost faded blue cloth. The soft scrape of cloth and skin would lull Merced back to sleep.

In the morning before Plutarco awoke grunting for his breakfast, Pina's hands would be rolling and slapping the dough for flour tortillas on the wooden table until they flattened into perfect circles. Merced and her sister Cleófilas, half asleep but dressed, would put on their aprons and start making the *té de canela* and setting the clay dishes out for their father, who would get up as soon as he smelled the chorizo frying in the skillet.

Merced would shove more wood into the iron stove to bring the clay pot to a boil and then throw in sticks of cinnamon. The woody spice would fill the kitchen, pushing the women into finishing the morning preparations.

For special days, Merced would grind coffee beans. She would bend down and bring out the small but heavy grinder and fill it with the dark, roasted beans. She'd then grip the crank and pull it around until the beans were finely ground and then pour them into the boiling water.

"What a beautiful aroma," Cleófilas would usually say, taking a deep breath before tearing the chorizo apart to be fried.

"The best smell in world," Pina would invariably respond. "Next to the rain."

Once the coffee was brewed, they'd sit and enjoy a cup before Plutarco got up and disturbed their moment of peace.

As soon as the chorizo started sizzling, Pina and Cleófilas would steel themselves for Plutarco's entrance.

❀❀❀

The morning she finished Merced's dress, Pina dressed her up like a doll. From the plaited ribbons in her hair to the clean leather shoes on her feet, Merced's transformation from a farm girl to a woman seemed complete. Merced hated it.

"Why do I have to dress up to go to his store? It's stupid," Merced grumbled as Pina smoothed out her hair with the brilliantine she kept hidden in her cosmetic box.

"Just put on those shoes. You need to look nice."

"For what?"

"Never mind for what. You'll thank me later."

When she stepped back, Pina realized that her niece was closer to womanhood than she had thought. The soft blue cotton dress she had been secretly taking in for weeks draped Merced's body like the dress form at Doña Margarita's studio. With its puffed sleeves accented with white piping, the dress retained the semblance of the school uniform Pina rescued from the waste can behind the Carrasco house. At night, while her nieces slept and her brother drank at La Panocha's, Pina cut open eyeholes in the fabric for a lace-up front, which would hook into an eye at the top. One day, on seeing a young woman stepping off the bus from Chihuahua, a tiny breast pocket on the top right of the woman's tan dress caught her eye. A miniature silk square peeked above the seam. Along with the puffed short sleeves, Pina noted the pocket for her sewing later that night.

"Do you ever sleep, Tía?" Cleófilas asked her one time while working on the dress at the kitchen table.

Pina rubbed her eyes and shook her head. "I'm like those cats out at night," she laughed. "*Nunca duermo*."

"But even the cats sleep during the day."

Pina yawned and blew out the candle burning on the kitchen table.

On the night before she had completed Merced's dress, Pina opened her door and saw Merced expose her breasts to her brother. She saw him hand his own daughter a clattering tin box of coins. Pina closed her eyes and held her breath, then stepped back into her bedroom. She opened the linen curtains to the full moon's light and saw Merced run out through the back door. Pina returned to the kitchen and her sewing. She nipped the dress' waist with a wide waistband and sewed gathers around the bust. Quickly, she cut and trimmed the buttonhole for a button back at the waist. To better accentuate Merced's shape, she added two rows of decorative red buttons down the hips.

❁❁❁

"Why are you doing this, Pina?"

Donaciano couldn't understand Pina's plan. Why would he ever want to marry someone he didn't love, when the woman he wanted could just say yes, were it not for that stupid promise she had made to her mother.

"You don't know Plutarco," Pina said as a way to explain her bizarre plan.

"I know we don't have to stay here."

Donaciano reached over the counter for Pina's limp hand and placed it over his mouth. With closed eyes, he kissed the calloused palm and fingers. The store was empty and cool, and in shadows. Outside, the breeze blew through a napping El Sauz. For a moment, Pina saw herself in Manzanillo with Donaciano, the waves breaking over and over to the rhythm of her heart. Their breathing was the only sound until Donaciano moved, jingling the coins in his pocket. Instantly, last night's image of Plutarco and Merced jolted Pina.

"He'll destroy them," Pina said, jerking away her hand.

Pina's black eyes seemed to grow larger with each word that Donaciano could barely grasp.

"You have to marry Merced. It's the only way."

Donaciano wanted to refuse, wanted to call her idea incredibly stupid or worse, an abomination of love. He knew running away wouldn't change her mind. Her promise to her dying mother held her like a leash in her brother's grip. Just like Doña Margarita's had held him.

The day Donaciano asked Plutarco for Merced's hand, Pina's heart broke. Donaciano had gotten up early one Sunday morning to bathe, iron his clothes and shine his shoes. He had even bought a new fedora for the occasion. He knew Merced, Cleófilas and Pina would be at the church. As he walked the long dirt road through the village, the white-washed houses glowed beneath the hot Chihuahuan sun. Plutarco sat outside his house, smoking, a floral-print cloth wrapped around his head, covering his left eye.

Plutarco raised an eyebrow after Donaciano asked him for Merced. "*¿Y por qué?*" Plutarco asked, puffing deeply on his hand-rolled cigarette.

"She's very pleasant," Donaciano put forth gingerly.

"Ugh, she's such a bitch," Plutarco said, then took another deep drag.

"Really?"

Plutarco covered his eye, then looked away from Donaciano's puzzled face. "Just because I wouldn't let her see some *pinche* movie, she threw lye in my face."

Donaciano remembered that night well. It was the night the itinerant movie company had featured *Santa*. It was the night he first saw Merced in all her young prettiness. As the movie flowed from the innocent romantic exploits of Santa and her soldier boyfriend to the inevitable seduction, some of the older and married women left. Instead of dying of shame and poverty, Santa becomes a celebrated prostitute. In the end, she dies of cancer. Donaciano should have known then: What kind of a decent woman admires a prostitute? But then again, even he couldn't resist the fantasy of a courtesan with a heart of gold. Some of the younger women were dragged away from their seats by their sisters, aunts and mothers, but most of the men stayed.

After their wedding night, Donaciano learned that Merced had thrown the lye on Plutarco's face to stop him from watching her as she bathed.

❀❀❀

When Merced asked Donaciano for the velvet bolt, he laughed.

"White cotton would be better," he said, tapping her nose with his forefinger. "You'll be roasting in the summer heat."

Merced wanted a glamorous dress that felt rich, just like the dresses that María Félix wore in *Doña Diabla*.

"Don't be silly," Pina said. "You'll burn up in that material."

But Merced had to have the blue velvet, no matter the heat. And she wanted it long enough to cover her old *huaraches*, because she couldn't afford heels, which she'd have to buy in Chihuahua. The thought of walking into a fancy department store in her old clothes and shoes made her almost cry. If the dress was long, maybe no one would notice. Of course, everyone did.

On a warm July morning, in the small church in El Sauz, Merced's family gathered to see Plutarco's daughter marry the town's richest man.

As Plutarco walked her down the aisle, votive candles twinkled in the dark corners while late morning light streamed through the purple stained glass. Instead of a cool spongy cloud, the velvet felt more like warm fur to Merced. As she stood next to Donaciano, the wedding lasso snug against her left shoulder, she nearly fainted.

It felt like it had happened yesterday, but it had happened fifteen years ago.

"What are you thinking?" Rufina asked Merced.

"About my wedding," she said, still staring at her ring. "It was so hot that day."

"I remember."

"*Ay*," Merced blurted out, "what an idiot. Both of us, idiots."

Merced laughed as she threw something into a field full of grass and grazing cows.

"*¿Por qué?*" Rufina asked. "You could have sold that ring."

Merced shrugged. "Water under the bridge," she sighed and changed the subject. "Let's stop at Ahumada for cigarettes."

"I don't smoke," Rufina said, shaking her head. "It makes everything stink."

Merced rolled her eyes. "How about gas? You need gas, don't you?"

The fuel needle pointed close to the "E" on the dial. Rufina leaned in, squinting hard. "*Hijo de la chingada*," Rufina growled. "How much money do you have?"

"I won't have any money until we sell those *chiles*," She said, flicking her head to the truck's bed.

She took Rufina's hand and pressed her wedding ring into her friend's palm. "Take this."

"*¡Cabrona!*" Rufina laughed. "You really had me fooled."

Merced laughed at the blue Chihuahuan sky, empty except for its white bright sun.

Rufina tilted her head toward her. "What about your girls?" she asked, gripping the vibrating steering wheel.

"They'll be fine," Merced sighed. "They'll be fine."

To calm herself, Merced pulled out the black leather clutch Leandro had bought for her on their first date. She opened it slowly, caressing its edges. When she found the red lipstick, she noticed the silver band around the top of the tube. It reminded her of her wedding ring.

When Donaciano had slipped that ring on her finger, it had felt so big, she thought it would fly off as soon as she slammed the wash against the rocks by the river or broke a chicken's neck on the giant stone outside the house. But it never did. Instead, it tightened over the years of marriage, especially after she gave birth to her daughters. She remembered the date of their marriage, *27 de julio de 1935*, engraved inside. That was how she knew how to read the word *julio*.

The heat of her wedding day came back to her. The small, gloomy church lit up with votive candles. Her father quickly walking her down the aisle. Even her aunt Pina, the woman who had made Merced do laundry ever since she was five years old, had soaked, sewn and gently brushed dry her wedding dress, the long-sleeved blue velvet gown. Merced had never seen such a blue. Like a thief, in Donaciano's store, Merced had quickly checked to see if anyone was watching her. The early morning rush of customers was gone and Donaciano was in the back room working on his accounts. She leaned into the bolt, rubbing her cheek against the plush cloth. It felt just like a cloud, or what she imagined a cloud would feel like, spongy and cool. It smelled like the warm cotton balls growing in the neighbor's fields. It smelled like freedom.

❀❀❀

Merced first saw the couple in the Catedral del Sagrado Corazon in Chihuahua City. They were newly engaged, she could tell, and coming to see the priest about getting married. The girl wore an engagement ring with a diamond, not too big but not too small. In her other hand, she held a small bouquet of red roses. As the couple knelt down in front of la Virgen de Guadalupe, Merced heard the young woman ask the *Virgencita* for Her blessing.

Yes, Merced thought, *you will need it.*

Merced had just divorced Donaciano. In the process, her lover Leandro, who had promised to marry her in this very church, had left for Los Angeles.

"We'll marry in October, when it cools down," he had told her, squeezing her hand.

Merced was aware that a divorced woman could not get married in a Catholic church.

"How will they know?" Leandro asked.

They wouldn't, not her father, not the priest nor Donaciano. One day, they both went to the church office and asked about getting married in October. The secretary, a young blonde woman, looked them over.

"The charge is twenty-five dollars," the secretary said, writing down their names in a square for the month of October on a hanging calendar.

Merced knew that Leandro did not have the money.

"I have ten," he told the secretary, who stopped smiling, then erased their names.

Merced looked down at her feet. She was too embarrassed to look into the secretary's eyes.

"Don't worry," Leandro said. "I have a plan."

Otro *pinche* plan. These plans usually cost her pesos or pain. This time, she knew it would be the later. As they walked down the church steps, she saw a squirrel scurry up a tree. Its mouth bulged with an acorn. Winter was coming, and the squirrel was getting ready for cold and hunger. Merced shivered.

"How about a ring?" Merced asked about the gold ring he had promised.

"*Mira*," he said, "I heard about some jobs in Los Angeles. The shipyards need men like me."

Leandro had heard about the shipyards from Rufina's brother Moti. He had worked with him at a car dealership. Moti and Leandro bonded over their hatred for their *gabacho* boss, who never paid on time or underpaid them. Moti had hopped on a train to California, an empty freight with dozens of other veterans after the war. There was a need for men, now that the war was over and women had to go back to cooking and cleaning.

"I'll get the money in no time," he said.

That had been a year before. Rufina had heard from Moti that Leandro had taken up with a Mexican-American woman from Los Angeles.

As Merced watched the couple rise from the kneeler in front of the Virgen, Merced squeezed the beads on her rosary. This was her punishment for sinning against the Church and against Donaciano. Now she had to suffer.

The couple placed the bouquet of roses at the feet of the *virgen*. The girl crossed herself and looked down at her clasped hands. *She's looking at her ring*, Merced thought with a twinge. While the girl prayed, the fiancé looked around. When Merced caught his eye, he smiled at her. Merced's heart shrank. The girl missed that look. Merced flashed her eyes at him, pulled her *rebozo* tight around her head and shoulders. She knelt down clutching her rosary, pressing them to her head.

"*¿Por qué? ¿Por qué?*" Merced whispered.

She knew why. Leandro had found another woman. She swallowed hard, then looked up at the altar. The couple had disappeared. Merced pressed her head to the top of the wooden pew in front of her but wouldn't let herself cry.

"No!" she said.

The whisper bounced off the walls of the church. Some of the other women who had come for morning Mass looked back at her. Quickly, Merced got up and started walking toward the aisle. Before genuflecting, she looked over at the portrait of the *virgencita*, her face bent down toward the bouquet, her eyes sad but the shadow of her mouth tilted up into a smile. Suddenly, she saw the face of the man who had smiled at her. Instead of kneeling and crossing herself, she walked straight down the aisle, past the holy water. The sunlight almost blinded her as she pushed through the cathedral's wooden doors.

CHAPTER 10
Atchinson, Topeka and Santa Fe

It didn't take much for Leandro to leave Merced. He had
to get out of El Paso, had to follow that trail of men chasing
the Atchison, Topeka and Santa Fe. It was easy. He just had
to wait in the night with the others, by the railroad tracks near
the outskirts, near the factories where the trains unloaded
their cargo. Most of the men were really boys, some barely
thirteen, but others, like Leandro, were fully grown.

"You have to run real fast and, once you get on, you have
to help the others get on," Rutilio, a bartender from the Dome
Bar, told him.

"But what if he's too slow?" Leandro whispered.

"Then let him go."

When the bright light of the engine came down the tracks,
it slowly pulled out of the train yard, gaining speed little by
little. Leandro and the others crouched, ready to run. As soon
as the engine passed them, he knew the train would speed up
quickly. They ran beside the freight cars, looking for wide
open doors. Otherwise, if partially opened, the doors would
slam on their fingers. The first car was shut tight, the second
was wide open but there was no one to help the men hop on.
Leandro kept running until he heard Moti yell and get pulled
into the car behind him. As the car pulled up beside Leandro,
he grabbed it, running faster than he ever had. He leaped but

could not get in. Instead, he dragged a little before falling back onto the gravel. He felt his ribs crack as he watched the caboose stream out of El Paso.

"How in the hell did this happen?" Merced asked as she taped Leandro up after his failed effort.

"I was trying to throw out some *borracho cabrón* from the bar," he said, wincing at the pain.

She bought the lie but then she saw a postcard from Moti mailed to Leandro from a city far from El Paso. Even though she could only read Moti's and Leandro's names, she knew it was important. She could tell from the photo of the shipyards that he would be leaving soon.

"Why?" Merced asked as she placed the postcard on Leandro's chest.

"Why what?" Leandro said. "I need a better job than bartending at some *gringo* hotel where all my tips go to the white bartenders."

"But, what about . . ." Merced stopped.

Leandro knew that Merced wanted to ask, "What about me?"

What about her? It was not that he wasn't grateful for her. She had dumped her old man in El Sauz to live with him in El Paso. But he had to live his life, too. He wasn't ready to settle down for one woman, even if she did look like María Félix. Merced was ready to lay down her life for him, but he wasn't ready for that. He was only twenty years old and had his entire life ahead of him.

It would be six more months before Leandro tried freight-hopping again. By that time, Merced had brought her daughters from El Sauz to help her earn more money. She had her oldest, Norma, working the Juárez hotels and Alma doing housekeeping at the El Paso del Norte and La Plaza, the fanciest hotels in El Paso.

One day, while Leandro was enjoying a bowl of Merced's *pozole* in their small kitchen, she laid a thick envelope with his name scrawled on top of it. It looked like a child had written it.

"For the rent," Merced whispered, kissing the tip of his ear. "I need to pay you for the last six months."

The bills of fives and tens added up to three hundred dollars, flat.

"My daughters and me . . ." Merced continued as she took his bowl and ladled in more *pozole* from the clay pot. "*Mis hijas y yo* are making more than enough, so you don't need to go."

Leandro winced as he shoved the envelope into his pocket. That night, he knew he had to leave.

CHAPTER 11
Angry Blood

When the red-headed housekeeper from Mexico City came around to inspect the floors, Merced didn't blink. Did the *chilanga* think this was Merced's first time training a new hotel worker? She'd done it many times before. The only difference was that this time she was training her daughter Alma.

Under the *chilanga*'s watch, Merced showed Alma the best way to wipe down the toilet with the rags La Plaza had given her as part of her cleaning equipment. She polished the heavy imported furniture with circular hand motions, slowly vacuumed the thick wool carpet, maneuvering the brush-topped hose into the dark corners and dusted the silk lampshades by hand.

"Careful," Merced warned. "Supposedly, this furniture is from Italy, so you have to treat it like a baby."

Alma's rag slowly wiped the top of the deeply carved desk, then the porcelain base of the lamp. Her hands shook so hard she nearly dropped it.

One by one, Merced shared all of the standard rules for La Plaza's housekeeping, plus a few of her own. All the while, Alma nodded and blinked as the *chilanga* watched her with those glassy eyes of hers, wary that Merced would give her daughter special treatment. As soon as the *chilanga* left, Merced got down to the real job: whoring.

"You think I got these nice tips just for just making beds?" Merced snorted. "You think these *desgraciados* ask for me because I'm so good at cleaning toilets?"

Alma's eyes grew wide, but she did not blush. The full blush would come some weeks later when Merced would lay down the rules of hustling, along with a glass of Presidente brandy and the room number of a waiting john.

For now, Merced kept it simple. Fold the top sheet underneath the mattress tight and smooth. No wrinkles, no creases. Those will come later when the couple who rents the room has sex. Or maybe when one of those Fort Bliss soldiers with a weekend pass comes through with one of the *cabareteras*. All along, Merced didn't mention how her eldest daughter Norma helped support the family with her job at the Tivoli cabaret in downtown Juárez. Norma spoke only of the soldiers and their whores, groping and whispering in the halls of La Plaza before slipping inside the rooms. It didn't matter now that the war was over, had been over for five years; these Bliss men had more money than ever and they spent it all at La Plaza.

Alma blinked, taking it all in as her mother rambled on.

After the training period ended, Alma worked on her own, and one day simply rolled into the next for Merced. Beds, beds all day long. So what if the hotel was installing these new contraptions, "televisions," or whatever they were called, in the penthouse suites? So what if people like the mayor of Juárez or the governor of Texas stayed there, supposedly the finest hotel in El Paso. They were all the same.

"Pigs," Merced whispered to herself as her wet hair dripped onto her rag of a uniform.

She stripped the soft cotton sheets from the bed, and a used condom fell on her rubber-soled shoe.

"*Pinche* john," she whispered. "Whore," she said as she wiped the mirror above the dressing table and finger-combed her wet hair. She barely had three minutes to wash her crotch and *culo*, but that was time enough to fog up all the mirrors in the penthouse suite.

Merced emptied the wastepaper basket quickly and rushed into the marble-floored bathroom. It was bigger than her apartment in the Segundo Barrio. She inspected the room quickly. Water puddled near the clawfoot tub, and the canvas shower curtain was a little ripped at the brass rings, but that wasn't her doing. Only God knew what else grew in the deep scratches. Merced sucked her teeth in disgust, remembering she had put her feet down on that piece of porcelain just minutes before. She would have to scrub her body raw when she got home, then powder her toes with the athlete's foot remedy Leandro had left behind three years ago. Merced quickly wiped down the bathroom mirror, and her plump arm flapped like a little wing.

She looked at the clock. In four minutes she had to meet Alma at the service elevator. She rushed to powder the tub with Ajax and wipe it down. High class hotel my *nalgas*. The white powder ate away at her hands, making them itchy and stink of chlorine. After so many years as a chambermaid at the hotel, all she had to show for it were cracked, bloody hands and a heart as empty as the money jar Leandro had left in the middle of the wooden floor of their tiny apartment when he fled down Highway 80 toward California. All the neatly rolled American bills in the mason jar had disappeared into his pocket. What a *pendeja* she had been for telling him about her dream for a house, a home of their own. Even stupider was revealing the jar's hiding place. All the hard-earned savings from her paychecks at La Plaza were gone, and with them her dreams of a home of her own in the Sunset neighborhood.

❊❊❊

With just a half-day to make up six floors of rooms, Merced and Alma had to push their loaded carts hurriedly down the narrow hallways and in and out of the service elevators. Sometimes, to get her mind off her blistering feet, Merced would pretend she was one of the high-priced whores she'd seen sitting on the bar stools or stretching out their silk-stockinged legs in the windows of the cabaret she passed by on the way to the Mercado Cuauhtémoc, their shiny high heels and peroxide-blonde hair glowing in the sunlight. Juárez women had a name for that color: *Juareña* Gold. It was a harsh, yellow-orange color, but Merced wanted it for her own hair, even if it meant being called a whore herself. *Why not?* she thought, smoothing out her thick black hair. These days she practically was one. Already she'd made $10 fucking an old man who was a regular at the hotel.

"There's my little spitfire," the old *sinvergüenza* had told her, pulling her into room 303. "My little María. *Qué bonita.*"

Merced rolled her eyes at his reference to María Félix. She'd heard it many times before, once even from Leandro when they first met at the Mercado Cuauhtémoc when ahe was selling her *chiles*.

❀❀❀

Carefully, Merced stripped off her uniform and hung it over a chair. The *chilanga* would kill her if she saw her working in a wrinkled or ripped dress. Worse, she would probably dock her pay just to have the uniform pressed, just like that one time she docked Javi after his mother forgot to iron his fancy suit covered with brass buttons and satin trim.

Luckily for her and Alma, they wore the same brown-gold potato sack with plastic buttons every day. Merced looked over at her flat uniform as the old man split her legs open and entered her. Of course, fucking the old man was nothing like when she was with Leandro. For him, she took her time, caressing his face, kissing him. How she loved to look into his eyes and trace the outline of his lips, stopping at the mole dancing above his upper lip. Afterwards, if there was time, she would re-fry some beans with the leftover bacon grease and make him some fresh flour tortillas with lard.

"Just like my grandmother's," he would say, sopping up the last of the beans with a fluffy, warm tortilla. And then Leandro would laugh and talk about Los Angeles.

"Everybody from El Paso is going there. There's work in the shipyards. I'll go ahead and as soon as I find a place in East LA, I'll send for you and the girls."

Leandro never sent word or money. Merced had to come up with a way to support her daughters on her own. She considered herself lucky to have met a young soldier about five years ago, a Bliss man hungry for love. And then it came to her one day as she worked her rags and cursed under her breath, if she could make ten dollars in a morning off these rich *gringos*, then her two oldest daughters could make as much as fifty a night.

"C'mon, you can do it," she told them one morning while they each ate the last of the beans and tortillas in the cold kitchen. Suki had already left for school. "You're big girls now, *grandototas*."

"*Ay,* Mamá," Norma started, "it's too early for this."

When Merced narrowed her eyes and stepped toward her, Norma shut up.

"You're not even pulling in half of what you're worth in the cabaret," whispered Merced as she served beans out of the pot into Alma's bowl. "With the war over, lots of those *soldados* have a lot of money saved up. You should sleep so you can look fresh for them tonight."

Norma blinked her mascara-smeared eyes. "I'm too hungry to sleep."

Before Norma could dip her spoon into her bowl, Merced had emptied the last of the beans into it.

"*Cómetelos,*" Merced ordered. "You're going to need your energy today."

Norma nodded. The smell of cigarettes and beer danced around her as she shook her thick golden hair, trying to wake up a little.

"Today you'll need the brandy, too." Merced sighed as she opened a cupboard and pulled out a half-filled pint bottle of brandy. "El Presidente has to come, too."

"*¿Por qué?*" Alma asked as she looked at Norma, but her sister had covered her eyes with her hands.

Merced cursed Leandro again under her breath and motioned for her daughters to eat.

❀❀❀

With the *rebozo* tightly wrapped around her shoulders, Merced walked to the hotel with Alma. The shawl was a gift from Leandro during their first year in El Paso. She pulled it tighter across her shoulders and thought about the ones she had left back home with Donaciano. In the distance, the Franklin Mountains glowed in the pink dawn. It wouldn't be long before snow covered them in thick blankets. She needed a coat. And so did the girls. They needed so many things. And now there was a way to get them.

Merced had experience selling sex. She was thankful to the first Bliss soldier who had initiated her. After the tenth john, it wasn't so bad anymore. Today, Alma would learn. Today would be her first day earning real money, just like she and Norma. As soon as they reached the La Plaza's supply room, Merced and Alma began loading their carts. The *chilanga* stood by, eyeing them while mentally counting the cleaning supplies. They headed to the elevator and saw one of the bellhops, Javi, carrying heavy leather-bound suitcases behind a pair of men in thick long coats. They nodded a greeting to each other before he went through the revolving doors. As the elevator pulled Merced and Alma up to the fifth floor, Merced shut her eyes and remembered what she had learned during the last five years.

First, you ask for the money right up front or the *cabrón* could take off on you. Second, make sure he takes off all of his clothes first, just to check he isn't armed. Third, don't eat or drink anything he offers you. You never know when these

men will try to poison or drug you. You have to be safe.
Fourth, the moment he's done, you put your clothes on right
away, shower and clean the bathroom. That's the only time
you can do this because later on, as you clean more hotel
rooms and maybe fuck more men, you want to be a little fresh
but don't want your skin to get all dried out with rashes. For
the past five years, Merced had repeated these rules like a
prayer every day. She shared this prayer with her daughter as
they walked down the carpeted hallway to their next rooms.
Alma just nodded her head and stared at her feet.

"And ask them for twenty dollars, *m'ija*," Merced said.
"You're young enough, you can ask for more. How old are
you telling them?"

"Eighteen."

"Tell them sixteen. These *descarados* want to feel like
they're young studs again."

Merced could tell her daughter was biting the inside of
her cheeks.

"And you better not cry," Merced said. "That'll scare
them away."

Merced took out the brandy and twisted the cap off. Even
after a week, it was still strong. "Take two long gulps," she
instructed her daughter. On such a skinny girl, Merced knew
the alcohol worked much quicker.

Alma did not spit it out the way Norma had the first time
she received a shot of her mother's brandy. Maybe Alma already drank on the side, sneaking after hours into the hotel's
fancy Dome Bar, like Merced did sometimes. Maybe Norma
had already warned Alma. Whatever it was, Merced was glad.
It made her life easier, having at least one daughter who liked
to drink.

"*Y no te rajes*," Merced warned her. "If I hear any
screams and he's not killing you, I'll make you wish you
weren't born."

Merced looked at her daughter's face and saw her ex-husband Donaciano's black eyes. *Ese cabrón*. He had to pay for

sticking her with these ingrate children. He was the one who wanted the children in the first place, not her. But what did she know? Merced had only been fifteen when she married him. They had lived in a proper house in El Sauz, right across from the town plaza, and he had wanted a family of sons to fill it. But the son wouldn't come. God just cursed her and her old husband with two daughters. *Ni modo*.

"One day we'll leave El Paso," Merced promised Alma. "As soon as we get enough money to buy a house."

Alma pulled the Presidente brandy from behind the linens and took a long swig. As she leaned her head back, Merced saw herself tilting back her first brandy at the El Paso del Norte Hotel's Dome Bar on a date with Leandro. Her eyes watered when she remembered her burning throat and the way Leandro gently stroked her face as she coughed. How he had cupped her hands, and blewn on her fingers. How he had kissed her throat, tipping her head back again. Up above, she saw a glass dome made by some famous New York company. Pieces of stained glass fitted in metal whirled above her.

"*Tifanis*," the bartender had informed them.

Against the night sky, purple and blue glass glowed with moonlight. A jungle of green leaves reached toward the center of the dome, making Merced feel like she could almost fly through the center into the stars.

"Don't get drunk," Merced warned Alma. "Men want you awake and doing something."

Merced did the sign of the cross over Alma's head before she walked into the room.

"Think of me," Merced told her. "And hurry up. We don't have much time."

Merced watched the door close behind her daughter, then pressed her body up close, waiting until she heard Alma's muffled cries blend in with the john's murmurs.

"Okay . . . okay . . . okay?" the john kept asking.

Damn, Merced thought, pounding her fist into her thigh. Just fuck her and get it over with. Didn't the john know the rules? Why was this *gringo* so soft on her daughter? He should just break her into submission and be done with it. Just like her first time with one of those traveling salesmen, a *viejo* who'd just come out of the shower. He was quick. No questions. No answers, just money.

Merced walked over to her cleaning cart and pulled out the bottle of brandy and swigged from it until she heard the elevator announce its arrival on the fifth floor. Before Javi, the bellboy, and a *gringo* couple could reach her, Merced slipped the bottle back into the front pocket of her cleaning cart, where she kept the rags and industrial cleaners. Wrapping her fingers around the cold wooden handle, Merced leaned into the heavy cart and pushed. The cart rolled slowly down the carpeted hallway, passing doors with little wooden "Do Not Disturb" signs hanging on chains. Their doorknobs gleamed like giant diamonds under the hallway lights.

"*Cabrones*," Merced whispered.

The couple, a man in a long wool coat and a woman in fur and silk, passed by Merced, leaving behind a trail of perfume and cologne. The man winked at her as he passed. The perfume lingered, then faded as Merced kept pushing her cart back and forth over the same hundred yards of carpet.

"That *gringo* . . ." Javi said when he caught up with Merced. "The wife's a bitch. But he's a good tipper."

Merced stopped pushing her cart and stared at the bill in his hand.

"Not really."

Javi's face fell. "What do you mean?"

"You're only twenty," Merced laughed. "What do you know about tipping?"

"I know a dollar is better than fifty cents," Javi said, snapping his bill. "His wife came with him this time."

Javi started batting his eyes, putting his hand on his hips in imitation of the woman with the fur stole. Then he screeched, "I don't want these Mexicans stealing from me, so you better tip him good."

Merced and Javi's laughter could be heard down the hall-way, making one guest poke his head out of his room.

"We better leave," Javi giggled. "Before they catch us."

"You're such a clown," Merced sighed. She went back to pushing her cart.

Merced took the brandy bottle from her cleaning cart once more. Even before she unscrewed the cap, she felt her blood warming up, rushing like love. *She'd have to get more bottles, now that Alma also drank*, she thought. The brandy's heat throbbed through the cotton of her dress with every step down the carpeted hallway.

When Alma came out of the john's room, she looked ghostly, her black eyes now a gun-metal gray.

"How much?" Merced asked, holding out her hand.

Alma put a tightly folded square into Merced's palm.

"What is this?"

Alma reached over and unfolded the tight little square until three ten-dollar bills fanned out, almost covering her outstretched hand. Merced nodded at the money. She had never earned that much from one john in her life. She care-fully rolled the bills up and slipped them into her front pocket, where the roll hung heavy.

"Let's finish up the last room together," Merced told Alma, who barely nodded. She floated down the hallway in front of her mother.

The brandy bottle banged against Merced's thigh, re-minding her to finish it up before they left the hotel for the night. She hoped the guests in their last room had left behind a pack of cigarettes. They would go well with her drink. Once inside, she went straight to the nightstand and found a pack of Pall Malls next to two tumblers half-filled with golden water and nearly melted ice. One whiff and Merced knew. Tequila. Expensive tequila. She gulped both glasses down and pulled the bottle from her apron.

"Go shower while I finish the room," she told Alma.

The tequila burned her throat. Merced reached for the pack of cigarettes and the book of matches, but before she could light up, Alma called from the bathroom with a voice that was low and desperate.

"*Amá*. Come here."

"*¿Qué?*"

"I can't do it," Alma sobbed.

Merced rolled her eyes. *Now what*? She entered the bathroom and looked down into the toilet water.

"Just flush it, *mensa*," Merced told Alma, who tried to squirm away from the blood.

"I can't."

Merced grabbed Alma's hand and pushed it toward the toilet handle. But Alma pushed back, knocking Merced into the sink. Merced relented and flushed the toilet herself. Alma went to the bedroom and laid down on the bed. She was soon sound asleep.

Merced found a can of Ajax with bloody fingerprints and worried about Alma getting pregnant.

One day, instead of a bottle of brandy, Merced put a Coke bottle in front of her daughter.

"Remember to use this at the hotel," Merced told her before leaving for work that morning. "Then when you get home, we'll give you a good bath with parsley."

Norma reached over and brought the bottle up to her face, wondering what it was for. She would find out soon enough.

"I don't need it," Alma said.

"Ajax's not going to work," Merced informed her. "Men don't want a girl who smells like a cleaning lady. Men like innocent, pure girls."

"Like Coke?" Alma asked.

Merced picked up a wooden spoon and smacked her across the face. If she broke her nose, she didn't care. Soon, Merced would have to remember to leave Alma's face alone. Every man wanted a pretty face. The body could be bruised and bloated, but the face had to be clean and clear as a diamond.

Luckily, both Norma and Alma had inherited her clear skin. No pimples, warts or scars.

Merced counted out the money she and Alma had earned that day. Almost fifty dollars. Already she envisioned the house she would buy in Boyle Heights with Leandro. A house with a porch and a large, master bedroom.

When Alma and Merced reached the hotel, the *chilanga* told them to hurry up with the rooms. "Sales convention," she informed them. "Lots of men waiting."

Merced pushed her cart toward the elevator doors, nodding grimly. Alma followed behind her. In the 10th floor hallway, Merced pushed Alma into a room to clean with her. Merced made her way to the edge of the bed and grabbed a pack of Pall Malls the previous guest had left behind. She unwrapped it like a belated gift.

"My tip," she laughed out loud and lit a match that made a nice, sharp cracking sound as it ignited.

She took a deep breath. The cigarette smoke burned deep and long in Merced's lungs. Before she knew it, she felt herself fall back on the bed, the sheets' musky smell rising and mixing with the cigarette smoke. A small string of smoke rose from the bedspread and spread toward the ceiling.

Alma's dark eyes spread wide like a child's.

"*Chingado*," Merced yelled. She jumped up and yanked the bedspread up and threw it to the floor. She stomped on it until the smoke dissipated. The hole with its burned edges looked like a burnt-out eye socket. Merced knew the hotel wouldn't care, especially if she told the *chilanga* it was the hotel guest who had burned the hole. She also realized that she couldn't keep this life up. Sooner or later, the hotel would figure out her little side job. Quickly, she rolled up the bedspread and tucked it under her arm like a baby.

Then Merced took the cigarette from her mouth and slowly began burning a hole in the white cotton sheet. She relit the cigarette and burned another, then another until the sheet looked like it had a dozen bruised eye sockets and the room smelled of burning cotton. The smell followed Merced into the hallway, where she kept burning holes in the sheet until the perfumed couple's door opened. Merced didn't look down. Her eyes followed the couple walking toward her, their perfumed smell mixing with the smoke.

Before they could reach her, Merced threw her cigarette on the floor and rubbed it down into the thick carpet with her rubber-soled shoe. She kept staring at the couple, especially at the woman, who looked at her with raised eyebrows and a red mouth frozen into an *O*. Then Merced snapped open the sheet with its many eyes and laid it on the carpet in front of the couple, who looked down at her and then at the sheet and then at her again.

"Mamá!" Alma said as she looked down at the sheet.

Merced followed her gaze. The burned-out eyes stared back at Merced, bruised and empty.

"To hell with this fuckin' hotel," Merced told the couple.

The man stepped out in front of his companion, her blonde head peeking over the man's shoulder every third or fourth step.

"We're leaving," Merced told Alma. She grabbed the bottle of Presidente from the cart and headed away from the service elevators. "Today."

By the time she and Alma reached the lobby, the couple had already called the front desk. Merced wished she had taken the pack of cigarettes from her last room because at that moment she felt every eye in the world looking at her. From behind a stack of suitcases, Javi's gaze winked a good-bye. The *chilanga* yelled out to her, but Merced never looked back. Instead, she drank the last of the Presidente and dropped it with a crash in front of all the *gringo* and Mexican guests and workers.

Outside the sun glared down on her, on Alma and everyone walking toward and away from the Plaza Hotel. A car honked as Merced inhaled the smell of tacos from the restaurant next door.

Somewhere out in Los Angeles, Leandro was waiting for her, and she had to get to him soon or she would kill somebody. Merced looked at her daughter, still and silent under the white-hot sunshine. For a moment she saw Donaciano, and then she remembered what she herself looked like as a fifteen-year-old.

"Let's go get Norma and Suki" she told Alma. "We have to start packing for tomorrow."

"*Pero* . . ." Alma started, but Merced just kept walking away, her eyes on the horizon of brick and white stone buildings, the Franklin Mountains between her and the pulsing sky.

CHAPTER 12
Sentimental Journey

Merced had never hitchhiked in her life. She had seen other people, mainly men, with their thumbs out on the sides of El Paso's streets. Without a car or money for a bus ticket, she had to get to Los Angeles one way or another. All morning she had trekked along the highway with her small bag of clothes and twenty dollars tucked into her bra. The rest she had left behind with her daughters until she could find Leandro. When she did, she would send for them. But for now, it was easier and faster to travel alone. As the Texas sun burned high over her head, a truck slowed down.

"Where you going?" the driver asked through his open passenger door.

"Los Angeles!" she shouted.

He nodded, and she climbed up into the cab.

"Cigaretto?" the driver asked and waved a Lucky Strike pack at Merced.

She smiled and took one. He pulled out the hot lighter from its socket and held it up to her. She pressed the end of the cigarette into the igniter's glowing red center and sucked. Smoke streamed out of her nose. The driver put his hand on her knee. He squeezed and rubbed it, all the while smiling. Merced smiled back and pressed her cigarette into the pale skin of his hand. The trucker's dark eyes bulged. He banged his fist on the steering wheel and was about to swing his arm her way when she put the cigarette close to his eye. He abruptly held back the swat he was about to give her.

"*La próxima*, I burn you *ojo*."

"Okay, okay," he said, sweat trickling down the side of his head. Slowly he placed both of his hands on the steering wheel.

Merced lowered the window to calm herself. She knew it must have been close to eleven, because the winds were blowing hot, and she started craving the sugar she usually had after lunch. But there was nothing in the truck, just an empty Coca-Cola bottle rattling around on the floor.

The trucker played with the radio, tuning it to a variety show in English. Over the thrashing winds, she thought she recognized the squeaky sound of Charlie McCarthy, that stupid puppet and his stupid puppeteer, Edgar Bergen, who had no idea he was not funny. The doll reminded her of a wooden midget. Merced sighed and leaned her head against the window. She thought about the time she had caught Leandro with a peroxide blonde, a *juareña*. She imagined them lying together in his bed, her arm around her waist while she lay face up, awake and excited. Merced rubbed her eyes but she still saw them, especially the *juareña*'s blonde hair, glowing in the morning sunlight that came through the windows in Leandro's apartment.

Merced reached over and changed the program from Bergen's nasal voice to a soft singing voice. It was "Sentimental Journey," her favorite, sung by Doris Day, some *gringa* with a mellow voice. The song reminded her of the nights she had cleaned the Dome Bar at the El Paso del Norte Hotel. Sometimes, she could hear the bar's piano player warming up in the afternoon while she mopped the tile floors in the lobby nearby. Sometimes she would know the melody from the songs she heard on the radio.

When Leandro told her what the words meant, she thought the song even more beautiful. She could feel the driver smiling through his mossy teeth. Then she heard him singing. When she thought the trucker wasn't looking, Merced watched him. His nostrils flexed slightly as he stared at the road, then at her. Scarred and thin, his dull face looked half asleep, but he had a nice mouth without a thin moustache like Mexican men wore in Juárez. It wouldn't suit him anyway with his blonde hair. Merced took the cigarette from in-between his fingers and smoked it.

"Name?" he asked. His voice sounded like that puppeteer.

"No," Merced shook her head. "No *nameh*."

They listened to the radio for about an hour before she dozed off and dreamed that Rufina and Leandro were in the truck helping her find a clean bathroom. The smell of salt woke her up.

"*Oye*," she said. "*Tengo que mear*."

"What?" the driver asked. "Speak English."

Merced leaned back and tried to remember the word for bathroom in English but only *baño* kept popping up. Then she remembered: "Pee pee."

The driver smiled.

"Okay," he said. "But first a *bay so*."

Pinche cabrón. Merced knew he had her, would have her. She couldn't jump out of the cab without killing herself. She didn't see any other cars driving down the black highway. No gas stations. She'd have to wait.

"*Ay, Dios*," Merced whispered, closing her eyes, thinking of Leandro and his smooth dark brown face, dark hair and fedora. Her body became wooden. Suddenly, a white sign outlined in black popped up, "Los Angeles, 300 Miles."

"Okay," she said, her fist jammed into her open palm. "Okay."

The driver leaned down sideways toward her, reaching over the stick shift. Merced stretched her neck and rolled her face toward the driver. His salty stubble stung her lips and chin. She quickly fell back into her seat before his hand could grab the back of her head. She shook her head.

"*Uno*," she said. "*No más uno*."

"No pee pee then," the driver shrugged.

Merced almost cried. It would serve him right if she pissed all over his seats like an angry tabby cat.

"*Más*," he said, pointing to his cheek.

This time she leaned over and bit him. The truck swerved into the next lane, then back.

"You crazy bitch!" he said, trying to backhand her again.

Merced wondered if he would pull over and throw her out before they reached Los Angeles. If she could only get to a city or town to meet a man who could help her, then she wouldn't have to rely on this *cabrón*. She grabbed his Lucky Strike packet sitting in between them and lit up a cigarette.

"*Sohrri*," she said and placed the lit cigarette in his mouth.

His eyes wrinkled with his crooked smile. He sucked on the cigarette hard before throwing it out the window. This time, Merced didn't move his hand from her knee. This time, she let him massage her thighs. This time, she promised to fuck him if he let her pee like a human instead of in her seat like an animal.

Merced stared into the white-bright desert, his hand crawling into the crack between her legs. She tried to stiffen her muscles and numb her skin.

The driver had already passed a rest top but then pulled into a truck stop. Other trucks lingered by the side of the road. When Merced jumped out of the cab, an oven-hot gust scorched her face, awaking her from the wooden stupor. She walked around the back of the station to the restroom. It was locked. She waited, in the heat. The bathroom's stink seeped through the wooden door. Merced gagged, then spit at an oil puddle near her feet.

"Leandro, Leandro," she prayed.

The driver, whose name she now knew was Edgar, approached her, waving a wooden slab, a key swinging from a short chain.

"You're gonna need this."

Merced grabbed the key and opened the door. Relief overwhelmed her as she urinated. It felt like forever. Then, just as she was pulling up her panties, Edgar pushed into the restroom. Before she knew it, the trucker had pushed her inside and bent her over the sink. Merced closed her eyes.

She numbed her body and then realized it was no different from what she and her daughters did in Juárez. Edgar kept grunting.

Edgar finally came. When he pulled out, she opened her eyes and looked down into the rusty sink. She heard him zip up his pants and sit down on the toilet next to her. With the bathroom key, he uncapped one of the bottles of Coke he had managed to bring in with him and set on the floor. He took a large hearty swig. Suddenly, Merced felt thirsty and she grabbed the bottle and drank the rest of it. Edgar did not look at her. He uncapped the other bottle, but she grabbed that one, too. Instead of drinking it, Merced pressed her thumb over the opening and shook it hard. When she stuck it inside her, she could feel its warmth whooshing up into her vagina. Edgar watched in disgust, then ran out, slamming the door behind him.

As the burn set in, Merced thought of Norma, who had told Alma about this remedy American girls used to keep them from getting pregnant.

The thought of any woman shoving a bottle into herself had made Merced nauseous, but she was glad her daughter had learned to keep herself safe. An abortion was too expensive and dangerous. A reliable and skilled midwife was hard to find, even in cities like Juárez. And forget Texas. Those in El Sauz apprenticed and learned from their grandmothers. Merced had learned from aunt Pina about ways to get rid of a baby but, disgusted with the idea, she paid little attention. Merced thought men, of all people, would know that they would be the ones desperate to stop a baby before they married. But no. Men just left when a baby came along.

Merced poured water from the faucet into her cupped hand and quickly wiped herself before pulling up her underwear and fixing her skirt. The driver was waiting for her in the cab of the truck. When she climbed in, Edgar said nothing. Without looking ar Merced, he held out a cigarette. She took it without a word.

As soon as the truck engine started, Merced felt wooden again. Edgar drove all day and into the night, feeling her up and swallowing little white pills that he shared with Merced. They made her feel like jumping out of the cabin and running all the way to Los Angeles. They rode for a few hours without talking. They drove down the shiny black highway sparkling with diamond-like twinkles, and for the first time since the truck stop, Edgar spoke, calling out the names of buildings and bridges. Merced saw a black stream flowing between cement banks.

"Los Angeles River," the trucker said.

As they made their way through downtown, in the cool morning, Merced could not believe the height of the buildings, which dwarfed the ones in El Paso. On the street level, crisscrossing wires were connected to the red trolleys.

Cars sped by in front of them while other trucks, some carrying sailors, roared beside them. Merced, dizzy from the pills and the rumbling, closed her eyes, then quickly opened them. The road looked soft and wavy, like the ocean. As Merced looked over the broad streets, she imagined herself sitting beside Leandro in one of those cars without a roof.

"Olvera Street," the trucker said, and Merced indicated that she wanted to get down from the truck.

Edgar stopped the massive vehicle, and Merced jumped out, but not before taking the pack of Lucky Strikes and the dollar bill he had tucked in between the stick shifts.

She found herself in front of Casa La Golondrina, the Mexican restaurant Leandro had mentioned in one of his letters to her. It sounded like the lyrics of a song when read by the woman she had paid to read it aloud. She felt like a swallow, the bird that travels back and forth between homes. Covered in swallows and the colors of the Mexican flag, the restaurant looked like one of those colonial style houses she'd seen in Chihuahua. A mural of a volcano was painted on one wall while the other glorified the Virgin of Guadalupe. Los Angeles was already starting to feel like home.

❀❀❀

Leandro had left Merced for another woman while the *café de olla* was still sitting in the clay pot. He just took all his clothes out of the closet and stuffed them into a drawstring bag, the one Merced had used to carry his dirty clothes to the laundromat. He pulled out his few pieces of underwear, balled them up and shoved them into the bag. Merced clenched her toes inside her red velvet shoes as she watched him from the kitchen. He would not look at her, only focusing on his clothes, the bureau, anywhere but her.

Merced felt like one of those saints at church, stiff but in pain, always in pain. The harder she tried not to scream at Leandro, the harder she dug her toes inside her shoes.

The worst thing was that he did come back. But not to her. He came back to El Yuma with his friends from the steel plant. He would see her, nod and then go back to playing pool.

Merced's friend Rufina had taught her many things, including some spells Merced thought she would never use. Praying to the Virgen wasn't helping. Neither was going to church every morning and reciting the "Act of Faith" along with the rosary every night.

When her period came, Merced remembered Rufina's spell for winning back a lover or husband. "*Sangre de luna*" she called it. The woman saves her monthly blood and then mixes it into her potential lover's favorite drink. Her sister Cleófilas tried it as an experiment once, mixed her menstrual blood into a *champurrado* during Christmas. And just like that, Rufina's brother, Hernán, kissed her while they rode in his truck, and soon he became her fiancé.

Through the days of her period, Merced kept saving the strips of bloody cloth, laying them out in the sun, on rocks, hoping none of the neighborhood dogs or cats would chew on them or make off with them. After they dried, she stuffed them in a burlap sack.

On the last day of one of her periods, before heading out to El Yuma, she layered fifteen pieces of cotton stiff with blood at the bottom of her biggest clay pot and poured water over them. As the rags boiled, Merced prayed. With each whiff of the sweet blood, she made the sign of the cross over the pot. After letting the water cool a little, she ladled the liquid into a baby bottle she'd bought at Woolworth's.

All the way on her walk up to Indiana Street to El Yuma, the bottle stayed warm like a little heart pressed against her thigh, beating hard and slow through the leather of her purse. Merced smiled. Its warmth made her walk faster. If it stayed warm until she made it to El Yuma, then Leandro would love her again, would come back. He would leave Gertrudis with her peroxide blonde hair. It would be like the movies: she would be María Félix again, beautiful and content. And Leandro would be hers. Nothing would diminish her happiness. But Merced promised herself that she would keep this man, not throw him away like María Félix did in the movies and in real life. When she touched the bottle through her purse, its warmth made her walk faster. Just a little bit of this into Leandro's usual can of Tecate would bring him back. She could feel it in her veins.

Even in the dark cold of El Yuma, the bottle warmed her. As she put on her apron, she saw Leandro come in, a blonde head bobbing behind him. Gertrudis. Why would he bring her to El Yuma? Wasn't she supposed to be too high class for this place?

Cigar and cigarette smoke burned Merced's eyes as she poured brandy into two thick glass tumblers and uncapped two bottles of Schlitz. As the pool balls clacked, she laughed harder with the men sitting in front of her. She watched Leandro closely whenever he left Gertrudis' side. Once, she could have sworn he flicked his chin at her. Merced nodded back, reached under the bar and grabbed her little bottle and rubbed it, warming it in the grip of her fingers. The blood seemed to pulse with the *cumbia* playing on the jukebox. The waitress came to the bar with her little tray and told her Leandro's order: Tecate with salt and lime. She took a can from the refrigerator behind her and pulled open the tab. As the bloodied drops fell into the Tecate can, Merced was breathless. Would Leandro taste her blood through all that beer? Would he smell it? Leandro was talking to Gertrudis like she was the only woman in the world.

Merced whispered one more *"Ave María"* before she sat the sweaty can on the tray along with wedges of lime and paper packets of salt. When the waitress walked the tray over to Leandro, Merced turned around and looked at herself in the mirror. She could still see the Tecate's red and gold can floating between the other men and women like some lost soul, heading toward the pool table where Leandro was leaning over with his cue stick. The can floated down in front of him. Leandro gulped down some of the beer, then kissed Gertrudis. Merced smiled, wondering if Gertrudis could taste the blood, Merced's blood. She could just see Gertrudis fluttering her eyes, trying to look like one of those helpless women in the movies. Leandro stood up, grabbed a cue stick, leaving Gertrudis with her peroxide hair and fluttering eyelids. Merced heard herself breathing hard above the juke playing *"México Lindo,"* above the laughter and the smoke. Now, Leandro was sitting at one of the little tables talking to Gertrudis. Merced saw him squeezing the lime wedge between his long brown fingers, the little drops of cloudy grayish juice dripping down into the can's hole. Her heart stung when he sprinkled salt into the opening. Merced wiped her eyes and watched Gertrudis drink the last of the beer.

Gertrudis shouldn't have been at El Yuma. The only women who came to El Yuma were women like Merced.

The blood was working its way through Leandro's veins and arteries and soon into his heart. Merced tried to remember what Rufina had told her about how this love potion would work.

Nothing happened. Men kept walking by, coming in through the doors and still, nothing happened.

Gertrudis walked over to Leandro, who kept shooting pool balls. He looked around at the other men like he'd won some kind of prize. Moti, Rufina's younger and useless brother, sat there in front of Merced, asking her for another beer. Suddenly, Merced felt cold and her feet hurt. She slipped off the velvet heels and massaged one foot with the other. Her soles stuck to the sticky wet floor, but it cooled her sore, hot feet. Gertrudis came up to the bar and asked Merced for another Tecate for Leandro, as if Merced was just another barmaid. Then Leandro came up to Gertrudis and asked if she had his beer ready. The juke played "*Los Chucos*" by Lalo Guerrero. Leandro took the beer and held his hand out to Gertrudis.

Before she knew it, Merced had thrown a velvet shoe at Gertrudis' peroxide blonde head. Most of the patrons did not see it, except for some men in the corner, who whistled and clapped.

"*¡Otra!* One more time!" they cried.

So, Merced threw her other shoe at Leandro, who slapped it away. He laughed, but Gertrudis didn't. She grabbed Leandro's arm and pulled him toward the door and out into the warm summer night. Someone tossed Merced's shoes back to her. She guessed it was Moti. She left them on the floor until closing time, kicking them out of the way when she walked over them. Later, when she put them back on, the shoe edges cut into her swollen feet, pinching her toes and heels. Nothing hurt so deliciously as those shoes that night, especially later, when she danced with Moti at the Diamond Club down the street. Her feet throbbed when they walked back down the hill on Indiana. She kept them on through the night, through Moti's fucking, sleeping with them on her hot, fat feet. If Merced could just get through the pain, Leandro would come back.

CHAPTER 13
I Hate My Name

I hate my name. What the hell does Lucha mean, anyway?

"To fight," Grandma Merced tells me.

"To kick ass," Tía Suki laughs.

But really, it's just a name most people make fun of. George, my boyfriend, tells me I should change it to Lucy, just like he changed his name from Jorge to George. But everybody's always known me as Lucha.

"*Qué Lucy ni que nada,*" Grandma scolded me when she overheard me talking to George on the telephone. "Your mom gave you that name and you have to stick to it."

Actually, Merced gave me my name. I know this because Tía Suki told me on her last visit. We were sitting in the kitchen. I remember because I was near death with the flu and was just getting over it. Suki had promised to make me a *caldo de albóndigas*. And I remember feeling hungry for the first time in a week, when I smelled the meatballs cooking in the thick soup.

"*Ay,* Lucha," Suki said, "more and more you're looking like Merced."

Great, I thought. Not only do I have a crappy name, now I'm starting to look like an old hag. Grandma is the last person I want to look like ever.

"Is the soup ready?" I asked Tía Suki. "All Grandma ever makes for me these days is Spam and eggs. Or beans."

"Almost," Tía Suki said, lowering the flame and dipping her big spoon into the soup. "Your grandmother likes her *albóndigas* right away, too."

I just wanted to eat and go back to bed so I could dream about George and his beautiful brown hair and eyes. When Tía Suki put the bowl in front of me, the soup steamed up into the peeling paint of the ceiling. I didn't wait for her to serve herself before I started slurping up the hot broth. The more meatballs I ate, the better I felt.

"Just like Merced," she laughed, looking at me. "You know, she's the one who named you."

I just looked down at my *albóndiga*, a big brown boat in a sea of rice, cilantro and potatoes. I kept eating.

"She named you after your mom left Don Pedro," Tía Suki said, then gulped down the rest of her soup.

Grandma had told me about my mom and Don Pedro, this guy she had met at El Yuma bar. She ran off with him to Las Vegas without telling my grandmother. He had been way older than Mom, but I think that's why she liked him, because he was old and quiet. Not like Grandma Merced, skanky and loud. But they hadn't lasted, and soon she was back.

"But she hadn't named you yet," Tía Suki told me, handing me a tortilla. "She just called you '*muñequita*.' I kind of liked that."

I tried to finish my soup quickly so I could go to bed with my thoughts of George, but Tía Suki's voice was low and deep and crawled into my ears, then into my brain. Before I could finish, she told me that one day, when she had come to drop off some herbs from her garden, she found Merced and her neighbor Dolores in the living room, singing to some *ranchera* song on the radio.

"Lucha Villa," Tía Suki told me. "Merced and Dolores were singing '*Amanecí en Tus Brazos.*'"

Merced was holding a picture of Leandro in one hand and me in the other. Yeah, soap opera stuff, but I believed it. She's been hung up on that guy for so long, I don't think she'll ever get over him.

"Lucha still sings," Tía Suki went on. "Not as good as Lola Beltrán, but she is good."

"She still sings," I said rolling up the last tortilla in my hand. "Good."

"And beautiful, too," Tía Suki said. "Long black hair. Brown skin."

I stopped eating. I knew what Tía Suki was trying to do, and it wasn't going to work. No way was I falling for that Chicano pride crap. I knew better. That shit was over. This was the 80s and I was an American. So, over the soup I whispered, "Lucy," and watched my breath and steam float up into the peeling paint.

Next year, I remember thinking, when I started at Roosevelt High School, I would start using my American name, just like George. I would make the teachers remember my name and soon, I knew, Grandma Merced would call me Lucy, too.

❀❀❀

The minute I walk in, they hit me—Aqua Net hairspray and Miss Clairol or whatever they use in this tacky salon to color hair. Caesar's Hair Salon always looks empty when I walk by on my way to Griffith Junior High, but today it's totally full of so many yapping *viejas* and music, it sounds like a party. Some of the women, mostly old ladies my grandmother's age, are waiting, gossiping while ripping through hair books, *La Opinión* newspaper or that bloody *Alarma* magazine. Some are in the back, getting their hair washed, laying back on their chairs like their heads have been cut off. Other women sit in big fat black chairs, white plastic helmets on their heads. From the boom box sitting on the counter next to the cashier, I hear Los Bukis' singing "*Me Muero Porque Seas mi Novia.*" Except for the *viejas* and Los Bukis, it's almost like a disco in here, with big mirrors shaped like stop signs hanging against walls covered in foil wallpaper with black and red velvet flowers.

I drop into a chair right next to a woman reading a *fotonovela* with pictures of women in bikinis and big eyelashes. I don't know why I'm here except that I don't know where else to go to get the haircut I want. Ever since I can remember, it was either Grandma or her neighbor Dolores who cut my hair, but it was always in the same boring style: long hair to the shoulders and straight up bangs. I am so sick of my flat, little-girl hair—the Lucha hair. I want something for Lucy. American Lucy. At first, I think maybe I can get my hair permed like Brooke Shields or some other cool movie star, but then I remember this girl in my history class who got one and looked just like a walking Brillo pad. So now, that's what we call her. And you can hear the boys call out to her: "Hey, Brillo! Comb your hair." "Brillo, need a perm?"

It's pretty shitty. So, when a hairstylist with hair the color of mangoes comes up to me and asks what I want, I point to the feathered model in the *Women's Style of the 80s* hair book. She introduces herself, but I can't hear her name over the din of gossip and the *norteño* music. I show "Mango" the picture of the woman with the Farrah Fawcett feathered hair. This is the style I want to wear in September when I get to Roosevelt, or Rosy, as everybody else likes to call my new high school.

"Hmm," Mango says. "*La* Farrah."

"*Sí*," I say. "*La* Farrah."

But this is going to be *La* Lucy, and I have to do it before Grandma Merced gets back from the hospital and figures out that I took ten dollars from her purse. Mango leads me to the little black sinks and wraps a towel around my neck. She leans me back. The water feels hot, but I don't say anything. When Mango starts rubbing the shampoo, she looks down and asks me about my grandmother. I can barely hear her through the water rushing over my ears. She says something about Grandma's hair and asks when she's going to come back to get her hair done. I want to tell her that Grandma now uses Miss Clairol's "Turkish Night," and her hair isn't mango-colored anymore. Now it's black-black, like Elvis' hair. It doesn't even shine, it's so black. And she has Dolores cut it in the middle of the kitchen with newspapers laid out on the floor.

I don't tell her anything, just smile and close my eyes while Mango rinses my head. I try not to think about Merced, only of Lucy. Everything feels soft, even the hard plastic against my neck melts under me. Before I know it, Mango is straightening me up, wrapping a towel around my head, squeezing it a little to get out the extra water. She walks me over to one of the clear plastic chairs facing a stop-sign mirror. Los Tigres del Norte are singing *"Un Día a la Vez."*

"Ready?" she says smiling.

I nod and smile back.

A black cape whips around my neck, and Mango takes out a comb with a thin pointy handle, combs my hair flat against my skull, her scissors flashing under the fluorescent lights. Black chunks fall around me, and my head feels lighter. The feathered model's face floats around me. Yes, I nod. Yes. Soon I'll have my American hair.

"Hold still, *m'ija*," Mango says, holding my face between her soft wet hands.

They remind me of my boyfriend George's hands on my face when we kiss. I imagine him kissing me, my new feathers looking good against his shiny brown hair. Mango starts cutting again, her face close to mine. I look at her hair, little dried wisps like the fibers that stick out of mango pits when you're done sucking on them. If I could reach out from underneath my cape, I know I would break the ends. I close my eyes, waiting for my feathers to spread out. I can hear Mango rattling around in her little black drawer, and when I look, she's pulling out a big round yellow brush. The hair dryer revs up, whining like a little airplane. I can feel Mango rolling my hair around the brush, pulling, burning my scalp.

Then, what I've been waiting for, she pulls out the smaller round brush from the pile in her drawer. The bristles scrub against my skin, pulling my hair by the roots. Suddenly, the blow dryer stops. I keep my eyes closed, knowing that when I finally open them, I'll see the model from the hair book in the mirror. The blades squeak in my ear, cut more of my hair off. And then the blow dryer starts again. And it's like this for the next half hour, first the blow dryer, then the scissors. Dry, cut, dry, cut—the rhythm scares my eyes open.

I almost scream. The hair on my right side is thicker and longer, one perfect wing tucked against my head. But the other is so short, my ear looks like a little *saladito*. Instead of the beautiful Farrah model, I see a Cabbage Patch doll with a fat face and a balding head. Shit. And the Belvedere kids? Forget it. American Lucy is screwed. I can just hear it now.

"Hey, Cabbage Patch, where's your hair?"

"*Saladito* ears! You need a lemon or what?"

"I need to trim the other side," Mango says.

Good thing for her the cape keeps my hands from reaching out and ripping her hair out. Really, I want to rip out my own hair, cover my head, set it on fire, anything but show it to the Griffith Junior High students, especially not to George. He won't kiss me for sure after this. He'll probably dump me for one of those cha-cha girls who don't look like Brillo pads and wear those skintight bubble-gum pants.

Again, Mango starts trimming my one good wing until my other ear sticks out. I just watch my wing shrink, my face getting redder. I'm trying hard not to cry, but one tear starts rolling down the side of my nose. When Mango hands me the little mirror and spins me around so I can see the back of my head, I jump off the chair. I reach for the ten dollars in my back pocket, throw it at Mango and run out of Caesar's Salon down First Street. I don't stop running, not even to wait for the cars speeding down the street. One car almost hits me, but I don't care. I just want to die and never go to Roosevelt or any other high school for as long as I live.

When I get home, I lock myself in my room and turn on the radio to the beginning of "Blue Monday." When I hear the phone ring, I turn up the music, knowing George is trying to call me. When the ringing stops, I walk into the bathroom and look at myself. Pimply faced and almost bald, my head looks like it's ready to explode. I go into the kitchen and grab the scissors from one of the drawers and watch my hair fall down into the sink. Little by little, my head feels lighter and lighter. In my room, Duran Duran sings "Girls on Film" while I swear I can hear someone, maybe George, yelling "Hey, Lucy!" I just keep cutting and crying.

⚜⚜⚜

I can barely hear the female announcer.

"The Mighty 690," call out upbeat singers, followed by the deep voice of a woman announcer: "Tijuana, Mexico."

It is the best AM radio station in East LA. It doesn't compare to KROQ, the only FM station to play real British New Wave and punk music, but it has a signal strong enough to drown out the morning sounds of the *ranchera* music screeching from the transistor radio sitting on the kitchen window.

"This is Rob Tonkin with the Mighty 690," and then the thrumming sounds of Lover Boy's "Working for the Weekend" blare through the sponge coverings of my headphones, one of two gifts from George. The other is a Dodgers baseball cap. He bought it and the bootleg Sony Walkman at Thrifty's with the change he saved up from the grocery shopping he does for his grandmother.

"Do you like them?" he asks me when I unwrap them.

"Now you don't have to be embarrassed when we're at school." My heart goes cold for a minute because I know he's the one who's really embarrassed. But I don't want to think about that so I smile up at him. He wraps his arms around my neck and leans down close to my face. And at that moment, I decide I love George with his feathered hair and pimpled chin. So, I kiss the peach fuzz on the side of his cheek. He smiles at me, then takes my face in both hands and pecks me on the lips. I can smell the fries from today's school lunch.

After our first kiss, I wear those headphones around my neck, sometimes plugged into my bootleg Walkman. One time, I listened to my Stevie Nicks cassette all night. By morning, my batteries had died, so I had to use the batteries from the transistor radio. Grandma Merced was so pissed she gave me a couple of swats when I got back home from school. After that, I just listen in the mornings and after school.

This morning calls for some loud music to drown out not only Grandma's *rancheras* but also the neighbor kid's boom box version of "Angel Baby." Luckily, Olivia Newton-John's "Heart Attack" plays next on Rob Tonkin's pop list. She's my favorite singer and has just come out,with her second "Greatest Hits" album, which I can't afford to buy.

"I'll get it for you," George says as we walk hand in hand from school.

Before I can ask how, a car blasting "Cutie Pie" thumps toward us. Inside, Yoli Zamudio and a group of girls scream "Cutie Pie" at George. He smiles back and waves. Like a *pendeja*, I say nothing.

CHAPTER 14
Malflores

One time, Aunt Suki lost control. It was the time her girl-friend Lily, the lawyer she had met at her medicine store, La Malinche Botánica, came over to our house. I had just come home from school, when I saw Tía Suki at the kitchen table with this beautiful woman with very long black hair and brown eyes, wearing bright red lipstick, just like Crystal Gayle, the singer.

Over the back of Lily's chair there hung a black shawl embroidered with roses as red as her lipstick, with long black tassels that touched the floor. She laughed as she held Suki's hand.

"Then I grabbed this gun," Tía Suki continued.

Lily stopped sipping her tea. "What? A real gun?"

"A BB gun," Tía Suki explained, laughing. "It looked so real, those kids just split the moment I pointed it at them."

When they finally saw me at the door, Tía Suki waved me over to her side.

"Lily, this is my niece, Lucha," Tía Suki said. "Lucha, this is Lily Valdez."

"It's Lucy," I corrected. "Remember?"

When Lily took my hand, I could smell a light perfume, like the gardenias in the bushes planted near our porch. Silver rings bulging with turquoise shined from her fingers while a silver bracelet molded into a feather wrapped around her wrist.

"I see you like the Dodgers," Lily said.

I touched my baseball cap as if she would reach up and snatch it off my sweaty head, then pulled it down tight.

"She never takes that cap off," Tía Suki teased. "Her boyfriend bought it for her."

"He's not my boyfriend," I said. *Not anymore*, I thought.

Before Tía Suki could grill me, Lily jumped in. "You have a nice collection of books."

Lily must've seen my room, because I kept my books in a wooden milk crate next to my bed.

"What are you reading now?" she asked.

Suddenly, I blanked. All I could see was a woman who was like those aliens on *Star Trek*. She didn't belong in our modest little house with all its sadness. Lily's face glowed like the flame on those white votive candles Grandma Merced keeps lit at the top of her dresser.

"*Are You There God? It's Me, Margaret*," Tía Suki answered for me.

"Judy Blume," Lily said, nodding.

"I'll be right back," I said and slipped into my room.

The afternoon sun had warmed the room up from its icy morning levels. Tía Suki's bed was still unmade. She usually made it first thing before she left for her store. As I brushed my hair out, I heard a soft romantic song coming from the kitchen radio: "*¿Cómo fue? No sé decirte, cómo fue.*"

I'd heard Grandma playing that song over and over on my record player when she was in one of her "*novela*" moods. And by *novela*, I mean *muy* dramatic *y muy* drunk. But Tía Suki and Lily weren't drunk.

I walked up to the kitchen doorway and saw them dancing close. Tía Suki buried her face into Lily's black hair and whispered into the strands. They reminded me of the couples at school dances. At fourteen, I wanted to be one of those couples so badly. But George didn't. Now that he was cheat-

ing on me with Yoli Zamudio, I would never be one of those
couples who got to dance close and slow with their true love
at the Halloween Dance, Sadie Hawkins, the Winter Formal,
Spring Fling and, finally, the biggest dance at Griffith Junior
High, the Tower Dance.

I leaned against the doorway, crying like a baby, watching Lily and Tía Suki dance. Maybe they couldn't hear me
bawling because the music was so loud, or they were just too
into each other. I couldn't hear my grandmother, who'd come
home early from her shift at the bar. She came up behind me
and stood watching Lily and Tía Suki dance. Then she jerked
me away and shoved me into my room and slammed the door
shut.

"*¡Malflores!*"

Bad flower? What the hell does that mean?

"*¡Cabrona!*" Tía Suki yelled,

Suddenly, grandmother's body crashed through the door
and fell hard in front of me. Suki screamed curses at the top
of her lungs, and Lily tried pulling her away from her as she
lay on the floor gasping for breath. I tried to help Grandma
up, but she just pushed me away. As Grandma caught her
breath, she opened her eyes and looked straight up at Tía Suki.

"*No quiero tus pendejadas en mi casa,*" Grandma snarled.

"Don't worry," Tía Suki said, wiping blood from her nose
and mouth. "I'm leaving."

My chest tightened, and suddenly I couldn't breathe.
Don't leave me, Tía Suki, I thought. Suki looked up at me.
Lily whispered something in her ear.

"Not now," Tía Suki said, shaking her head.

By this time, my grandmother was sitting up, but she
didn't move. We watched Tía Suki and Lily walk out the door.

"Don't even think about leaving this house," Grandma
warned me.

All the while, the radio kept playing songs of love.

CHAPTER 15
Girls of Summer

Whenever my mom, Alma, isn't working at El Yuma or cleaning the houses of *gringos* in Pasadena, she wanders around the house like a ghost, pretending to clean, sometimes switching on the radio to her favorite station, listening for a few seconds, then quickly turning it off. As the days get hotter, she goes outside and waters the roses. Sometimes, I join her, sitting on the cement steps of our little house.

"Did you finish your homework already?" my mother asks me.

"Yes," I lie.

She stares into the rose bushes budding pink, peach and red.

"O my Luve is like a red, red rose," I start reciting before I catch myself.

Mom squints at me. "Why do you say that?"

I look up at the clouds, those soft, pinkish and purple cotton balls. Soon, my mom will leave to meet Grandma at El Yuma and leave me alone in the warm, dark house.

"I have to memorize a poem for class," I finally tell her. "'Red, Red Rose.' That's the first line: 'O my Luve is like a red, red rose.'"

"Is it about *la virgencita*?"

"It's about love," I say. "It's about a man separated from his love."

Alma nods, watering the rose bushes and flooding them until the water spreads into the lawn. Shaking herself awake, she walks over and twists the handle of the faucet off and stays bent over.

"Are you okay?" I ask.

Mom shakes her head, then stands up. Her mouth opens a little, like she's about to say something, but stops herself. She walks over and sits down next to me.

"Can you recite the rest of the poem?"

I close my eyes. I think about George cheating on me yesterday. Then, his face blends with Suki's, then Lily's. Before I know it, I'm reciting the entire poem. I know my mother doesn't understand a word of it, but I'd like to think she's enjoying hearing my bad Scottish accent.

"That's good," my mom whispers. "You sound like Suki."

We go back into the warm house. She flips on all the house lights and the house glows. When she opens the door to leave for El Yuma, music spills out into the warm night.

※※※

Today, George and I go to the library across the street from Griffith Junior High School to do our homework. We sit at our usual spot, the round table near the plaster copy of the Aztec calendar encased in glass. I put the orange cushioned headphones attached to the thin metal band over my ears and press the play button, starting the next song on Stevie Nicks' *Bella Donna* album.

"Outside the rain, the heart skips a beat," Stevie warbles so loudly, I don't hear skidding noise. George pushes his chair back.

He points to the restroom and mouths that he'll be right back. But as the minutes tick on, George still doesn't come back. By the time Stevie and Tom Petty start "Stop Dragging My Heart Around," I know that he has gone to the park just outside the library. Slowly, trying not to drag the chair's metal legs across the linoleum floor, I push myself up and walk over to one of the floor-to-ceiling windows that face the park. Its large shallow pond shines blue and purple under the late afternoon sun.

"It's hard to think about what you've wanted. It's hard to think about what you've lost," Stevie quavers to Tom.

At the far edge of the pond, I see them, two slim figures walking slowly, hand in hand. George and a girl with long black hair reaching down to the back of her butt.

"Stop draggin' my heart around," Stevie and Tom over and over until I back away and walk back to our table. Instead of finishing the algebra homework, I stare at the stone face on the Aztec calendar. Its tongue hangs out of its mouth, and geometric patterns encircle the carved animal and toothy snake heads, trapping me in a never-ending pattern.

❀❀❀

"For these last few days, leave me alone," I sing into the cold water, trying to do my best Bernard Sumner from New Order. Far away, seaweed floats and bobs like strands of hair on bath water.

Along the shore, a dog and its owner splash in the ocean. It's the first time Tía Suki takes me to the beach, the first time since Grandma Merced kicked her out of the house for being a lez. We walk for an hour, kicking at the foamy water. We're close to the Santa Monica Pier. It's closed today because of a sewer leak.

"Why's the ocean so foamy?" I ask.

"Because of all the sailor spit," Tía Suki says, then laughs after I jump out of the water. It's something George would say.

Tía Suki looks down at her watch, a shiny brass one with a thick leather strap. Lily gave it to her for their first year anniversary. I can't believe that it's already been a year since she left home. I look down at my brown, sandy toes, remembering how George's feet looked when he walked away from me. Right now, he's probably with his new girlfriend.

"Are you hungry?" I ask.

"Hmm, I guess I could eat something."

From the half-buried Styrofoam cooler, I pull a bean burrito wrapped in foil. The moment I unwrap it, the corners fall apart.

Suki also picks out a burrito, the fattest one Grandma made this morning—stuffed with chopped fried potatoes, scrambled eggs and chorizo. She unwraps it and takes a big bite. I look at Suki with her mouth full and laughing.

Behind us, a high school boy and his girlfriend set down their towels and ghetto blaster deep into the thick sand. The girl wears a black bathing suit cut high like those leotards on the Solid Gold dancers. When she walks up to me, her boyfriend just keeps watching her ass.

"Can you watch our stuff?" she asks. "We're going for a swim."

I nod and watch her go back to her boyfriend. A white bow sits low above her ass, the white ribbons slapping her cheeks with each step.

When the couple are far enough away, Tía Suki pulls their radio out of the sand and brings it closer to us. She changes the station to KRLA, the only one that still plays lame *cholo* music like "Angel Baby" and "I'm Your Puppet."

A newsman announces something about Gerald Ford and "increasing the immigration quotas for Mexicans desiring to come to the United States."

"Holy shit," Tía Suki says. "Maybe we can finally get your grandmother her green card, a real one."

The sand whitens, almost blinding me. When I look out toward the water, the sky pulses bluer.

"Who cares? She's lived without it this long," I say. "Ready to leave?"

Nothing's helping me today. Not the beach, not Tía Suki. Right about now, George is probably making out with Yoli, his hands gripping the back of her neck just like he used to grip mine.

CHAPTER 16
Gringolandia

God, I hate chamomile tea. Even worse is *yerbabuena*, but that's what Tía Suki wanted me to drink to help me sleep, to stop the nightmares making me jump out of bed almost every night. And it's always the same dream. It's the middle of the night, and I'm in the garage. There's a bunch of *cholos* drinking, playing cards, clicking dominoes. I can't see their faces. Then one of them comes running toward me. I try to run, but my feet stick to the dirt floor. I slowly pull my legs off the dirt, but before I can reach the sliding door, one of the *cholos* grabs me. I scream. And before I know it, I'm jumping out of bed, heading for the bedroom door. Tía Suki's up, grabbing me by the waist.

"Where are you going?" Tía Suki asks.

I'm catching my breath, looking around. "I have to get away."

Tía Suki leads me back to the bedroom.

"*Cholos*," I tell her "The *cholos* in the garage."

Tía Suki laughs. "What garage?"

"The one in the back," I say.

When I was thirteen, I remember seeing a *cholo* there with one of the neighborhood boys, smoking a joint, laughing. When they saw me, the *cholo* smiled and waved me over.

I ran. He was some girl's boyfriend. Her name was Jessie, a wannabe *chola* who bragged about drinking beer.

"C'mere, Buckwheat," the neighbor boy yelled.

He made me angry and scared me at the same time. I stuffed down my anger and ran into the house through the back door, bolting it and turning the key. As I lowered the shade, I heard the *cholo* laughing thickly. I'd heard stories about *cholos* from Grandma, who said that sometimes they'd try to get into the Yuma Bar.

She cursed one out when he tried to get in by pulling a steak knife on her. "The *pendejo* looked like he still wore diapers," she said.

I didn't tell her about the *cholo* in the garage.

"You know what I did?" Grandma asked me. "I just took it from that *escuincle* and threw it into the street."

It turned out that *escuincle* told Jessie, who called me "big ass" and "*nalgona*" at school. She'd follow me as I walked home, yelling those words, right up to the door. It was just annoying at first. Then, I saw a movie with George at the Golden Gate about the *cholos* who cruised Whittier Boulevard. In one scene, they try to rape a girl. I close my eyes for the rest of the movie, but George watches it all the way through.

"Why are you closing your eyes, Lucy?" George says, tapping my shoulder.

My heart beats like I've run a million miles. I just shake my head, keep my eyes closed.

"Are you okay?" George asks and pops a Milk Dud.

"I gotta go to the bathroom," I say.

In the bathroom, I splash water on my face and take off my Dodger cap. With my wet fingers, I flatten my fucked-up hair so that the feathered hairs can't fly out. Then, I press the cap down, tucking in the feathers tight, until both sides of my head look smooth. I walk out to the snack bar for more popcorn. For the first time, I notice the giant cement clam shell behind the bar. It looks like it would swallow all the candy and the girl behind the counter. I stay in front of the clam shell until the movie ends.

As soon as I see George exiting, I wave him over.

"Where'd you go?" George asks.

"More popcorn," I say, shaking my half-empty bag.

George grabs a buttered handful.

"How did the movie end?" I ask.

"Everybody dies," he says in between bites.

"Even the girl?"

"What girl?"

I can't go on.

While George and I walk down Whittier, I think about the girl and her wide-open eyes as she thrashes against the men pinning her down. It's Friday night and the low-riders soon start cruising the street. George loves to watch those cars. I usually keep an eye out for that one low-rider painted Dodger blue with the "LA" logo on its hood. This time I just want to go home.

"Well, you go," George says harshly. "I'm gonna stay here and watch."

I don't understand. He always walks me home.

"But I wanna go home."

"So go," he says, then turns around and walks down the boulevard.

I catch up to him and stare at the *cholos* and their cars, wondering how many have raped a girl. I watch them with their black shades, thick black hair and thin moustaches. They look like those men in the movie, but some also look like the men in the old movies my grandmother and mother love to watch.

When we finally start to walk home, George won't hold my hand.

"I think we need to break up," he says, looking out at the boulevard.

He won't look at me. I press my Dodger cap tighter around my head. I don't want to ask why because I'm afraid he'll tell me it's because of my fucked-up feathers or my big ass. The reason will be mean, and I'm too scared to hear it.

"Okay," I say, then walk myself down Whittier Boulevard to our house.

As soon as I see a *cholo* walking on the other side of the street, I run to the house, past the kitchen where Suki sips coffee with my mom, and I go straight to bed. That night, I have the nightmare. The next night, Suki makes that chamomile tea. It tastes like dead flowers.

❀❀❀

After my night terrors, my mother never asks me why I almost run out of the kitchen door screaming. She barely says anything, just rubs my arm.

"Are you okay?"

"Yeah," I say. "Stop touching me."

She pulls back like I burned her or something.

"It's just that you've been rubbing my arm for a long time."

My mom covers her eyes with both hands. "You're still thinking about that boy."

I don't tell her about the *cholos* threatening me. That's worse than telling her about my breakup with George. Mom starts stroking my arm again. She's starting a new job, working with my grandmother and Tía Norma at some white family's house in Pasadena. "Rose Parade Pasadena," I call it.

"We won't be home until ten," my grandmother tells Tía Suki and me. "Make sure you cook the *frijoles* and leave some for the rest of us."

Tía Suki nods, but I know I'm the one cooking the beans.

"We'll have some fun," Tía Suki says.

No, we won't. Tía Suki's just here to pick up the rest of her stuff and then she'll book it to Redz, the lesbo bar down First Street.

"Don't worry," she says, like she knows what I'm thinking. "I'm going to show you something."

Instead of cooking, she takes me to her garden beside the garage, in the little side alley where she grows parsley, rosemary and thyme. Just like the song by those ugly guys, I think. The ones who sing "Mrs. Robinson" and "Sounds of Silence." She hands me some funny looking scissors with huge handles and tiny blades and tells me to cut some of the parsley.

"Is that for dinner?"

Tía Suki laughs at me. It seems like she's always laughing, not just at me but at the whole world.

"Believe it or not," she says, smiling in the bright sunshine, "this is my most popular plant."

"Popular for what?"

This is when she gives me the paper bag filled with the parsley and waves at me to follow her into the garage. I hold my breath, thinking about the *cholos*. I stop.

"What are you afraid of?" Tía Suki says, pulling my arm. "The *cholos* won't get you."

She pulls out a little brass key from her back pocket, inserts and twists it into the chunky lock. As she lifts the wooden door, cool dusty darkness blows out. The afternoon sun reveals all the cardboard boxes filled with Grandma Merced's crap from El Paso along one of the wood-slatted walls. On the other side, bookcases with little curtains in front of them line the wall. Behind the gingham curtains, neatly arranged are jars filled with Tía Suki's collection of dried herbs.

At first, I'm excited and then I see more curtains strung on a rope hanging from one end of the garage to the other. Tía Suki pulls one of the curtains aside and jerks her head at me. I step behind the stiff green cloth. It's dark, but she knows her way around. Suddenly, there's a click. A green lampshade glimmers in the middle of the dark space, and the shadows disappear. Under the light, a green wool blanket covers something. Tía Suki gently lifts the blanket, uncovering a blue table with metal rings on each side. We stay quiet, listen to the sounds of sirens and cars speeding down Indiana Avenue.

"That's an exam table."

I touch the sky-blue table with its silver rings.

"Those are called stirrups," she whispers. "Women put their legs on them."

Before I can ask why, Tía Suki tells me that she uses it to examine women and help them with her herbal treatments. I'm so shocked that I almost forget about George dumping me.

"You're not a doctor," I say.

Tía Suki's brown eyes seem blacker under the green light.

"When you were a baby, not many of us could afford a doctor," she says. "Some couldn't afford babies."

For the first time ever, I see her start sweating. I can smell it. Tía Suki never sweats . . . or stinks. She's the calm aunt who smells like lavender and laughs, helps you know the world is not so scary. She still looks like Linda Ronstadt but older and sadder. At this moment, she looks and smells serious.

"Some didn't want babies," she says, patting the table like it's a faithful dog. "Sometimes, I helped them not have babies."

By this time, I can't look away from the silver stirrups glowing under the light.

"I still help them sometimes," Tía Suki says, knowing my struggle. "With parsley and other things."

I let her words sink in but still wonder where she learned to take care of women and their babies. After a while, she snaps off the light, and I follow her out from behind the green curtains to the bookcases. Tía Suki reaches for some jars filled with dried plants. At first, I think they're ashes, but their labels have words like "*perejil*" and "*yerba de la perdiz*," herbs from her garden."

"What's this for?" I say twisting the lid off one jar.

"It's for babies," she says. "It's the dried parsley."

I wait for more, but Tía Suki's mouth becomes a line. Her black hair glows orange with the sunset, like she's thinking hard about something she doesn't want to tell me.

I slide the jar back with its sister jars. I remember a movie I saw a few years ago with the actress who played Nancy Drew on TV. Instead of solving a crime, she commits one by having an abortion. The movie was supposed to be funny, but Nancy Drew was just mean to her sweet friend, who crushed on her. He loves her so much, he's willing to lie to her father for the money Nancy needs. That's love.

"You've fallen in love with Jorge," Tía Suki finally says. "So, you've got to be careful."

I freeze. She doesn't even ask. She just tells me how I feel.

"I'm not in love," I practically yell. "Jesus."

I hate that. Even if the person's right, I hate being told how I feel. Even if the person's Tía Suki, the one person I love even more than George, I hate that she's right.

❀❀❀

Our house is haunted. Ever since I can remember, I have felt her: the ghost of a young *rancherita*, as Grandma likes to call Mexican women who have crossed the border without papers. At least, I think she's a *rancherita*, even though she dresses like an American. I've only seen her once, looking through the living room window between the green curtains. She has long brown hair that hangs loose over her shoulders, scarred cheeks and a black leather jacket worn and torn with travel and work. At first, I thought she was one of Norma's friends, so I opened the door to see if she wanted to come in and wait. I walked out to find her sitting on the peacock chair, the one that looks like the one Morticia Addams sits on, but this one looks like it'll turn into dust if you touch it.

"*¿Dónde 'stá m'ija?*" she asked in this little girl voice.

She stared at me hard and crossed her legs. She was wearing these flared white jeans. When she asked me the question again, a bright red star-shaped stain near the bottom of her fly grew larger and larger until finally her pants were covered in red. She touched the wet stain and jumped up. The skinny woman looked down at herself and then at me. She reached out to me with her stained fingers, but before she could touch me, she disappeared. I screamed, ran back into the house. Mom came out in her pink quilted bathrobe and asked me what was wrong. When I told her about the woman on the porch, she grabbed my arm and pulled me close to her. She whispered that it was La Tilica and started praying the "*Ave María.*"

"Who's La Tilica?" I asked my mom while she prayed.

She turned to Tía Suki, who had also come out, wearing nothing but her T-shirt and shorts.

"What happened?" she asked, rubbing her eyes.

As soon as my mother told her, Tía Suki went straight to the kitchen and grabbed a jelly glass. She scooped two tablespoons of sugar into the glass, filled it with faucet water and stirred like it was one of those cocktails served at El Yuma.

"Drink it," she told me.

I gulped it down, but I was still trembling, although not as much.

Ever since Tía Suki moved out to Santa Monica back in December, I feel La Tilica is on the porch and sometimes in the garage. Just before I get my period, I see her again, sitting on the wicker peacock chair on the porch, watching people pass by. When George visits me, he asks me about the "skinny woman."

"What skinny woman?" I ask, hoping it's not the same girl who's haunting me.

"The one on the porch," George says.

I freeze, and he grabs my hand and takes me out to the chair. "She's sitting in that Addams Family chair watching people go by."

George and I look at the chair that's been on the front porch since my grandmother and Leandro bought the house fifteen years ago. Of course, it's empty.

"She was here." George points to the peacock chair. "I swear, I saw her."

All that's there is gold-brown wicker so old and rotten, it looks like nobody can sit on it without the chair disintegrating. What's new is the dark brown stain on the seat.

La Tilica haunts us both. George almost spends the night with me. My mom is in Pasadena tonight, earning extra money babysitting for a family, and Norma is out with her latest boyfriend. Because Grandma Merced will be at El Yuma until late, I let George stay and watch the "Elvira Mistress of the Dark" show with me in my room. Tonight's movie is *The House That Screamed*. It's about a boarding school for troubled girls who begin to disappear after the arrival of the headmistress' son. It's the first time I don't watch the whole movie because I let him kiss me and rub his hands up and down my legs, my back and the sides of my boobs. I want him to stay all night, but when the movie ends, he twists his head away from me and shoots up from the bed.

"What was that?" he says, jerking his head around.

I jump up. "A spider?"

"Cold air," George says, grabbing the back of his neck. "Did you feel the cold air?"

I look around. All the windows and doors are shut tight. On the floor next to us, the small electric heater vibrates in and out of its red hot glow.

"I better go," George says, barely hiding his urge to run.

"My grandmother won't be back for another hour," I say, looking up at him.

He shakes his head and slips his shoes on.

"Are you scared or what?" I ask him, trying not to show him how scared I am.

"Scared?" George says, smiling, holding my hand. "I'm not scared of jack shit."

But he is afraid of something. Maybe it's La Tilica or maybe it's Grandma.

After he leaves, I go to bed. Later, I hear the dishes in the dishrack next to the sink rattle against each other. In my dreamy mind, my grandmother's come back and prepares her usual late-night snack of Jack cheese quesadilla, but the dishes just keep clacking like they're swaying back and forth, back and forth for like forever. And then I hear the phone start jerking on its holder. I run into the living room, thinking George is trying to call me.

"George?" I whisper into the phone.

Nothing.

"Grandma?"

"Suki," a faint voice whispers, then hangs up.

I drop the phone, run back into my room and lock the door.

The next day when I'm walking home from school, the neighbor lady named Tencha tells me all about La Tilica and Tía Suki, how one day, about fourteen years ago, the girl had come to Tía Suki's house for an herbal massage called a "*sobada.*"

"It was no kind of *sobada*," Tencha says, grimly hosing down her rose bushes. "I knew what your aunt was doing."

I don't understand her but I just nod.

"*Pobrecita*," Tencha says. "Suki was just trying to help the girl but just couldn't do it."

When I try to walk away, Tencha talks louder.

"*Pues*, you know the girl died at your house, right? She died trying to get rid of her baby."

I stop breathing. The roses glow bright red, and the hose water crashes over the leaves like two cars wrecking up on each other. And from the corner of my eye, I can see a hippie girl sitting in the peacock chair watching Tencha and me, her head nodding.

"But how . . ."

"I don't know how they did it, but the poor girl's mother was so ashamed, she didn't want anybody to know, not even the police."

❀❀❀

"I need to pay her," the woman says, barely breathing. Her voice sounds distant like she's calling from the other side of the world. "Suki saved my life."

At first, I think she's the ghost from one of those women Grandma Merced has told me about, the ones who died in childbirth. She swears some of them were too country-folk backward to go to the hospital and have their babies.

"Who is this?" I ask the woman on the phone; afraid she's going to tell me she's a ghost.

The woman coughs so hard, she nearly blows out my ear. In the background, I hear a machine pumping. Her scratchy voice pronounces a name, but I don't understand.

"I'm sorry," she wheezes. "I'll have to call you back."

When she calls back, her voice sounds clearer, more human.

"Are you Suki's daughter?" she asks.

I tell her I'm her niece, but I'm not sure I should tell her that Tía Suki has moved to Santa Monica to live with her girl-friend.

"I never came back to pay her, but I want to, now," she says. "Tell her to expect something from the 'Hippie Girl.'"

The next day, I hop on the bus to Santa Monica. There's no way I'm going to chance speaking to Tía Suki with my mother, grandmother and Norma in the next room. It's already warm and sunny in Boyle Heights but gets colder and foggier as the bus gets closer to the beach. I find my aunt in her slippers and bathrobe, very relaxed. Good. I'm hoping my news about "Hippie Girl" doesn't scare her. When I tell her about this woman, she almost falls out of her patio chair.

"*Ay, Dios*," she says. "I didn't think I'd see her again."

"Who is she?" I ask. "Why does she need to repay you?"

Tía Suki takes a deep breath and sips her chamomile tea. "She's a *gringa* who had heard about me through Jane."

"Who's Jane?"

Air sucks through her clenched teeth, reminding me of the sound the *huizache* tree makes during a rainstorm. She shakes her head like she's shaking out memories.

"It was a group of women who helped each other back when abortion was illegal."

At the word "abortion," I remember the TV movie with Nancy Drew. She's sixteen and pregnant with some rich boy's baby. Her guy friend, who's secretly in love with Nancy, pays for her abortion by a medical student. When she's done, another girl holding a little brown teddy bear goes in after her. They show her lying down, her arms wrapped around her teddy bear. I think she dies, but I can't remember. Then I imagine the ghost of La Tilica with her bloody pants bumps out the teddy bear, and I see her reaching for me.

"What about La Tilica?" I ask.

Tía Suki nearly chokes on her tea. "*Ay*, Lucha," she sighs. "Her name was Alicia, from Puebla. Her husband had come out here first and was up in the San Joaquin Valley for the grape harvest."

"Sounds like how Leandro came out here leaving Grandma behind."

"Yeah," Suki agrees. "Alicia was in love, but she was scared."

"Scared of what?"

"Everything . . . Americans, *La Migra*, doctors, especially male doctors."

I wait for more, but Tía Suki looks spaced out, like she's dreaming. Is the chamomile tea spiked?

She jumps up out of her seat, walks through the sliding glass doors to the living room and brings me a photo of Alicia, who is wearing an apron and stirring something in a big cast-iron pot. She's also very pregnant in the photo.

"She wanted me to help her with her baby," Tía Suki continues. "She was too scared to go to the hospital here because of *La Migra*, and her husband was who knows where. But your grandmother found him."

She quiets again, takes a few breaths, then starts again.

"He was working the fields up in Delano. He had been waiting for Alicia to come up to help, *pero* . . ."

Cold, salty air grips my body as a foggy breeze whips by. I know what happened but ask anyway. "Did she die in our house?"

Tía Suki nods, sips her now cold tea and looks out at the dark green ocean, dull with the fog.

"The baby too. On Grandma's bed?"

We both stare into the ocean, the water roaring and the seagulls calling out for something.

"Her husband, I think his name was Cuco, came down and took her and the baby back to Puebla."

The sun has finally come out, but the ocean in the wind sprays over me and fills my eyes.

CHAPTER 17
Reclaiming Space and Time

Sometimes, Norma fucked around with the family she worked for, especially when the mother made her babysit her daughter for hours. Just because the lady of the house was Mexican, it didn't mean that Norma was her friend or her child's godmother. But the woman insisted on calling Norma her "*comadre*."

"*Ay, comadre*," the wife would say in her uppity Mexico-City Spanish. "Can you babysit the little one for a while?"

And then she would leave for her shopping excursion with her rich friends to Bloomingdales or to Rodeo Drive. And she'd be gone, until the night. Occasionally Norma would just make the last bus, leaving from the stop on the street three blocks away. At least the woman would drive her there.

The more Norma babysat, the older she felt. The little girl, a toddler, babbled away, following Norma as she mopped the floors, cleaned the bathrooms and made the beds.

"You know you're a shitty-diaper *gringa*?" Norma would ask in her most bubbly, gentlest voice so the girl would smile.

Every so often, after Norma changed the girl's diaper, she would touch the atomizers on the perfume bottles lining the vanity in the master bedroom. The freshly diapered little girl would follow her there, repeating the phrase "*Gringa caca*."

143

As Norma spritzed perfume on herself and over the little girls' curls, they did a little dance. Norma would continue laughing as she picked up the silver-handled mirror and inspected her face. She would notice how haggard she looked.

"*Pinche* Clorox," Norma would whisper.

"*Pinche*," the little girl would repeat.

Norma would lead the toddler into the master bathroom and from there into the bathroom. After adjusting all six shower heads and the water temperature, she'd strip herself and the little girl down and then guide her into the shower.

As she'd lather the little girl's hair with the Zest, she would remember Merced bathing her in the metal tub back in El Sauz. Back then, the water was ice-cold in the winter but tepid in the summer.

CHAPTER 18
Genius of Love

"*¿Qué onda, Jorge?*"

Shit. Not that guy again. But I knew if I walked down this street again, I'd see Mayo with his piss-yellow Toyota truck. His speakers blow so loud, they make the truck bounce to the rhythm.

"Call me George . . . I'm George, not Jorge."

"All right, homes."

The funny thing is he's my cousin.

"Don't pay attention to that *baboso*," Mom tells me. "He's jealous that you're so white and handsome."

Sometimes, she'll stroke my hair like she did when I was little after Mayo ganged up on me with my other cousins. They were all dark like him, but he was the darkest. And I never said anything to him. Didn't call him monkey or *carbón*, like the other kids at school did.

"I wish your *tío* would get him under control," my mom would say, "because one of these days he'll end up in jail."

Today, he just cruises beside me, hair sprayed up into a pompadour like those guys who hand out fliers for the house parties near the school.

"Hey, cuz," he says. "Where you jetting to?"

I'm not telling him that I'm going to see Yoli Zamudio. He dated her back in the day and cheated on her. He'd probably ask me why I'm taking his sloppy seconds. But, just to fuck with him, I lean into the window and tell him where I'm going.

"Get in, Jor," Mayo says.

He likes the way "Jor" sounds like "whore" but, according to Yoli, *he's* the whore. That's why she broke it off with him, even though it took her like three months. From the first day of school to Christmas, I saw Mayo cheat on Yoli right and left, especially when he dejayed at the house parties. He'd put on a twelve-inch "club mix," go to his car with some chick and then, in like ten minutes, he'd be back. The sad part was that Yoli knew and put up with it. She was like a fuckin' yo-yo going back and forth with Mayo. That's what Lucy called her behind her back: "Yo-yo Yoli." Sometimes I did, too.

One night, Yoli finally caught him. Not with just any skank. This time, she saw him with her best friend, Patty Landa. She finally broke up with him for good and gave me the chance I'd been waiting for since September. Then, for some stupid reason, I think she's still fuckin' in love with him. What's worse is that I'm a yo-yo too, because I still want her. Now I'm stuck in her ex's truck going to pick her up for a date.

"I'll take you there," Mayo yells over the music.

For some unknown reason, the asshole takes me the other way. We drive over the Sixth Street bridge, straight to downtown and park on an empty street next to the old brick factories and warehouses. I get a little scared. Before I can ask what's going on, he looks at me real serious and says I have to wait. At first, I think he's going to beat on me for dating his ex. When he breaks out a joint, I almost piss myself. After a couple of puffs, he hands it to me. "Genius of Love," my favorite song, comes through loud and clear on the door speakers. The bass and grass hit like an earthquake.

"Your girl's pregnant, Jor," he tells me, smoke filling me up when I'm just beginning to bop my head to the beat.

"What?" I choke out. "You shitting me? Who?"

"Yoli told me."

Mayo looks out the window like there's something out there more interesting than explaining himself. Usually, he likes to trip out on me when I'm feeling like shit. As smoke fills up the car, I think how easy it would be right now to grab him by his thick black hair and smash his head into the window.

"Why didn't she tell me?" I say.

"I'm sorry, Jorge," he says. "She came over that night to talk and, *pues*, you know how it is with the exes."

I finally get it. He fucked her. Fuckin' Yo-yo's still in love with him. I'm pissed but buzzed. I pull the seat lever back, close my eyes and mellow out, but only a little.

"You need to help her," Mayo says.

"Why should I help that cheating bitch?"

"Shit, dude," he says, "I'm not in love with her."

I open my eyes. By this time, Mayo's on the second joint and the smoke is so thick, I can't even see the street.

"No way," I say pulling my seat back up. "I don't got money for no abortion."

"Tell your mami," he says like I'm still a little *mocoso* he can pick on. "Her boyfriend's rich."

"She'll kill me," I say, then pinch the joint and suck out another drag. *No, first she'll kill Yoli, then she'll kill me*, I think.

Mayo laughs his devil laugh. "That's true," he agrees. "And what about that little Dodger girl you've been seeing? *¿La Luchadora?*"

Fuck. I forgot about Lucha. She really loves me too, *pero* . . . Yoli is way more fun. Plus, she's more of a babe. I feel the buzz coming on when "Cutie Pie" starts bumping through the speakers. I close my eyes and nod my head.

"That woman at La Malinche Botánica is a cutie pie," Mayo says just as I'm flying through the windshield.

"Lucha's aunt," I mumble.

"What did you say?"

"Lucha's Aunt Suki," I yell. "She runs that *botánica*. She let us smoke weed there once."

Suddenly, I'm flying over downtown, shooting straight to Whittier Boulevard. Over La Malinche Botánica, I glide through the windows with the foggy glass. Inside, Lucha stands by a woman who lies on a table, legs open while her aunt Suki inserts bushy green plants that look like parsley inside her. Lucha holds a steaming cup.

"Lucha," I say out loud, waking me and Mayo from our nice high.

"You just killed my buzz, homes."

Through my haze I tell him again that Tía Suki owns that herb store with magic potions.

"Is she a midwife?" Mayo asks loud and clear. His bloodshot eyes open just a little like he has an idea. A bad idea. "Maybe she can help you."

For some reason, that sounds real funny. Maybe it's because I'm the one cheating on Lucha and I need her for a change. Mayo laughs with me. We laugh so hard, we don't notice that a big blue boat of a car is coming at us from the side. I lower the window a little to let some of the smoke out.

"Why you do that, Jor?"

I stop laughing. The last thing I need is for him to call me that in front of someone at school.

"My name's George. Call me George, now."

"Whatever, Jor." Mayo waves his hands like I'm a fly. "You'll always be Jor to me. Just because you got pale skin, you ain't no *gringo*."

That's enough! I push his head into the window, but I'm so high, his cheek just mushes into the glass, and he laughs like a dumb ass.

"You're so weak," he says. "You better take care of your women."

All I can think about is the steaming cup and the grass inside the woman. Suddenly, the woman starts bleeding but smiles peacefully. While the blood pours into a metal bowl, Lucha gives the woman the cup. She drinks it, closing her eyes.

Zas! Zas! Zas! An old man in overalls taps at the car window.

"*¡Muevan esta carcacha, chamacos!*"

Mayo's truck is parked in front of his driveway. A sky-blue 60s Charger, like on the *Dukes of Hazzard* show, moves slowly toward us, it's white lights beaming high. This time I crank the window down all the way.

"Shit, Mayo."

He turns up the music when "A Fly Girl" pumps through the speakers. Mayo revs up the engine, then books it back to East Los.

❀❀❀

The next day, Yoli and I are at Belvedere Park, the one with the dirty lake and white ducks. We're feeding the ducks some stale bread she brought from her house. Our side of the lake doesn't stink as much as it usually does, because all the trees are covered in these purple flowers that look like little trumpets and smell like cotton candy. They had rows of them at Griffith Junior High. That's when I first spotted Yoli. She was a total babe then.

Yoli's already in a shit mood about Mayo telling me about the baby.

"You need to talk to Lucha about the *botánica*," I say. "Her *tía* Suki can help you."

"I'm not talking to that skank," Yoli says, all high and mighty.

God, but she looks hot with her bubble-gum pants and tight polo blouse, kind of like Brooke Shields in those jeans ads. Even though she's hot, I want to get back at her.

"She's not the skank who cheated."

I throw the last of the bread into the green water, and the ducks go crazy, flapping and quacking.

"Look who's talking," Yoli says with a flip of her long black hair. It's fried out in a perm she got from her friend but it's still beautiful. I want to make out with her, but now that she's preggers with Mayo's baby, it's like a fence between us.

"Talk to her *tía* Suki," I say. "She's cool."

"Why don't you stop buying dime bags and start saving some money so I can go to a real doctor, not some street witch?"

Then she starts rubbing her stomach, mumbling about how we need to get rid of the baby fast. How she can't go to college now because she's gonna end up like her sister Monica, who's tied down with three kids already. For a second, I think about asking her to marry me, to move in with Mom and me, but how the fuck would I even ask my mom?

A couple of kids ride by on bicycles. They stop at the playground and jump on the swings, yelling. Man, I wish I was a kid again. It's too much being sixteen. It's too much having two girlfriends, especially one that's pregnant.

I jump off the bench and walk to the street. I fuckin' give up with these chicks. How could Yoli be with my cousin, anyway? He's tall and has a car, but he's the ugliest one in our family.

"You're just like Mayo," Yoli screams. "You're all the same!"

"Shut up, Yo-yo!"

I shake my head as I walk down the sidewalk. I jump on the next bus home. Shit, I might have to ask my mother for the money. Or I could just blow it off. But people are gonna know.

❀❀❀

"What do you mean you want to go to Tijuana?" Mom asks. "*¡Qué idea!*"

"I wanna see my dad," I tell her.

I do, but I just need to get out of East LA and clear my head. TJ's not a long way but it's far enough.

"You're still in school. I'm not going to have an illiterate in my house."

I tell her I'll go to school in Tijuana. Even with my busted-up Spanish, I'd rather go to school in Tijuana than tell her about Yoli. Or maybe I could work with my dad in his jewelry store with his new wife, Coco. She's a total witch, but maybe Mom doesn't know the whole truth. Nobody ever does.

"Did you do something?" Mom suddenly asks. "Did Lucha make you do something you shouldn't have done?"

I go into my room, lock the door and open a window. I light up a joint and put on my headphones, the good ones that I'm not about to sell so some slutty chick can get rid of some other guy's baby. When I think of Yoli having a baby all by herself, I almost cry. So, I turn up the music.

"Cutie pie, you're the reason why."

Wrong song, but I'm stupid and I want to feel sad for Yoli and for me. Shit. And what about Lucha?

CHAPTER 19
La Llorona and La Malinche

Blues, every shade of blue can be found in the bathroom: powder blue on the walls, baby blue dots on the white tiles of the shower stall, royal blue towels, sky blue outside the windows. The sink, toilet bowl, cabinets and built-in wooden vanity all gleam porcelain white while knobs on the drawers and medicine cabinet sparkle sapphire blue. The white hexagonal floor tiles outlined in thick black goo cool me down after school while I wait for my grandmother to come home from her shift at El Yuma.

"Mirror in the Bathroom" by English Beat bounces off the wall as I step close to the mirror, bend over the thick white sink and squeeze the pores until the white heads push out like slugs. I know I'm not supposed to touch my face, but these pimples are driving me crazy. Red splotches with crescent indents pit my face. Tonight, instead of Oxy10, I'll rub halved garlic cloves on them because the last time I popped my zits, it left my face cratered like the moon.

"When are you getting outta there, Lucha?" my grandmother yells through the locked door and then pounds on it.

"In a minute!" I yell back, then turn up the radio.

I sit down on the toilet seat, finger the shaggy blue cover and close my eyes. If I wish hard enough, maybe my skin will heal itself, smooth out into a creamy white rather than acne scarred and charred brown.

Maybe the spell has worked. Maybe, like the mirror in "Snow White and the Seven Dwarfs," it will obliterate my image and reflect a clear, glowing white face. But this mirror is not cooperating. And I hate the thought of slathering on foundation, like the other girls who clog the high school bathroom between periods. Their cheap make-up powder makes them look like pink erasers instead of the glamorous models in fashion magazines. As the song ends, I get up and softly pound the mirror.

"Ugh!"

Before I know it, I'm slamming my fists against my reflection. But the mirror won't crack.

Before the next song plays, I kill the radio and open the door. Grandma Merced's fist is up in the air, on the verge of banging on the door again.

"It's about time," she huffs. "What happened to your face?"

"Nothing!"

I head for the kitchen, where I grab a knife and search through the basket of onions and potatoes for a garlic bulb. With each tear of the garlic clove's papery skin, I imagine my skin tearing off.

When Grandma walks out of the bathroom, her skin is heavy with the foundation she bought at Thrifty's, her lips pulsing bright red like a cracked heart. Miraculously, she smiles when she sees the garlic clove in my hand.

"You're cooking, what a surprise!" Grandma says. "Make sure you put the beans on low."

Before I can answer, she's out the door, heels clicking down the walkway. I slice the garlic clove on the beat-up cutting board and rub half of the clove on my face.

❀❀❀

Sometimes, I lie on the bathroom floor in my bra and panties while I listen to KROQ, the rock of the 80s. Richard Blade's sexy Australian accent rambles out of the transistor radio about some concert at the Greek or "Fabulous Forum." His voice bounces off the floor onto the walls and out through the thin panes of glass into the concrete courtyard. Then he spins the latest hits, "Shiny, Shiny" by Haysi Fantayzee or "Time Zone" by World Destruction. Weird but danceable.

Sometimes, a song's beat makes me jump up and twist the volume to the max so I can lip synch. I watch myself in the built-in mirror of the vanity. I lean in close, pretend I'm singing to John Taylor of Duran Duran or my boyfriend George. Before we started at Roosevelt High, he was Jorge with the corduroy vest and thick accent. The Fourth Street School boys made fun of him and called him a TJ. Not because he was from Tijuana but because he was Mexican. Never mind that all of our parents are Mexican, we're American and, somehow, better. But at Rosy, it's all about first kisses, dances and the "babes." According to my girlfriends, George is now a babe. No longer a TJ, it's okay for George to be my boyfriend.

During these summer nights, I need George the most. After dusk, when all of East LA cools down, I open the little bathroom windows for fresh air. Sometimes, especially on hot June nights, the stink of rotting pig blood drifts in through the windows, filling up the bathroom with gross death smells.

"That's the Farmer John Slaughterhouse," George says.

"Like the one from *Carrie*?"

"Same one," he tells me.

The moment he says this, the stink becomes glamorous. It's from Hollywood. I remember the scene with John Travolta killing the squealing pigs after Nancy Allen, his girlfriend, gives him a blow job. George and I kiss a lot, but he never asks or makes me give him a blow job. He just tells me to never hold his hand or kiss him in front of anybody at school. Now, he comes to stay with me in the little yellow bungalow until my grandmother comes home from her bar job.

"Don't come to my locker after class," he says more and more these days.

I know why. He's after Yoli Zamudio, the queen bee of Roosevelt High, who won't give him the time of day. The boys call her Miss Sixty-Nine, whatever that means.

❀❀❀

Grandma Merced is missing her boyfriend Leandro again. Once she gets started, she destroys anyone who tries to stop her. This time, she's coming after my runaway mom, Alma and Tía Suki, who moved out months ago to be with her lawyer girlfriend, Lily.

"No use crying over your children. What for? *Ingratas*."

Am I ungrateful too? True, I don't give Grandma any of the money I earn from working at the Jack-in-the-Box, but at least I'm not pregnant, like some of those other girls who come to Tía Suki's house for abortions.

Tía Suki and Lily have been running a clinic from their home in Santa Monica for a year now. Lily makes enough money to help cover expenses for some of the women who don't have the cash for a doctor and are too embarrassed to go to Planned Parenthood. At the kitchen table, Grandma Merced drunkenly tells me that Tía Suki and Lily are the worst ingrates because they do not share their good fortune, after all she has done for them.

"I took care of them," Grandma mumbles, fumbling with her Marlborough pack before shaking out its final cigarette. She catches it before it hits the floor, then floats it slowly to her mouth.

I try to focus on the beans simmering in the clay pot, but I'm afraid she'll throw the Bic lighter at me, like she did last time. After three flicks, a flame shoots up to meet the tip of her cigarette. She closes her eyes, taking a deep drag. I open the window above the sink to clear the smoke's stink. A slight breeze blows. I roll my eyes but turn back to the stove, stir the now bubbling beans, listening for another voice or the ringing of the telephone. George said he would call me about getting together to study. I know all he really wants is to make out, which I love but I also really want to pass my algebra class. If I say no, he'll go to Yoli. I set the heavy iron skillet on the stove, turn up the burner, then grab the half-empty red box of Farmer John Premium Lard from the refrigerator.

"I took good care of Alma and Suki," Merced shouts. She reaches over the table for her bottle of brandy. "And what do they do? They leave me for a broken-down old man and a *malflor.*"

At least they have love, I think. I spoon the *manteca* into the griddle and watch it melt, then ripple like the little waves at the lake. Slowly, I spoon in the beans. Thick fatty steam rolls up into the cracked ceiling. I stand back and watch droplets hang from the pale-yellow paint, ready to fall. I think of Grandma's face, then Yoli's, as I mash the beans into the griddle until they start to cream.

"*¿Me oístes?*" Grandma shouts.

"What?"

"I told you to start warming up the tortillas."

As I crouch down to pull out the warming drawer for the *comal*, the phone finally rings. I jump up but, even though she's drunk, Grandma's faster. She's been waiting for Leandro to call her for days and quickly picks up the receiver on the wall.

"No, she can't," my grandmother shouts. "She's busy." She slams the receiver down.

For a moment, I'm tempted to throw the pot of beans out onto the cement stairs outside the kitchen door. For a moment, I want to throw them into my grandmother's face. I don't. Instead, I bite the inside of my cheeks, feel the burning stone in my throat as I turn up the flame under the *comal* and watch a tortilla wrinkle its thin, sharp edges.

"It's too hot," Grandma yells. "You're going to burn them."

I lower the heat. My throat tightens, my eyes keep swelling and burning. Don't cry. Don't be a *pinche llorona*.

The tears drip, anyway. *Mocos* fill my nose until I use the back of my hand to wipe them away. I want to run out the door, jump on my purple bike and book it to the park. There, I can cry by the lake in peace until my body just dries up. Maybe that's what La Llorona was all about. Just crying until nothing of herself was left. Maybe she just wanted to lie on the riverbank and wait for her cheating lover to come back to her. Yes, I would wait for George to find me, pick me up and kiss me until his spit mixed with my tears. *Who am I fooling*? He hasn't kissed me in weeks, not since Yoli's been hanging out by his locker.

"Are the tortillas ready?" Grandma squawks.

At this moment, I want to slap her mouth shut. Just make her stop talking until this sadness blows out the window and into the purple dusky sky. At this very moment, I understand why La Llorona chokes her children. I open the refrigerator door, and the cold air rolls over me. I think of Suki and Lily near the ocean, the salty breezes carrying seagulls over their house. My face cools at the memory of throwing pieces of tortillas at them.

"I can enroll you here at SAMOH," Tía Suki said. SAMOH is her favorite name for Santa Monica High.

I said no then because I couldn't leave George. I loved him. I still do. You can't leave someone you love. At least, that's what the songs say. I know I'm only fourteen, but I feel empty whenever he's gone. How did that happen? Now that George exists, life at my grandmother's house is bearable, even without Tía Suki.

The corn tortilla sizzles on the *comal*, heat waves warping the air above it. Corn vapor and cigarette smoke mix with the steam of the beans, killing my hunger. As the tortilla edges curl away, I pinch the tortilla, then carefully flip it over.

After finishing her bowl of beans and tortillas, Grandma finally goes to work. I jump up at the phone and call George, who tells me he's "studying" with Yoli. Then I call Tía Suki.

"I miss the seagulls," I say, trying not to cry into the receiver.

❀❀❀

"Your *abuela*'s like Madonna," Tía Suki tells me the morning after I go to visit.

I laugh. What a joke. How can she compare the coolest queen of dance to a mean old woman who never wants her daughters or granddaughter to have a life, much less sex?

"They both have no sense of shame," Tía Suki says, "and don't care what anybody thinks."

We listen to Richard Blade, who's been broadcasting from the Live Aid Concert in Philadelphia. According to Richard, Madonna told off the men in the audience, chanting "Take it off! Take it off!"

"I ain't taking off shit today" Madonna said. Ha ha! Just because that gross man from *Penthouse* published her naked photos she took when she was a struggling dancer doesn't mean she's going to do it now.

Too bad my grandmother can't make money off of her shamelessness, like Madonna does. After bartending at most of the cantinas along First Street, Grandma is known as La Reina de la Primera by her customers, especially by the men.

"They call me the queen for good reason," she explained to me one day. "Staying loyal to one man keeps you decent. Too many men make you a *puta*."

Grandma thinks Tía Suki is shameless for running a successful *botánica* business out of the house she shares with Lily.

"She could've done it from here," she fumes.

Today, I help Tía Suki move her jars from the garage to one of the guest rooms in the little beach house.

"What are all these for?" I ask Tía Suki. She is labeling little jars filled with dried plants and powders. One of them looks like a little man who has sprung roots all over his body.

"That's ginseng," Tía Suki says, holding the jar closer to my face. "It's supposed to heal the whole body; it increases immunity."

Tía Suki climbs the stepladder to the top shelf of her medicine hutch, where she keeps the best and rarest plant samples.

"Immunity from what?" I ask. The jar hovers, then lands on the top shelf with other strange herbs.

"From anything," Tía Suki says.

"AIDS?" I ask.

She looks at me funny, but I have to know, because George's been bugging me about having sex with him. And I want to, but I know AIDS is out there. Even Madonna has a commercial about it. Suddenly the ginseng jar drops, explodes at my feet. Tía Suki scrambles down and holds my shoulders. Her hands squeeze me so hard, I pull away.

"You having sex with that kid?" she asks.

"No," I say.

Tía Suki's eyes widen. "Do you want to?"

When I don't answer, she yanks open one of the skinny drawers marked "SIDA." She hands me a purple plastic square with the word "Trojan" on it. The square has little white figures of men in those Greek soldier helmets all around its edges.

"Here," she says putting the square in my palm. "This will protect your body from AIDS."

"What . . . ?" I start, but Tía Suki's now laughing.

Before I know it, she's taken the square from my hand. She rips it open and jerks out a thin plastic circle. She pulls a little balloon tip, stretching the whole thing out until it snaps hard into her hand.

"It's a rubber," she says, suddenly serious. "Make sure he wears it on his *pito* before you go at it."

Little streams of sweat drip from my pits. She plucks out a couple more of the purple plastic squares and shoves them into my back pocket.

"If you're both virgins, then you're gonna need a couple of these."

She pats my butt and smiles down at me.

"Now let's sweep this mess up," she says.

❀❀❀

La Malinche, Tía Suki's new *botánica* on Whittier Boulevard, has it all. Love potions, charms, sacred waters, statues of saints and much more. She bought it last month from the owner, who was moving back to her home in Chihuahua.

"She was the best," Tía Suki says. "I'd always go to her with questions, and she finally told me to stop being a pest. So, I became her apprentice."

I guess *curanderas* have to learn from somebody.

"There are no schools for *curanderas*, as far as I know," Tía Suki says.

She not only makes her own stuff, she uses it. Mainly on women. Mostly, they're women who want a lover or a baby. Sometimes neither.

"For the ones who want a baby, I give them this special candle and water," she tells me.

Tía Suki pulls out a little brown bottle with a dropper. The water smells faintly of lilies and honey.

"They just place a few drops in their *té de yerbabuena* for twenty-one days."

Tía Suki wraps up the bottle in wax paper. She ties a gold elastic string around the top. It looks expensive.

"Is the woman supposed to drink it every morning?"

"After she makes love," Tía Suki says with a wink. She places the wrapped bottle on the top shelf of the glass showcase, where she keeps the most powerful and precious of her charms and potions.

"I call it moon water," Tía Suki says, turning the lock. "The moon is the mother of water and love."

Later, a woman with sunglasses like Jackie O. comes through the glass front door and asks for the moon water. A shiny black scarf with little gold "G"s covers her puffy brown hair streaked with copper highlights. Her black and white checkered suit looks tight but new. She smells like the make-up women at the nice stores in the Pasadena mall. I go to the little backroom in search of Tía Suki. I almost bump into her as she hunches over the copper coils sending little waves of heat up into the skylight. The faint smell of roses makes me a little dizzy.

"Some woman in a scarf wants the moon water. Where's the key?"

Tía Suki pulls it out of her back pocket and walks with me to the front.

"*Hola, comadre*," Tía Suki says, smiling. "You're back for the moon water?"

The woman smiles but does not pull off her glasses. Her lips glisten a soft pink even under the fluorescent light of the store.

"Yes," she barely whispers. "The lover's potion worked."

"Good." Tía Suki nods, opens the case and places it on top of the counter.

"Three hundred dollars," she says, writing up the receipt.

I suck in my breath and try not to widen my eyes. The woman keeps smiling as she reaches for her quilted leather purse hanging over her shoulder by a gold chain. She snaps open the two big gold Cs latching the purse. She pulls out a wallet, a fatter, slightly smaller version of her purse and delicately picks out three bills that look ironed and starched. This is the first time I see Benjamin Franklin up close and personal. Tía Suki recounts the bills and hands her the package.

"Does that potion really work?" I ask after the woman walks out and slips into her tiny, shiny grey car.

"What matters is the love," Tía Suki answers, tilting her head sideways like a bird. "Do you want to try it on Jorge?"

I don't bother with correcting her this time. Jorge will always be Jorge, not George, no matter how many girls he cheats with on me. Still, the thought of him sitting by the lake with Yoli, kissing her neck like he kisses mine, is too much.

I take the potion, but I hand back the condom.

"I don't think I need this," I say.

Tía Suki shakes her head and pushes the condom back to me. "Just in case."

Just then, Lili walks in, leading a girl by the arm. She looks like Yoli Zamudio from the side, but I'm not sure until she turns her face.

"She needs help," Lily says. "I found her at the bus stop down the street."

Yoli looks like she's been crying for days. Her greasy black hair looks stinky. The moment Yoli recognizes, me she trembles. Lily wraps her with the *rebozo* she usually wears around her shoulders and holds her tight.

"You're like ice," Lily says. "Can you get the *té de yerbabuena*?"

Tía Suki nods at me and I head back to the small kitchen. I pour water into the little enamel saucepan and put it on the hotplate. From the giant refrigerator, I find the jar of fresh mint leaves and rinse them under the faucet. I tear the leaves off the stems and drop them into a blue mug. Their sharp green freshness clears my head. As the water boils, I follow the steam up to the skylight. Tiny droplets float up into honey-combed glass and fade into the sky.

I grab a piece of ginseng and a grater. I pour the water over the leaves and grate the ginseng, then head back to the front of the store. When I hand the cup to Yoli, I crack a small smile. Her freckled nose wiggles at the minty smell.

"Drink it," Tía Suki says. "It'll calm you."

As she drinks, I can hear Yoli's breath slow down. Soon, I'm breathing along with Yoli. I know then I will still love George.

CHAPTER 20
Amor eterno

It always began with a shadowy figure. Just when Merced was about ready to fall into a deep slumber, in the dark, she could see a shadowy figure approaching her. Suddenly, she would feel like she was breathing through a straw and was paralyzed. She would jump out of bed, screaming, and run for the front door until someone caught her arm.

"Merced! Merced!" the shadowy figure would shout.

It was Leandro's voice awakening her. Slowly the outline of her bedroom would emerge from her dark nightmare. Her hard breathing would steady when Leandro's soft hand gently held her shoulder.

"Another nightmare," Leandro would say, leading her back to their bed. "Something or someone is haunting you."

Merced sensed that her ex-husband was haunting her for leaving him and their daughters. When she finally told Leandro this, his face paled in the glow of the streetlight streaming through their window.

"Why did you leave your children?" Leandro blurted out.

The question took Merced by surprise, especially after he had rescued her from another nightmare.

"They were better off in El Sauz," Merced said.

It sounded better than "I was just sick of them and their father." What kind of a mother would say that? A terrible one, she knew. And maybe she was terrible for not wanting her own children. She had never wanted any ever since her own mother died and left her, Tía Pina and Cleófilas for their father. Thanks to Tía Pina, she broke out of her father's grasp. Unfortunately, she had trapped herself with Donaciano, who offered her escape but for the price of children.

Leandro raised a thick black eyebrow. In that delicate look, Merced saw his judgment, even though he was the one who had encouraged her to leave, who had given her permission to leave, not only Donaciano but also her daughters. Yet, she couldn't throw this back in his face. She was trapped by lust and passion, like genii released from their bottles, that could never be stuffed back in. If they were, the bottles would explode.

"It's true." Merced tried to convince him and herself. "Donaciano could provide, I couldn't."

"Children always need their mother," Leandro said.

Anger flickered in her heart. Despite the chill of winter rain drumming outside their window, Merced grew warm. She rolled over to the table beside the bed and felt for the box of cigarettes and the metal lighter. Before she could light it, Leandro's arm pushed her hand down.

"I'm sorry."

It was too late. Anger gripped her heart, grew with each puff.

"*Pinche hipócrita*," she whispered. "I left them for you."

"I know," Leandro said, then kissed her shoulder.

His warm mouth made her skin goosepimple. Then she said something she didn't mean but knew Leandro would want to hear.

"We can have a baby, too," she said before her voice choked.

Leandro stopped kissing. "Are you sure?"

Merced nodded, but the thought made her stomach pull back on itself.

After they made love, she closed her eyes and tried to sleep. *I'm not sorry*, she thought, as she buried her face in Leandro's hair.

"I'd leave them again for you," she whispered, but all she heard in reply was Leandro's soft snoring.

⚛⚛⚛

When she first heard that her ex-lover Leandro was marrying Doña Gertrudis, Merced went straight out to Lerner's, the most expensive store on Whittier Boulevard, and bought the tightest and blackest dress she could find. Yes, it was summer, and yes, black was more a color for a funeral. But, so what? Black made her eyes glow like María Félix's. Black made her skin shine like it had been oiled up with passion. She even bought a shiny black plastic purse that looked like a little suitcase made of lizard skin. Everything had to be new: the gloves, the nylon stockings, the hat. Of course, she had to buy a new hat, the one that sat on the head of the dummy in the front store window, the one that looked like a black upside-down tulip with a netted veil.

Norma and Suki, who had just started her period, watched her get ready. From the little radio in the kitchen, Jorge Negrete's *"Ella"* rang through the bungalow, shaking the windowpanes. In the bathroom mirror, Merced could see her daughters' brown eyes, bigger and rounder than usual. Before they could finish asking where she was going, Merced cut them off: "None of your business."

The girls joined a napping Alma in their room and waited for Merced to leave.

Merced knew she was dressed more for a bar than a wedding. Knew that wearing the red velveteen pumps Leandro had given her when they had first moved to East LA would let him know about her passion. When the bus dropped her off at the bottom of the hill where the Santuario de La Virgen de Guadalupe sat, her heartbeat quickened. At first, she climbed the stairs quickly, but in the middle of the hill her feet began to throb as she took each step. By the time she reached the carved wooden doors, blisters stung her toes raw. Before walking inside, she rolled red lipstick over her peeling lips. In the darkness, holy water in the abalone shell looked cool but felt lukewarm as she sprinkled a few drops over her mouth before crossing herself. Merced was careful not to let the water touch her face, because it would ruin her foundation.

"*Ayúdame, señora,*" she whispered to the image of the virgen sitting behind rows of little white candles.

In the middle of the aisle, white paper tissue flowers hung off the pews like they were dead, and the white tiles looked bruised with purple light glowing from the stained-glass windows. When she stepped into the basilica, she heard Leandro's voice murmuring in the dark corners. He seemed to be whispering softly, "*Amor mío.*" Merced stood still, her blood humming in her head. She kept walking down the center aisle.

Incense burned Merced's nose as she proceeded clicking her heels over the rustling and whispering "*Ayúdame, señora.*" She knew her black shiny dress would glow under the purple light spilling from the stained-glass windows. Just as she turned right into the front pew, her foot slipped on its heel and she almost fell on the white floor, her hand slapping the cold tile.

"*Ay, cabrón,*" she cursed.

Some guests smiled at her. From the sacristy, a row of mariachis dressed in cream with matching sombreros filed in and stood left of the altar. The priest in his flowing robes walked over and stood in front of the altar. Merced's heart burst when the mariachi started plucking out "*Amor Mío*" on their violin strings and guitars, her fingers throbbed with each strum. Merced squeezed into the front row, pulling her veil tight over her face.

Leandro emerged from the darkness and stood near the altar, near her. When he turned her way, Merced's lips opened and before she knew it, she had begun singing with the mariachi, looking straight at Leandro: "*Amor mío . . . Tu rostro divino.*"

Nobody could sing like Merced. Not even Lola Beltrán could make stained-glass windows vibrate or the crucifix shake so hard that the priest had to hold onto its stand. It was like an earthquake in the dark. Nobody heard the bride's clicking heels coming down the aisle, not even Leandro. When the clicking stopped, the mariachi grew quiet. But Merced kept singing, even when the guests and the priests tried shushing her. Even when Leandro tried. Merced kept singing, her heels clicking on the cold tiles, her dress shining black and purple gliding past the wilting flowers and out through the church doors.

Once Merced got home, she took off the pumps and threw them in the corner of the living room. Suki and Alma ran out the door toward the store on the corner without saying a word. Merced said nothing. *Let them run*, she thought. *Cabronas*. But she could wait. Her shift at El Yuma would be starting soon, and she could already taste the sweet deadness. What a shame she had to work tonight. How would she face all the women and men in the room? They had been at the wedding. They had heard of her heartbreak. In the kitchen, the radio played the latest song by that greasy Elvis. When she changed it back to KWKW, the first song she heard was "*¿Cómo Fue?*" and she clicked it off quickly before the music had sunk into her.

The linoleum tiles felt warm against Merced's feet. She opened the refrigerator and saw a mason jar filled with a tangle of orange-yellow hair shaking like Jell-O. Merced had persuaded her hairdresser at Ceasar's Salon with an extra ten dollar tip to collect Gertrudis' hair the next time she came in for a cut and color. The last time she saw Leandro before he married, he was dancing with Gertrudis. The *curandera* down the street had told her refrigerating the hairs would guarantee long nights of pain.

"Like a vice gripping her head," the *botánica* woman had said.

Headaches didn't stop Gertrudis from marrying Leandro. Merced would have to change into her tight skirt and low-cut blouse, her work clothes. Why not go in the black dress? Everyone would know, anyway.

Suki and Alma came back sucking on tamarind candy and Coke.

"Get dressed, Alma," Merced grunted as she pulled on the red pumps. "We've got to go to work."

Alma took her Coke and tamarind into her room and shut the door. Suki looked up at Merced like she was about to ask for something, but then quickly looked down before she met her eyes. A firetruck siren screamed outside the window.

"Wash the dishes and clean the kitchen," Merced ordered Suki.

When Alma emerged from her bedroom, Merced turned to pick up the pumps she had thrown in the corner of the room. The lipstick rolled on easily, especially after taking a sip from the Presidente brandy bottle she kept hidden under the sink.

In the purple-orange dusk, Merced and Alma trudged up Indiana toward First Street. Merced's blisters had burst, but she liked the way the pain felt and she dug deeper into the cement sidewalk with each step.

Alma said nothing until they reached the door to El Yuma. "You know he's in there," she mumbled.

"Shut up," Merced whispered.

They parted the dirty blackout curtain that blocked nosy outsiders from peering inside, and walked into the sounds of *norteño* music, the accordion cheerful yipping along with the snare drum and *tololoche*. Wedding guests packed El Yuma. In the middle of it all, Gertrudis and Leandro danced while a *conjunto* played in the corner.

"Here comes the singer," someone yelled.

The tight crowd opened a circle for Merced. Gertrudis and Leandro stopped cold and looked dizzily at Merced and her daughter. Gertrudis opened her mouth, as if to say something, only to start laughing. She threw her arms around Merced and kissed her on the cheek.

"*Gracias*," she said.

Merced's fists clenched, but before she could push her off, Gertrudis walked over to Leandro and put her arms around him. The moment they struck their dance pose, the accordionist began singing "*El Día de tu Boda*." What Presidente couldn't do, singer Gilberto Pérez finally did, stunning Merced into silence. She watched the couple dance close by, swirling and bouncing in the dark, surrounded by a drunken crowd.

CHAPTER 21
Café de olla

The soft crush of velvet always reminded Merced of her marriage to Donaciano. Her dress had been a blue velvet empire with sequined appliqúes of lilies on the bodice. As she rubbed the burgundy velvet of her new shoes, she remembered that hot July day.

What was I thinking, she thought, laughing at the fifteen-year-old girl who thought it would be so romantic to marry in one of the most luxurious, smothering fabrics that could be found in her new husband's store.

This time, it was Christmas, and Leandro had just given her a pair of the most luxurious shoes she had ever worn. She loved the way they caught the golden sunlight of the late afternoon sun. She twisted her feet in unison to the rhythm of Mayte Gao's "*Como un Reloj*," one of the few non-Christmas songs playing on the radio. Leandro had surprised her with the new shoes for their first date after she had arrived from El Paso. He spun her around, dissipating memories of her wedding day.

"You look like a ballerina," Leandro said.

❀❀❀

Merced woke up every morning those first few months she lived with Leandro in their little East LA bungalow in the bedroom she had painted blue. Leandro finally slept next to her, warm and brown like a giant loaf of bread. Merced wanted to swallow him up first thing in the morning along with her coffee. Instead, she pressed her nose against the back of his neck and inhaled deeply.

One morning, the rain drummed against the windows like a heartbeat. She rubbed his neck, then slowly traveled down to the small of his back. His skin was smooth, a brown crust before it was sliced into pieces. Leandro's chest rose up and down with each breath. Merced turned onto her back and stared at the ceiling, listening to him sleep deeply. His breath told her that he would stay, at least for a little while. Her lover Leandro was almost as good as a husband. For a moment, she pretended he was Santa's soldier and could be called away at any moment. Suddenly, Leandro turned over, his eyes shut, mouth smiling.

"*¿Cafecito?*"

Merced smiled down at him, held his face in her hands and kissed his eyelids. Outside the rain came down harder, pinging against the window, chilling the room. She pulled on her flannel nightgown and walked barefoot over the cold wooden floor toward the kitchen. Orange burst through the darkness when she flipped the light switch.

"*El mejor*," Leandro said after his first hot sip of the sweet cinnamon-spiced *café de la olla*.

Merced knew Leandro was comparing her coffee to another girlfriend's *café*, the one he had met while he bartended at El Diamante on First Street. She had heard at La Gloria Tortillería that her name was Gertrudis. Very pretty. Very white.

The bright orange of the kitchen's walls glowed under the dim light of the sole lightbulb hanging from the yellow ceiling. Merced turned on the radio to Sarita Montiel crying "*Perfidia*." Slowly, she pulled the tin of Café Kombate and set it on the counter with a hollow thump. Luckily the earthenware pot on the stove still had water leftover from yesterday.

So, she let him enjoy his coffee, let him sip slowly while she looked at hair and eyes. Who knew how long she would keep him?

"*¿Otro?*" she asked when he waved his clay cup at her. The little yellow and green mugs matched the colors on the pot, reminding her of Tía Pina's chipped *olla,* stained with years of coffee boiling, grounds and eggshells. When she brought the coffee cup to him, he wouldn't look at her, just at what was in his cup. Its black bitterness overwhelmed the sweetness of the *piloncillo.*

"Let's go downtown," she said.

Leandro shook his head and turned the radio on to a soccer game. Outside, she heard someone singing "*Los Laureles*" as the morning sun glowed through the dark clouds.

"Aren't you going to make breakfast?"

Merced stood up and went over to the ice box. Someday, she thought, when she had her own house, she would have her own refrigerator like those women on the billboards and magazine ads. It would have a freezer, and she would be able to freeze her tamales to eat in July. But without Leandro, what would it mean?

As she looked for the frying pan underneath the sink, she heard Leandro step outside. A cool breeze blew in the smell of mint and wet dirt.

"Leandro," she heard one of her neighbors greet him. It was Moti, Rufina's brother and the man she had fucked months ago. He hadn't told Leandro anything. Or maybe he had and that's why Leandro hated her this morning. As she cracked the egg, she thought of Moti's fumbling sweaty body on top of her and then remembered her ex-husband back in El Sauz.

"*Mensa,*" she said to herself out loud.

Leandro came in and hugged her from behind. But the man wasn't Leandro, it was Moti. Through the window she saw Leandro walking down Indiana Avenue. He was going to see Gertrudis.

"What did you say?" Moti asked.

Merced pulled away and looked at Moti with his thick black hair and white smile.

"Forget him," he said. "He's going to see *la otra vieja*."

Merced poured coffee into the cup Leandro had left behind and handed it to Moti.

❀❀❀

On Sunday morning, the rain had cleared cold with a sun that cut the blue sky. Leandro's face glowed under the icy light, his forehead pinched and lips pursed. Merced stroked his cheek, kissed the stubble and breathed in the musk in the hollow of his neck. If only she could hide herself in there.

Leandro turned his back to her. The sunlight burned her eyes, but she opened them again and saw the blood-crusted crescent moons cut into his brown back. Pressing her cheek against his back, she started kissing them, then sucking on them, stopping now and then to see the purple bruise spreading over the cuts. Merced wrapped her leg around Leandro's waist. He pushed it away but could not help admiring her firm muscles. She pushed her leg back on him.

"What are you doing?"

"I know," Merced told him.

Leandro said nothing.

"I know about her," Merced whispered into his back.

By then, Leandro was snoring.

❀❀❀

For the first time in the twenty years since she had left El Sauz, Merced washed herself in a bathtub without hurrying. In the white-tiled bathroom, in the glow of the blue painted walls, Merced grabbed the Camay soap she had stolen earlier that day from the First Street Store and dunked it in the hot water. Perfumed steam spread around her. Water splashed softly against the sides of the tub as she rubbed the soap on her neck and her chest. Her breasts felt tender, and she knew her period would be coming soon. Foam spilled between her palms, bubbles floated around, and she reached for her long black hair. She imagined it the golden color of the cabaret vedettes and of Gertrudis. Then she remembered her father, who used to sit in a straight-back chair and pretend to cut thorns off the cactus pads. He'd sit there for a minute before he'd look up and stare straight at her, then down at her breasts, which had grown like those on a movie actress she had once seen. At first, she felt happy when her *tía* Pina pointed it out to her, but when her father also stared at them like the other boys in El Sauz, she no longer took her time enjoying the steam and hot water.

Merced snorted and dunked her head under water.

If only she had died with her mother at birth. As soon as her head rose out of the water, she heard Leandro come into the bathroom.

❀❀❀

Merced knew she was really in trouble when she saw Leandro standing on her porch with Gertrudis, the peroxide bitch. After two years he had finally come back, but not for her. Suddenly, Merced remembered the deed to her house was under his name, despite the fact that she and her daughters had worked their knees, hands and backs at hotels and bars to buy it.

Merced had seen the TV news stories about the Dodgers and how Gertrudis told the reporter that she and her La Loma neighbors were losing their homes to the new stadium.

"You have to let us in," Leandro said.

Behind Merced, Suki hovered like a ghost, pale and silent.

"You can't take my house," Merced yelled through the door.

"It's *my* house," Leandro yelled back. "Let us in."

"Just you, then," Merced's voice cracked. "Not her."

"She's my wife now," he said quietly. "This house is my right."

CHAPTER 22
Crawl Space

"Why would she want such a crummy house?" Norma
asks after I finish reading the special delivery letter from the
lawyer who represents a Mrs. Gertrudis Franco. It came in a
special envelope I'd never seen before. The envelope looked
scarier than a letter from school.

"Don't be stupid, Lucha," Grandma Merced sneers. "It's
my house. She knows Leandro loved me, not her. He only
married her for . . ." She stops before she can say the words.

"Here we go again," whispers my mother.

I wonder the same thing: Why does Gertrudis want this
old bungalow? True, Grandma Merced works her ass off bartending at El Yuma and cleaning houses in Alhambra and
Pasadena to pay the mortgage. She works my mom's ass especially hard to punish her for running off with, then divorc-
ing Don Pedro, my father. Aunt Norma ran off long ago but
now she's back cleaning houses with my grandmother and
mother. Aunt Suki also sends her money. So really, the house
belongs to all of them. Maybe it even belongs to me, too. Ever
since I left my job at Jack in the Crack and started working for
Tía Suki, I give Grandma a share of my money too. She supposedly uses it to pay the bills, but I know she uses it for cigarettes, brandy and sometimes a new dress or a necklace.

175

Now that Leandro's gone, Gertrudis wants the house he shared with my grandmother in the early years of their love.

"Was your name on the deed?" Norma asks as she taps out the last cigarette from the red and white pack of Winstons.

"Of course it was," Grandma huffs impatiently. "Do you think I'm a fool?"

"Where's the paper? Do you have a copy?"

Grandma Merced paces the floor, her right hand pulling and ratcheting the Virgen medallion around her chain until it comes to the clasp.

"Leandro buried it somewhere under the house," she says, not taking her eyes off of the floor, her brows pushing together, her mouth a straight line.

Norma and Alma look at each other, roll their eyes. Lucky for them, Grandma is looking hard at the gold Virgen, as if it's the Mother of God's fault that Leandro had chosen Gertrudis over her and not her daughters, for a change.

I knew Leandro had dumped her for Gertrudis a while ago, had abandoned her to live high up in Chavez Ravine instead of down here in Boyle Heights. Boyle Lows, really. But then they lost their house to the Dodgers, and Leandro and Gertrudis had to move into the Maravilla Projects, which is way worse than Boyle Heights. All along I kept thinking that Gertrudis was a skank, but I met her once when she and Leandro had come to claim the house. She was younger, smaller than my grandmother, the complete opposite of my *abuela*, even down to the blue eyes and blonde hair. She was the *güera* my grandmother could never be.

"*Puro* peroxide," Grandma had scoffed then, but I could tell by her straight mouth that she felt "moded and corroded" just like when George had dumped me for Yoli.

At least, I hadn't bought him a house.

❀❀❀

I have no choice. I want to cry the moment I feel the cool moldy air hit my face. I pull my hood over my head and climb

in headfirst through the black rectangle, making sure the
flashlight doesn't slip out of my hands. Some daylight shines
through the little grates that cover up the other three holes.
They're supposed to keep out the rats and mice, but some of
the wire mesh has been chewed out. My fingers sink into the
soft dirt. At least it's not muddy, but my Vanderbilt jeans will
be ruined. Good thing I wore my UCLA sweatshirt. I keep
crawling, trying to find the glass bottle shaped like a pig with
a cork for its nose. Inside there's supposed to be some kind
of contract my grandmother says was written up by a lawyer
Leandro met at El Yuma. I don't gag when I see the bones. I'll
barf for sure if I think they could belong to a baby, a cat or
some other kind of once-living thing. Right now, it doesn't
matter because my grandmother promises she will kick my
ass if I come out of that crawl space without that contract.

"Did you find it?" she calls out.

So far no, but there's still the other side of the house to
check. As I crawl toward that corner, the stink of shit gets
stronger. I just keep rewinding my new Hall and Oates tape
and play it until Daryl Hall sounds like he's singing under
water. This is the only way I'll keep from barfing or fainting.
Grandma Merced and her corny ideas. Let Gertrudis have the
house! There are plenty of nicer houses outside of East LA.
Houses in Whittier, Montebello or Alhambra.

"Too many *chinos*," Grandma says every time Norma or
Alma mention those nearby neighborhoods.

"Fuck," I want to tell her. "Why stay in this noisy neighborhood where every Saturday night you can hear every single house party up and down the street. Imagine, no more
helicopter noise and spotlights at night looking for some
bleeding *cholo* on the run. No more rotting-blood smells from
the Farmer John meatpacking plant in Vernon."

"It's there," she says. "Leandro gave it to me."

Yes, I know the house means memories of her passionate
love for Leandro, but he never came back to her. He's dead.
What kind of crazy love is that? No matter. My grandmother

wants to stay in the house Leandro bought for her when she first came to LA. It's like this fake Walkman that George gave me. I'll keep it until the day I die.

Besides rat shit, spiders hang from dusty webs. I try avoiding them but can feel them snagging on the tip of my hood. I yelp.

"Did you find it?" Grandma asks again.

"No."

"Don't come out until you find it."

I cough into the soft sweatshirt arm and wish I had brought a bandana to cover my mouth and nose. The closer I crawl to the middle of the house, the softer and wetter the dirt gets. I see something soft and brown sticking up. I hope it's not a turd. I pull my flashlight out and focus on what looks like a snake with its head and tail buried. I see more of these snake backs around it. Then I realize they're roots from the huizache tree planted out in front. I'm so relieved, I blow out a sigh. Then I see it. Some glass shining right underneath the middle of the house. I get excited until I realize it's a tall glass votive candle, the kind you find in church with images of the Virgen de Guadalupe, San Martín de Porres, San Judas Tadeo.

As the stench gets grosser and the ground gets wetter, I find the cork. I dig with my hands until they hit the glass, cloudy with dirt and grime. I dig as much as I can. The bottle's halfway out, and I see it's hopeless.

"Did you find it?" Grandma Merced asks again through the uncovered grate.

"I need the gloves and the little shovel."

Norma throws me a pair of yellow gloves and a shovel. By the time I dig through the dirt and crap, I realize I can't pull this thing out while lying on by stomach. I look up at the floorboards above me. I forget about the rat shit, dead mice and spiders. I close my eyes and then open them up to the image of San Ramón, protector of midwives and babies, painted on a little door. I reach up and trace my finger over the image. I try to push it up, but it won't budge. Something's weighing on top of it. I roll over and try kicking through the little door. My foot punches through the cheap flooring and into a dark room. At first, it looks like I've punched into outer space, but it turns out I'm just in my grandmother's closet.

"Holy shit," I say.

"*¿Qué pasó?*" Grandma yells.

"I think I found it."

"Well, start digging, *mensa!*"

The little door I've smashed in leaves a space big enough for me to crawl through, and I go up into the closet. I lean down through the space and start shoveling around the glass pig's nose. Now I can finally see that *pinche* pig. At first, I just want to smash the smile off the pig's face with my flashlight, but I don't want to deal with the broken glass. It takes a while, but I finally get a grip on the nose and loosen the cork. I flash the light into the glass belly of the pig. Instead of a paper deed, I find a metal, mint-green box.

It's not heavy but it clatters when I pull it from the pig. The box's color and condition scare me, and I quickly say a prayer to the Virgen. Let her know that my grandmother made me do this. I also vow that this is the last time I'll ever crawl under the house again for anyone. Ever. I get up and pull off my sweatshirt, spreading dust, mice shit and spider webs all over the floor. My jeans look gray with dust. I pull them off and throw them in the washroom. I grab another pair and head back to the closet.

"Where are you, Lucha?" Grandma yells. She still thinks I'm in the crawl space.

I don't answer and sneak around to the back.

As I come up behind her, I remember something that made Grandma Merced look really bad. It was when Leandro came to pick up some things, and she brought him in. What was terrible was that she was crying. I'd never seen my grandmother cry before. She was wailing. I'd never heard it but read about it in books about women who lived a hundred years ago in England or Massachusetts. Or about ghosts of women who wailed after their lovers or lost children.

"Don't leave me," Grandma Merced wailed in Spanish.

As she held on to his arm, Leandro looked down at her. He didn't say a word, just squinted down at her, moved his arm like he was about to stroke her hair but put it down. Then he just turned around and left. My grandmother came into the house and sat down on the floor, placed elbows on the coffee table and covered her eyes with her hands. She wailed like a ghost. I sat there on the couch, wondering if I should hug her but, really, I didn't know how. We never hug. We never touch one another, except to hit or snatch things away.

Grandma Merced sat there alone, and I went into my room, put on my headphones and turned on the Walkman. I pulled out *Pride and Prejudice* for the tenth time and read for two hours until my mom came home.

She came into my room and asked, "What's wrong with your grandmother?"

I told her about Leandro.

She shook her head and sighed. Then, she lay down on the bed and fell asleep. We stayed in our room until Grandma lifted herself off the table and went to bed. The next morning, she was making *menudo*, smoking her cigarette, not making a sound while "*Paloma Negra*" played on the radio. I didn't say a thing because both my mom and grandmother said nothing. It was the quietest morning in my life.

And now, here I was, sticking my hand into a glass pig looking for a piece of paper. I pull out the metal box, cutting myself along its sharp edges. Inside, there's a folded, yellowed paper. I unfold the sheet of paper and see a scrawled signature, the faded typewritten ink declaring in English legalese the house belongs to Merced Carrasco Fierro. I run with the paper and give it to my grandmother.

"Look, look," she says. "I told you!"

She barely reads Spanish and can't read any English, but she knows her own signature, knows her name: Merced Carrasco Fierro.

❀❀❀

Grandma Merced wants her citizenship. After nearly forty years living in the United States as a *mojada*, she decides to finally get her act together and get her *mica*.

After that big fight with Tía Suki, Grandma had the nerve to ask her if Lily, Suki's own girlfriend, could help her fix her papers. I could hear Tía Suki laughing over the phone. While she waited for her to stop, my grandmother lit a cigarette.

"Why?" Tía Suki asks.

"For my house," Merced whispers, thinking my mother and I can't hear her. "That *piruja* Gertrudis wants to take away my house."

I can hear Tía Suki laugh harder.

"Is your name on the deed?" Lily asks.

Tía Suki's laughter can still be heard in the background.

"Yes . . ." Grandma Merced hesitates. "But I don't have a green card."

"Oh," Lily says in a low tone. "That's a problem. Does Leandro have legal residency?"

"*¿Qué's eso?*" Grandma asks. "*¿Papeles?*"

"Yes, papers. Does he have them?"

My grandmother smiles as she tells Lily that Leandro was also a *mojado*.

Laughter bursts from Lily. "How in the hell did you get a house?"

"Long story . . . *cuento largo*," she tells her then takes another drag. "Can you help me get my papers or not?"

For a long time, Lily breathes low and slow. Merced holds her breath. Everything's quiet, even the cars outside stop running.

Lily finally speaks. "I'll need your birth certificate."

❀❀❀

As Tía Suki presses the gas and speeds up the I-10 on-ramp, in the back seat Grandma Merced slaps her daughter's headrest. "You're going to fast!"

Tía Suki presses on, going faster than fifty-five miles per hour. Merced leans back into the leather seat and pulls out her box of Marlboro Lights.

"I said, no smoking in the car," Tía Suki snaps, eyeing her grandmother from the rearview.

Grandma Merced pulls out her Cricket lighter, clicks it quickly and lights up. Tía Suki rolls her eyes, twists her mouth ready to snap again, but Lily quickly turns on the radio. David Bowie's "Let's Dance" rises out of the speakers, tinny but rhythmic.

"Turn that shit down," Grandma tells Lily, who ignores her.

Tía Suki reaches over and turns the plastic knob until the volume is on full blast. Lily quickly lowers it.

In all of this, I poke the button to roll down my window, stick my hand out, palm pushing against the wind. Hair whips around my face, slashing at my cheeks. It feels good. I'm excited. We're finally going to visit my grandmother's home-town. It'll be the first time I see other parts of Mexico that aren't Tijuana. And I for sure want to see El Paso and the fancy hotel where my grandmother and my mom used to work.

At the Morongo Indian Reservation, we stop for gas and a bathroom break. I heard about Indian reservations in my history class but they never went into deep detail. Now I know why. There's nothing, just empty desert. Maybe a few scrubby bushes and the San Bernardino Mountains in the background. Tía Suki parks the car in front of the Super Shell gas station. "It's more expensive," Tía Suki says, "but has cleaner restrooms.

"Lily and I will go get snacks," she adds. "Go take your grandmother to the *escusado*."

This time, it's my turn to roll my eyes, but Tía Suki and Lily have already opened their doors, and desert heat blasts away at the cool, conditioned air.

"*Aquí viven los indios*," Grandma Merced informs me as if I haven't noticed the off-ramp sign. Then I remember, she can't read. I walk her over to the restroom behind the gas station. I knock on the door.

"Just a minute," a man's voice calls out.

While we wait, Merced recounts the time she hitchhiked from El Paso to Los Angeles. I can't believe it.

"Ask your *tía* Suki," Grandma says. "She'll tell you."

"How come you didn't take Alma, Norma and Suki with you?"

"Not enough money, or time," she says. "Your mom was still working at the hotel. Your *tía* Norma was married to some soldier and Suki was going to school."

Before I can ask her why she couldn't just pull Tía Suki from school, a tall dark man opens the restroom door. He looks us up and down, then looks at me with a little smile before walking away.

Merced juts her chin at the man. "*Ese es indio*," she says, then pulls me into the restroom.

I want to wait outside, but she seems convinced the "*indio*" will take me. At that moment, I wish he would.

CHAPTER 23
El Yuma

Merced knew she was home the moment she stepped through the faded velvet curtains of El Yuma. Then, through the curtains, Merced heard it. Lola Beltrán's rendition of sobbing "*Paloma Negra*" sounding just like the mourning doves Merced would hear outside Leandro's window.

As she made her way up to the bar, she was deafened by balls banging each other on the pool tables, the laughter of couples on the small dance floor and the blaring of the Wurlitzer jukebox. Merced immediately recognized Leandro's erect back and thick stiff black hair.

Before she could touch his shoulder, "*La Enorme Distancia*" by José Alfredo Jiménez cut through the rumbling laughter. Leandro turned around. His black eyes darkened, but he smiled under his thin moustache. In the flickering darkness, his hair shined with the same brilliantine he wore back in Juárez when she first met him at Mercado Cuauhtémoc. He stood up and offered her his stool. Merced sat down without thinking and nodded when he offered to buy her a drink.

❁❁❁

The chipped aqua blue walls of El Yuma bar glowed under the white-hot light of the late morning sun when

Merced arrived. Small windows the size of shoe boxes squinted like they had just woken up with a hangover. A picture of a Yuma Indian with his bare chest cut like a diamond thrust forward and his flexed arms at his side gleamed on the plastic sign jutting over the red wooden door. Red, green and white feathers stuck out from the top of his head, and his long black hair poured over his shoulders and down his back. Merced loved that *indio*, who reminded her of Leandro when he would strut around naked in their bedroom.

Inside El Yuma, the vapor of days-old smoke, sweat and stale beer swirled around Merced. Red vinyl stools on chrome legs lined the black padded bar. A small black and white Zenith TV was forever broadcasting a boxing match or soccer game between Mexican teams. On the walls hung posters of blonde women in black velvet bikinis smiling behind Canadian whisky bottles. Others had Mexican women with long black hair and tight short dresses, sitting on their knees, kissing a tall can of Coors. Merced's favorite was the big red and gold Tecate can, shiny with water droplets making the metal look like gold and rubies.

Merced made her way to the tiny backroom, picked out her mop and bucket and headed to the women's restroom. For some reason, the owner thought it would be sexy to install a red light bulb above the mirror.

"To glow with a woman's passion," he had said as he rubbed her knee.

Merced had quickly pressed her cigarette into the back of his hand, just like she had done a long time ago to the truck driver who had given her a lift into Los Angeles.

The owner had almost fallen off the stool, but he laughed and told her that if she cleaned the restroom every morning, she would earn an extra ten dollars. Merced wondered if it was worth the money because whenever she entered the cold damp red room, she felt like hell. Every time she wiped down the scratched-up mirror, Merced looked like a demon glowing red, a black cloud of hair waving around her face. And she felt like one, especially when she was drunk and missing Leandro.

Outside the restroom she could hear *rancheras* playing on the jukebox. At least the owner kept it stocked with the latest records by Vicente Fernández, Lucha Villa and José Alfredo Jiménez. Whenever the jukebox went silent, Merced would drop in a dime or a quarter just to fill the place with some joy, even if it lasted for only three minutes. When Leandro came to visit her before finally leaving her, he had sung "*Paloma Negra*," her favorite, right there on the corner stool. She had sung it with him. Little did she know that he was already planning his escape.

❀❀❀

I'm singing with Olivia Newton-John as I sweep up the cigarette butts from last night's *pachanga*. Grandma Merced has sent me to El Yuma to take over her afternoon shift.

"Hey, young man! Where the hell is Merced?"

Suddenly, Olivia's gentle crooning stops as the manager yanks my earphones off. Luckily, my Dodger's baseball cap hasn't slipped. I push the stop button. The manager just stares at me, puffing on his cigarette. I didn't have time to wash my hair, so I just tucked it under the cap. I know my cap makes me look like a boy.

"I'm covering her shift tonight," I tell the manager.

He looks me up and down. "Do you know how to serve drinks?"

I nod.

Grandma had warned me ahead of time that he would test me. To prove my bartending skills, I walk behind the bar and pour a shot partly filled with water, just like I do at home. The manager takes a sip.

"Yep, that's right way," he approves. "Make sure you mop the bathroom up. Some *güey* pissed all over the floor."

I slip on my headphones again and click play on the Walkman. As I sweep the butts, dust, used matchbooks and crumpled napkins, I know I'll never want to live my grandmother's life. Nor my mother's, for that matter.

CHAPTER 24
Coffee Time

My mom gets up every day at four-thirty in the morning and starts boiling water for coffee. I smell it the moment she opens the Hills Brothers Coffee can, the one with the old man in a yellow dress and white turban.

After she leaves, I make coffee for myself. I'm not supposed to because Grandma Merced always gripes about how coffee's so expensive. I never drink too much, just enough to have with sugar and milk. The condensed milk is best, but if I punch open the can with the pointy end of the can opener, Grandma will know. So, sometimes I make powdered milk then pour it into the coffee, add two or three teaspoons of sugar. Then I go to school, ready to take on Patty Landa and Yoli Zamudio, the queen bitches of Roosevelt High.

One morning, I dream the aroma of coffee and wake myself up. But Mom and the coffee aren't in the kitchen. I open her bedroom door and find her still in bed, eyes red, nose running.

"I'm sick," she says and she pulls the blankets over her head.

This is the first time I know of that she'll miss work. She never misses, even when she's sick. Later, I find out she's been crying all night and every night for the past week because the Pasadena woman laid her off with no warning.

By this time, I need my coffee. Already the headache's coming on. The last time I missed my morning coffee I almost threw up, my headache was so bad.

Grandma pokes her out of her bedroom just as I pull the Hills Brothers from the freezer.

"¿Qué haces, Lucha?"

"I'm making my mom some coffee," I mumble.

"Alma's not going to work," Grandma says.

"I know."

I quickly pour the ground coffee over the boiling water.

Grandma scrunches her face. "Coffee's expensive."

I nod, while the grounds sink into the water. Soon it will be brown, and that deep coffee smell will take over the kitchen. As soon as Grandma closes the door, I pulled out a can of condensed milk and my stained coffee mug.

The next morning, Mom's still in bed. I open the freezer and the Hills Brothers is gone. I open all the half-empty cupboards, even the one's under the sink, and there's nothing except a can of Comet and an old Hills Brothers coffee can filled with bacon grease. I knock on Mom's door.

"What?"

"Did you take the coffee?" I ask, opening the door.

"What coffee?"

I start sweating. "The Hills Brothers? The can in the freezer!"

Mom twists her mouth, gets up and closes the door.

When the door reopens, she's holding the Hill's Brothers can. "This?"

Before I can grab it, she pulls it away. "No more coffee until I get another job."

My head starts throbbing. I want to cry right then and there. Instead of leaving for school, I sit down at the table and massage the sides of my head, sharp pains shooting through my eyes.

An hour later, Grandma comes out of her room, hair wet from her shower. I'm asleep at the table, the side of my face wet with drool.

"Why aren't you at school?" she asks, lighting up one of her Winstons.

"I have a bad headache."

Grandma sits down across from me and lights up another cigarette, puffing at it. "Here," she says, putting the filtered end of her cigarette close to my face.

I lean in and start sucking a little bit of smoke, feel the burn. My eyes water, but I keep sucking. Grandma laughs but I know she's impressed. I inhale a little more smoke and quickly blow it out. Slowly, my headache starts to go away.

My mom, dressed but red-eyed, walks into the kitchen. "What are you two up to?"

"We're smoking," Grandma answers, smiling.

The smoke tingles my lungs. Maybe cigarettes can substitute for coffee.

Just like that, my mom snatches the cigarette away from me and throws it into the sink. As she runs the faucet, she looks out the kitchen window, making sure the neighbors are not watching.

My headache's coming back, and Grandma lights up another cigarette but before she passes it up to me, Mom puts the familiar red can between us.

"This is cheaper," she says.

Before long, water rushes into the chipped enamel pot. Mom sets it over the dancing gas flames, and soon the water is singing with heat. As soon as the hot water soaks the grounds at the bottom of the pot, the pounding in my head softens a little. The grounds float to the top. I can't wait, so I dip my cup instead of using the ladle. I don't bother with the milk, just the sugar. Black-brown darkness makes the cup bottomless. As I swirl the coffee around my mouth, I make a wish. Never run out of coffee.

❀❀❀

Don Pedro, my father and owner of El Yuma, buys me a bicycle for my twelfth birthday.

"Why purple?" I ask.

"Because, Lucha, he didn't know if you were a boy or a girl," Grandma says.

"Why not?"

"Because Alma never told him."

Don Pedro has sad eyes and a big round stomach. He looks like a tomato Santa Claus with his white fluffy hair and his bright red face. He's a white man, but his face looks like it's always on fire.

"Where have you been?" Grandma Merced asks Pedro as she leans against the doorway of El Yuma's kitchen, smoking.

I can tell from her voice that she wants to yell at him but doesn't. I just want to take that bike and ride far away.

"I've been traveling," Don Pedro says. "Traveling around Tijuana, checking on my businesses."

Grandma Merced blows smoke out of her nose like those angry bull cartoons I used to watch when I was little. Suddenly, she looks at me like I had just popped up from the ground.

"Why don't you go ride your new bicycle somewhere?" she says. "See if it doesn't fall apart like the other toys."

Don Pedro's jaw bulges out, but he says nothing. This is the chance I've been waiting for. I roll the bike out the door just as my mom is walking up the cement path.

"What's that?"

"My new bike," I say proudly. "Don Pedro gave it to me."

"Oh."

Mom's mouth turns down. She stands still, then walks around toward the back of El Yuma to enter through the kitchen door. I take off, ride my purple bicycle down the street, avoiding the boat-like cars parked on both sides. I hit Arizona Avenue, which turns into Mednik. I pump my legs up past Griffith Junior. High and finally reach Sheriff's Park. I'd been there before, on a school field trip to the library. Some families are hanging out, little kids stagger up the hills, trying to keep up with their brother and sisters. One girl and her father are flying one of those long-tailed kites that looks like a dragon.

I ride on the cement paths circling the shallow lake. In a few weeks, he'll attach a white basket to the handlebars. It will be covered in shiny plastic flowers. Attached on its front with copper wires will be a little metal license plate with my name, "Lucha."

CHAPTER 25
Cleófila's *Botánica*

After parking in El Paso, we cross the International Bridge to Juárez. The smell of mangoes and smog hits me. The Mexican border guards with thin little moustaches wave Grandma Merced, Tía Suki, Lily, Tía Norma and me through the turnstiles, and soon we're on the cracked sidewalks of the Mexican city. Of course, they give Lily, whose wearing her shorts and off the shoulder blouse, a once over. Lily just smiles and flips her hair like it's nothing. The guards liked Tía Suki too, but she's wearing pants and her caftan blouse with the big sleeves. Grandma looks pissed. She wanted the guards to look at her, but she's not young enough for these guys.

As if she's been living in Juárez all her life, Grandma walks straight to a beat-up taxi driven by an old man.

Grandma gets into the passenger seat next to the driver. My *tías*, Lily and I squeeze into the backseat. Before I can put on my lap belt, the taxi jerks forward and speeds down the cobblestone street toward a row of brick buildings that look like something out of Masterpiece Theater with their brick walls and curvy roof tops. Although it's cold outside, our body heat makes the smell of old vinyl and Pine Sol from the green tree shaped car freshener stronger. I ask Tía Suki to roll down one of the windows, and soon the black truck exhaust almost makes me throw up.

As the sun goes down, the neon lights from the night clubs flick on, shining purple and pink words like Noa Noa, Juárez Turf Club and Tivoli. The thump, thump of DJ music bumps out the open doors.

"Look at the giant boobs on her," Grandma Merced shouts, waving at a woman dressed in platform heels and a low-cut dress. What's worse is that the woman smiles and waves back at my grandmother. The taxi driver's cigarette almost drops out of his mouth. I sink down lower into my seat but Tía Suki and Lily just laugh at me.

❀❀❀

"*¡Ay Dios mío!*" Tía Cleo yelps when she opens the door to my grandmother, Tía Suki, Lily, Tía Norma and me.

My lungs burn the moment Cleo opens the heavy metal door to her little house. The air rushes out with a mix of cigarette smoke, hair spray and roasted *chiles*. I get a little dizzy with the brightness of the yellow walls. On white wooden shelves and on dressers painted yellow-green with peach tulips, there are glass jars filled with dark and silver-green leaves curled into little fists. The thin frosted windows are reinforced with honeycombed wiring.

Virgen de Guadalupe statues pop out from rows of jars, oils and candles. Inside a glass counter are *milagros*, *rosarios* and pendants with golden saints. My mother should be here but she had a fit when Grandma told her about the trip.

"I can't go back," Mom said. "No."

Then she went back to our bedroom and locked the door. It was a miracle that Grandma didn't pound the door down. I knew there and then I would have to corner Tía Suki later to get the real story. Tía Norma would never spill the beans unless she was drunk, and I didn't have the money to get her high. What I have, I had to save up for my calls to George back in LA.

Tía Cleo walks over to me, her long gray braid swishing like a horsetail behind her back. Her brown fingers scrub my cheeks, and her soft black eyes tick side to side, examining every inch of me, trying to find something. Maybe a trace of my mom? I can't look away, even though it feels like Cleo's about to put me in a jar with all the other dried out leaves.

"She looks like her mother," Cleo finally says to Grandma.

"At least she's thin."

Tía Cleo twists her mouth, nods while she pulls on my hands until my arms stretch out.

"Yes," she nods. "Like Alma."

I don't ask for more about my mom because I know I'll regret it. Before she says anything else, I pull out the Kodak and start taking pictures.

"She's doing my life story for her school," Grandma explains.

Tía Cleo's left eyebrow arches, but then she takes my hands. "*Una artista*," she says.

She's wrong. I'm no artist, just a reporter. Actually, the pictures will be for a special edition of my school paper, "The Family Tree" edition. Grandma Merced is family, but not like the other students' *abuelas*.

"Come through here," Tía Cleo says, walking through a little archway leading into a smaller kitchen painted orange. On a small round table, clay mugs surround a plate of *conchitas*, *marranitos* and *empanadas*. The white tablecloth almost blinds me, it's so white and starchy. We haven't eaten since we got to Juárez. The moment we crossed the bridge, Grandma was too excited to stop at any of the restaurants or food stands. I reach for an *empanada*. Tía Norma takes two. Tía Suki and Lily drink cinnamon tea Tía Cleo serves us from a hot ceramic saucepan. A cool breeze blows from the open backdoor leading to a backyard. After eating my *empanada*, I make the mistake of stepping through the door. My body freezes when I see a freshly gutted pig hanging upside down from a tree, slowly dripping blood. Tía Cleo says it's for to-morrow's celebration. I go back to the table, pick up the mug and sip my tea. My hand shakes a little.

"And how's the *botánica* going?" Tía Cleo asks Tía Suki.

Grandma cuts off Tía Suki before she answers. "How do you know about . . ."

Lily winks at me, then I aim my camera at Tía Suki. It's a good moment, because Tía Suki walks over to Tía Cleo and hugs her from behind. Click. Flash. Crank the film with my thumb. Click again.

"She sends me her recipes and recommendations," Tía Suki says, then kisses Tía Cleo on the cheek. Click. Flash. Crank.

"Really?" Tía Norma asks, spitting out the crumbs from her half-eaten *empanada*. Click. Flash. Crank.

"Tía Cleo's been running her own *botánica* for years," Tía Suki says. "She learned it from Tía Pina."

"She learned it from me," Grandma Merced says matter-of-factly.

Tía Cleo folds her arms and leans back in her chair.

"No way," Tía Cleo says, getting up to pour herself more cinnamon tea from the enamel saucepan. "She learned it from me and Tía Pina after you ran off with Leandro."

"True," Tía Norma agrees. "Suki was more interested in herbs than spells."

"*Malflores*," Grandma Merced mumbles.

Tía Suki nods, smiles widely.

Lily says proudly, "Suki's *botánica* is the most popular in East LA."

Grandma blows smoke through her nostrils. "Tía Pina never helped me," she mumbles.

Tía Cleo takes the now cold cinnamon tea back to the burners, pours more water into the saucepan and says, "She saved us from our father."

I know almost nothing about my great-grandfather, ex-cept that his name was Plutarco and that he was a hard worker. I know that Tía Pina took care of my mother and aunts when Grandma ran off to Juárez, then El Paso and then Los Angeles. When the water in the saucepan starts bubbling, Tía Cleo refills our mugs. It's the best cinnamon tea I've ever had, but too hot to drink.

Lily asks the question we're all afraid to ask. "How did Tía Pina save you?"

Grandma Merced turns her head so quickly from the window, her neck bones crack. She makes her lips disappear into a tight line but says nothing. I really want to take her picture, but it's too dangerous.

"She gave the love of her life to Merced," Tía Cleo states. We wait for more.

"So," she says, holding the earthenware mug close to her face, its steam rising. "What happened to Leandro?"

All of us are quiet, waiting for Grandma to say something. After a long pause, she says, "He's dead."

Tía Suki and I look at each other. Tía Norma shakes her head but says nothing.

"Not even a *pinche* goodbye?" Tía Cleo asks.

We all laugh except for Grandma, who looks out the backdoor. "What for?" she says. "He was already married to Gertrudis."

"Don't tell me," Tía Cleo closes her eyes. "A *güera*?"

Grandma Merced rubs her face and looks out at the busy street. I know this is a bad time to take a picture, but it's the first time I see Grandma's heart in her eyes. We sit on the plastic covered love seat and kitchen chairs, quiet except for the rush of buses and people. Tía Norma crosses and uncrosses her legs. Lily smooths out her skirt, while I hold my camera, ready for something to happen. When a horse clip-clops by the window, Grandma breaks the quiet.

"And Donaciano?"

"He still has his little store," Tía Cleo says, taking the cigarette Grandma offers her. "But he moved back to Chihuahua and also opened a woman's clothing store."

Grandma makes a face and starts coughing out smoke. Tía Suki slaps her back.

"He makes really nice clothes," Tía Cleo says.

To prove it, she brings out a cardboard box from a back room. From a cloud of light pink tissue, Tía Cleo pulls out a long navy-blue velvet dress with a lace collar and cuffs. At the sight of it, Grandma drops her cigarette. Tía Suki quickly picks it up before it burns a mark on the floor. Still, the ash scatters over the linoleum before she throws it into the kitchen sink, then scoots her chair closer to Lily.

Grandma rubs the hem of the dress between her fingers. The velvet's so thick, it almost looks like fur. "Looks like my wedding dress," she says so quietly I almost can't hear her.

"What?" Tía Norma says, then pulls the dress from Grandma's hands. "Why would you want this dress?"

Grandma grips the hem.

"Didn't you get married in the summer?" Tía Suki asks.

"It looked like the sky," Grandma whispers, then grows silent again. "The sky over the *huizache* tree."

Tía Norma hands the dress back to Tía Cleo. Later, when we're in bed, she tells me about the tree where she and her sisters gathered to play *Lotería*, tag and other games while Grandma and Tía Pina worked the *chile* fields.

"We'd spend hours just playing, sleeping while your *abuela* and Tía Pina picked *chiles*," Norma says.

I don't ask about my great-grandfather, Plutarco. I'd been shushed before. I take out the camera from beneath the little bed I'm sharing with Tía Norma, aim the lens at my face and press the lever. For a moment, the flash lights up the little room. Nobody wakes up.

CHAPTER 26
Pomegranates for Cleófilas

"The pomegranates are bigger in Mexico," Norma told the fruit vendor.

He nodded and picked out two of the biggest from the pile. Their tough red skin reminded Norma of her mother. They were perfect for the *chiles en nogada* Cleófilas planned on making for our family. It was hard to believe that anyone wanted to make a sumptuous dinner for Merced, but Cleófilas insisted the moment Norma called her and told her about Merced's mission to retrieve her birth certificate.

"You have to stay with me," Cleófilas said. "I'll make your mother's favorite."

Merced had many "favorites," Norma wanted to say but kept her mouth shut.

The thought of returning to the town where she first met, then lost Eduardo made her nauseous. The drive from Los Angeles was hellish enough, and now she was back in the city that almost tore her apart.

"*Gracias, está bien*," Norma agreed. "But we'll buy all the ingredients."

Cleófilas protested but Norma refused to defer. It was the least they could do. Cleófilas opened up her tiny house that faced Avenida de los Insurgentes for them. Lily and Suki opted for a hotel room at the Hotel Chula.

"Lucky them," Norma mumbled, hoisting her bag full of pomegranates, pears, apples and stew meat.

Suddenly, Eduardo appeared. Instead of an army uniform, he was wearing a blue *guayabera*. A little girl held his hand.

Norma could not believe her eyes. It *was* Eduardo, a little leaner and balder, but Eduardo. For a moment, all of the *mercado*'s overripe fruit, cheeses and raw meat overwhelmed her. The flayed cow heads in the butcher counter stared at her, recognizing her. The *mercado* spun around her. In her tunneled vision, she reached for a metal bench near the butcher counter and sat down, handing her basket to Lucha as soon as she returned from the restroom. Norma leaned over her knees and took a few deep breaths.

"Are you okay?" Lucha asked, rubbing Norma's back.

"I'm fine," Norma said, sitting herself up but keeping her eyes closed. If Eduardo was still there in front of her, she'd faint for sure.

Norma opened her eyes. The *mercado* was no longer spinning.

❁❁❁

Norma was looking forward to the party at her *tía* Cleo's the next day. But that was before she knew Eduardo was coming. Before she could ask why, Cleo said she was the godmother of his daughter, Sirena. From the back of her throat, the lump that had started when she first saw Eduardo at the Mercado Cuauhtémoc grew until it almost choked her.

"Why would he want to see Norma after she dumped him?" Grandma asked her sister.

"*¿Quién sabe?*" Cleo shrugged.

"Maybe it's because he saw her at the market," Lucha volunteered before Norma could slap her palm over her mouth.

Norma could barely breathe and ran out to the backyard, where the freshly butchered pig was hanging upside down from a chain. The branch of the giant oak tree swayed with the breeze and the slaughtered animal's weight.

"Sharpen your fangs, girl," Norma whispered to herself, using the phrase Nicolás, the owner of La Sirenita Cabaret, would say whenever the soldiers from Fort Bliss would step into the club to check out the crowds and *cabareteras*, including herself.

"Sharpen those fangs, ladies," he would shout into their dressing room. "We got some fresh meat tonight."

In the breezy silence, blood slowly dripped from the pig's throat into a tin tub, its bright cherry color darkening into a brown. The longer Norma stared into the pool, the wider the tub grew. For a moment, she stopped breathing.

"Norma!" Merced shouted at her. "You forgot the tortillas."

Norma kept staring into the reddish-brown circle until she felt like she was drowning. She finally pulled away when Lucha placed her hand on Norma's arm.

"I'll go," Lucha said.

Norma was still breathing deeply but said, "I'll go with you."

"Norma, you need to start chopping the onions and roasting the *chiles pasilla*," Grandma called from the doorway. "You need to get the *nogada* done by tonight."

Norma wiped her face but the lump in her throat was growing. Suddenly, everything went black.

❀❀❀

"And I don't want to hear her crying," Merced's voice came from far away.

The scent of roasted *chiles* slipped into her room. Norma woke to the blaring light of the streetlamp glowing down on her like a spotlight. For a moment, she thought she was back at La Sirenita.

"Sharpen your fangs," she whispered.

From the open window, she heard the cars honking and faint accordion music. It sounded like, *"Tiburón, Tiburón,"* Eduardo's favorite *cumbia*.

CHAPTER 27
Smoke and Bread

Smoke, always smoke somewhere in this *pinche* Los Angeles: cigarette smoke, mesquite burning, exhaust, smog, morning fog. . . . Always smoke. *Damn, I wish I had a cigarette*, Merced thought, but she was in a hospital. Everybody used to be able to smoke in hospitals, even the doctors. Now, the smoking section was out on the street. *I'd give my left* chichi *for a nice juicy Kent or Winston Light. Even one of those shitty Virginia Slims that look like chicken bones.*

"I'm going to die," Merced mumbled, turning her head toward her pillow, its whiteness amplified by the fluorescent light.

Before she could turn her head, a nurse walked in.

Merced knew the nurse would check her bed pan, but she'd find nothing, because as much as it pained her, Merced would make herself walk to the toilet. She'd rather sleep on it than let Nurse Nalgas, the nurse with the most enviable ass she'd ever seen, treat her like some invalid. On the first night of her hospital stay she forced herself to the bathroom, rolling the IV bag streaming its clear liquid into the vein below her elbow. She sat on the cold white seat and leaned her head against the vinyl wall and slept until she fell. Instead of crying out, Merced laughed at herself and crawled back to her bed. But she couldn't sleep. Suddenly the door opened. It wasn't Nurse Nalgas.

"Stop raising such a ruckus," Tía Pina whispered. "Go back to sleep."

"*No puedo.*"

Tía Pina reached for Merced's hand. "Would you like some tea?"

Merced nodded, closed her eyes. Before long, she could smell the cinnamon tea brewing in the room. She opened her eyes to a steaming earthenware cup she hadn't seen since she'd left El Sauz. It's sweet, spicy steam revived her, took away the pain in her chest.

Tía Pina held the cup to her mouth. "This is medicine for you."

Merced sipped, expecting her lips and tongue to singe, but it was just hot enough to warm her chest.

The next morning, Nurse Nalgas would find Merced asleep, breathing steadily, the IV bag nearly empty. As the nurse replaced the bag and adjusted the oxygen tubes, Merced's eyes opened slowly. A small dixie cup with pills shook before her.

"They're good for your heart."

"You know what's good for my heart?" Merced smacked. "A big bottle of brandy and a pack of Winstons."

Merced's indignation grew when the nurse started laughing. She leaned in close to Merced and put her hand on her cheek.

"You remind me of that actress my mom likes," Nalgas said "María Feliz."

It's Félix, idiota, Merced thought. *Not Feliz, because I'm anything but* feliz.

"She was tough," Nurse Nalgas goes on while keeping her hand on her cheek. "Just like my mom."

Before Merced could slap her hand away, she took out a packet of cigarettes from her front pocket and tapped it against her palm. After lighting one up, she sucked on it a couple of times, then handed it to Merced. For a moment, after her first puff, Merced tasted cinnamon, then hot brandy. Before Nurse Nalgas walked out, she opened the window and blew her smoke out into the smoggy morning air. Merced watched the cigarette smoke drift over her, thought of the first time she woke up with Leandro in their little house in Boyle Heights.

Back then, she loved the way cigarette smoke curled up into the white ceiling, floating like an angel. Then Leandro would be over her, looking down with his *chinito* eyes.

"I can see me," he would say, smiling. Then he would start kissing her again, and Merced would get lost in the cigarette smoke and warm bread that was his skin. Smoke and bread would fill the little house on Indiana Street, mixing with the *ranchera* music on the radio. A calendar with a picture of the Virgen de Guadalupe watched over them. The only other thing on the wall was a photo of Leandro and Merced, her hair short and black, just after she had had it cut and styled. They had taken that picture on their first date, when she was still married to Donaciano.

That house on Indiana was so small, but Merced loved it, with its tiny living room, yellow kitchen and bedroom the color of the sky. It had wood floors that felt like ice when it rained in the mornings but were shiny and smooth. Except for the kitchen, which had yellow linoleum that always felt sticky, no matter how many times she mopped it. Bright morning light beamed down on the tiny leaves fluttering on the branches of the thick *huizache* tree that grew close to the house. On the walls hung little clay pots and a calendar from La Rosa Bakery down on First Street. And there was always something cooking on that little gas stove: *menudo*, *chiles*, *albóndigas*. . . . Leandro loved to eat. And Merced would cook what he liked, even after hours of standing and serving beer and brandy to the men at El Yuma bar. No matter how much she had cooked or baked or smoked, Leandro would not stay.

Outside, the sky glowed dark red and orange. No more blue. Little squeaky wheels rolled down the hallway. The food that tasted like nothing was coming. Nurse Nalgas took Merced's cigarette stub and walked out. Merced closed her eyes. Leandro's eyes and skin filled the room. The tree's dark branches reached out for her. Before she knew it, the smell of rubbing alcohol woke her up again.

❀❀❀

When Lucha walked into her room, instead of saying *"Buenos días,* Grandma" or "How are you?" Lucha gave her grandmother the bad news that she couldn't go home yet.

"¿Y por qué no?"

"The doctor said so."

Merced closed her eyes and pushed herself deeper into her hard hospital pillow. "Go get me some cigarettes and a bottle of Presidente."

Lucha scrunched her face and walked out the door. Merced heard her granddaughter's voice but could not make out what she was saying. Then she heard Nurse Nalgas' laughter. Merced smiled, leaned back against her pillow. She waited for Lucha to come back, and finally after an hour, her granddaughter returned holding a mesh bag bulging with bottles of Fanta and Squirt. Buried deep in its corner, a little brown bag folded tight in the shape of a square gave Merced hope for her cigarettes.

Nurse Nalgas fluffed up her pillow while Lucha pulled out the package and said, "A little gift for the sick girl," and giggled.

The moment Merced heard it, she knew the package was a trick. Inside, she found a blue velvet case stuffed with cotton.

"¿Qué's esto?" Merced asked as she dug through the white fluff and found a gold chain with a pendant in the shape of a branch hanging from it. Its deep little grooves made the surface look like golden bark, reminding her of the sunlight shining on her beloved *huizache.*

"Put it on her," the nurse urged Lucha.

Later, when the nurse left, Merced pulled off the necklace and placed it back in the box.

"Here," she said, holding the box up to Lucha. "You keep it for me."

"I don't want it."

"Then sell it or give it to one of Suki's *malflor* friends."

Merced forced it into Lucha's hands while telling her never to disobey her grandmother again, especially when she was dying.

"You're fine, Grandma."

"I know, but one day, when I die, I need you to do something for me it's very important."

Merced took a deep breath, wishing it was smoke, not the rubbing alcohol vapors going into her lungs.

"When I die, I want you to take me back to El Sauz, back to my *huizache*."

Lucha stood quiet, like a tree, unblinking. "A whi-what?" Lucha stammered. "What's that?"

"*Ay, mensa*," Merced breathed, slapping her forehead and unscrewing one of the Fanta bottles. She took a long swig before answering.

"It's a tree, but it looks like a giant yellow bush when it blooms."

Lucha's face reddened. She crunched the velvet box in her hand. Merced ducked as it flew straight at her face.

"But what about the house? You made me crawl through all that crap so that you could get the deed, and we paid Lily a whole bunch of money."

Merced wanted to tell her that the house meant nothing, now that Leandro was not in it. Now that he had married another woman who was half Merced's age and who looked like one of those *gringas* who paid her crap to clean her mansion, what was the point?

"Just take me back," Merced whispered. "Tía Cleo will show you."

Lucha rolled her eyes. "What if she's dead?"

This time, Merced threw the box at Lucha, who ducked just in time to see it fly out the open window.

CHAPTER 28
Baby Doll

"Baby, what's wrong with you?"

I hate that. Hate, hate, hate when he calls me "baby" or worse, "Baby doll." I know that's what he calls the other girls working at the cafeteria. He even calls our supervisor, Enriqueta, a woman old enough to be his grandmother, "baby." Ugh. But Gary is handsome. God, Lucha, why are you such a *pinche* sucker for a cute guy? Didn't you learn anything dating Jorge? *Pinche mensa.*

I wish I was still working at the *botánica*. Talking with Tía Suki after school, that got me through my break up with Jorge. Even if I hardly saw him at Roosevelt, every fuckin' love song reminded me of him. Once I got to UCLA, I thought, I'll meet someone nicer, cuter. I'll meet my Tristan. What a *pendeja*!

Little did I know that paying for tuition was going to mean working my ass off at the cafeteria.

I have to work with this guy in the worst place imaginable: the dish room. Luckily, the garbage disposal runs so loud I can barely hear Sheena singing "Strut" on the tinny little speaker over my head. But today, since we're still waiting for the student brunch rush, I can hear Gary loud and clear. He moves in closer and circles his arms around me. His rubber hands climb up my cotton apron ready to grab me. Maybe it's because I'm tired from studying until two a.m. Or maybe I'm just sick of school. Or maybe I'm just sick of men right now, since Jorge dumped me. We're the only two student workers in the humid room filled with the smell of greasy eggs and bacon.

"C'mon, baby doll." His warm breath chills me.

I remember Grandma's advice whenever she was harassed at El Yuma. "Dig your elbow into his ribs." So, I do. Right in his tight little stomach. His yellow hair bumps down my shoulder and a sudden whoosh of stale breath blows around me. Gary's arms release and I turn around. I stand facing him, ready to kick his balls, but he holds his hands up. He coughs and walks out of the dish room. I turn off the garbage disposal so I can hear my breath and heart. I need to think.

"Strut, pout, put it out, is what you want from women," Sheena sings, a little louder now.

When Enriqueta comes in, followed by Gary, I'm ready to walk out, but not before I feel my throat swelling, tears filling me.

"*¿Qué pasó?*" she asks me.

"Can you do this in your office and in English?" Gary says as he towers over Enriqueta and me.

"Come after lunch," she tells me.

Gary keeps his distance, quickly wiping the leftover eggs, gravy, biscuits, oatmeal and other leftovers into the water running through the food trough. I'm rinsing each plate, cup and saucer as quickly as possible. At one point, he says "bitch" loud enough for me to hear. I just keep rinsing the dishes speeding along the conveyor belt. It's almost like that *I Love Lucy* scene with the chocolates, except with cold coffee and half-eaten food.

Behind her desk, Enriqueta settles back in her chair as if she knows this is going to take forever. She pulls out a long, yellow notepad, just like a lawyer.

"She elbowed me," Gary tells Enriqueta as he rubs his belly like he's rubbing a magic lamp.

"Why?" she asks, her Cuban accent clouding her question.

"*Por cabrón*," I can't help saying.

Enriqueta bursts out laughing. "*Sí*," she says. "I believe it."

Gary's face burns pink but he knows he's fucked. "I'm gonna report you," he says. "You can't . . ."

He stops when I put my hands over my breasts and show Enriqueta what Gary wanted to do to me in the dish room.

"Here's some English for you," I say.

"Is this true?" Enriqueta asks Gary, whose face has grown paler than it usually is.

Strangely, he looks even handsomer than before. Maybe it was fear or maybe the pale skin set off his thick, golden hair. Whatever it is, I feel safer than ever in Enriqueta's office and in the dish room.

"If this is true . . ." Enriqueta continues writing notes on her long, yellow notepad.

❀❀❀

I drink the last can of Jolt cola before walking back up to the stacks from the snack room in the bottom floor of the main library. Its two a.m. and I still have five more pages of my term paper on the *Merchant of Venice* to finish before the eight a.m. deadline. Then I have to trek over to the Mac lab, type it up and print the paper out. This summer, I'll work overtime at El Yuma to get myself a Macintosh computer and a printer.

I pause in front of a thick glass window in the stairwell. Outside, the spires of the English building glow blue under the cold moonlight. There are a few lights on, but I don't think my professor can be in her office at this time of night. The cement courtyard glitters like sugar, sparkling when I move my head back and forth. My fresh crush, Jeff, a me-

chanical engineering major, told me earlier when we met that
the minerals in the cement give it the diamond-like shine.

"Too bad," I said. "I liked to think they're actual diamonds in there."

"Are you kidding?" Jeff said. "This whole place would be
torn up."

My breath fogs up the window. I know Jeff is studying at
the Tech library across campus, not the main "libes," where
every English major is scribbling tonight. I make myself jog
up the stairs, but my feet weigh me down like they're carrying the shiny cement. Maybe Jeff's waiting at my carol, a liter
of California Cooler tucked in his backpack. I had left a note
on his door, but his roommate told me to forget it.

"Jeff doesn't study on Saturdays," he said. "He'll be at
the roach motel."

God, I hated that term. Roach motel. That's where I live.
One time, I asked my friend Myra why they called it that.

She made a face. "It's because we live here . . . All of us
black and brown folks."

When I finally reach my floor, I see it. Right behind the
door, a giant roach the size of one of those ugly duck boots the
sorority girls like to wear. I rub my eyes. Not only is the roach
still there, but it's getting bigger, its wriggling antennae length-
ening into the size of a fishing rod. The roach jumps onto the
wall the moment I scream. But it's so heavy, it falls on its back.
It shrinks back down to its duck boot size, then further down
until it's no bigger than a plastic pencil sharpener.

I scream louder, even while stomping the shit out of it,
crunching it into a syrupy pulp. I keep screaming until I hear
somebody running up the steps. For a moment, I think it's
Jeff, but it's only the pudgy security guard.

"Are you okay?" he asks, half terrified himself. "You really shouldn't take the stairs at this time of night."

Back at my carol, there is no Jeff.

CHAPTER 29
Zapp

After my sophmore year, I moved back to Merced's bungalow. No more roach motel for me. I start my day at five in the morning, with either Zapp singing "Dance Floor" or Blondie's "Rapture" on my jacked-up radio clock. I blow out the Virgen de Guadalupe candles that burned all night on the chipped blue dresser. Already, there's barely enough hot water to wash my ass, since Tía Norma got up an hour earlier than all of us so she could finish her homework before going to her cleaning job, then to her classes at East Los Angeles College. Grandma sleeps off her bartending shift at El Yuma bar on First Street. Mom's making burritos.

After showering, I get stuck trying to figure out what I'm going to wear. Not that there's much of a choice. I can wear those brown cotton pants with the big pockets and the white button-down shirt (but that would mean I'd have to iron and there's no time for that right now) or I can wear the cute, black baby T-shirt with my Gap khaki pants Mom ironed last night. Ugh. But they have that corny crease running down the middle of each pant leg, which my mother insists on ironing into all of my pants.

I warm up two flour tortillas in the microwave to wrap up the scrambled eggs with potatoes Mom made for me. Then, I pour some hot coffee into my thermos before hauling my ass into my Honda Civic. Last time, I forgot my lunch bag and had to trek out to the Farmer's Market and shell out ten bucks for a po' boy sandwich. And why? All because I didn't want my co-workers to think that I couldn't keep up with them when it came to eating out for lunch. Well today, I'm not forgetting my po' girl lunch: two egg and potato burritos, a juicy orange, a couple of cookies and my thermos of coffee.

By six a.m., my Honda is on the freeway, on the 60, then the 101, snaking through downtown with the rest of the east-siders. Usually, an hour is enough to get my ass to Television City, but sometimes, especially on Mondays, East LA gets farther away. Driving to that lousy news assistant job that pays about seven dollars an hour makes me wonder if I'll ever get a job that will let me move out of Grandma's house. By seven o'clock, all the crazy working stiffs are jamming the I-10 freeway, honking their horns, blasting their radios and getting into fender benders. *Híjole*, you'd think these people would learn how to drive already. But that's okay. Somehow, I manage to eat one of my burritos, roll on my new lipstick and rub on my eye shadow without crashing into anybody. Once my *pancita*'s warm with food, I can even sing along with Joey Ramone as he yips out "Rock and Roll High School." That Joey, he reminds me so much of my boss, Clare Darby, that I call her Joey behind her back. And it's not just because Clare's a crazy bitch. She really does look like him, with her big nose and long, black hair. And when she puts on those sunglasses, it's hard not to bust out laughing.

"*Buenos días, muñeca*," Ignacio, the cute Mexican security guard, says as I pull in and show him my freshly laminated badge.

"*Buenos días*, Nacho!"

One of these days I'm going to call him over and give him a real Chicano greeting, one of those kiss "hellos" all the other college-educated Chicanos did at school. Before UCLA, I never kissed anyone hello, because neither my family nor anybody else in our neighborhood did that. I thought it was some scam, so that these Mexican college dudes could just touch me for no reason. Then, someone (was it my girl-friend Terry?) told me it was a legit way to greet people, so I went along with it. Today, I wouldn't mind Nacho touching me, that's for sure. Maybe tomorrow.

As I make my way to the little back door to the news bu-reau, I see those crazy Midwestern tourists already in line for "The Price Is Right" tickets. I keep meaning to pop my head into the studio to see whether Bob Barker is around for an autograph.

What'll it be today? Man-on-the-street interview about Madonna's latest escapade? Another Tylenol scare? What does the *Wall Street Journal* say today about Chernobyl's nu-clear melt down? How about that new Oprah show? When I first joined the bureau, I thought I would be doing real, orig-inal stories about real, original people, but it's all a rehash of other news stories I've already seen on ABC, NBC, *LA Times*, *New York Times* or *People Magazine*.

The air conditioning blows cold as soon as I walk in. The in-box is already piled high, and my typewriter hums with electricity. It's gonna be a long day. Clare's on the phone try-ing to snag an interview with somebody named José.

"Jesus, Lucha," she says, "can you talk to him? He's at the Mexican consulate, and I need him for an interview about this whole amnesty deal."

¡Híjole! I had just talked about all this with Grandma Merced, who's been nagging Lily about getting her citizen-ship and going back to Chihuahua for her birth certificate again.

"I can," I say, trying not to show my excitement. This was why they hired me, after all—the only Chicana in the news-room and the only news employee who can speak Spanish.

Clare smiles and hands me the receiver. Right away, I know this guy won't give us the interview we need. I think about interviewing my grandmother instead if the Mexican consul refuses to talk. Grandma's applying for amnesty, too, so she can keep her house and start getting her social security money once she retires. I pick up the phone and start talking to the consular representative, who tells me he has no opinion on the legislation right now, since he hasn't reviewed it thoroughly.

Clare stares hard at me with her Joey Ramone face as I shake my head.

"Ask for someone else," she barely whispers, eyes opening wide. "Is there anybody else you can talk to?"

Yes, you stupid bitch! I want to scream: Merced!

I do as I'm told and ask the consular rep for another name. He suggests a Chicano Studies professor at UCLA, who then refers me to someone at MALDEF, who offers me one of their attorneys at their downtown office, who can't do the interview today. I know, sooner or later, Clare's going to want an immigrant, an "illegal." When I mention my grandmother, she squints her eyes.

"Are you sure she'll do it?"

"For me she will," I say proudly. "I can also find others to interview in Boyle Heights, in East Los."

"Okay, but I need the interview by three today."

"No problem, but I want to be on camera for the report."

Clare looks me in the eyes, runs her hand through her shaggy black hair.

I'm not used to asking for what I want, so I almost blink. "If I don't get the spot, I'm out," I bark.

Is that admiration in her eyes? No. More like disbelief.

"I'll think about it," she says.

Fuck her. But what can I do? Quit? I don't have to put up with this shit. If she doesn't recognize my value, I'm out of here.

She's back on the phone, taking notes on her long yellow pad. For a moment, my vision tunnels, TV snow blocks my vision. I lean over, head between my knees.

"Don't faint," I whisper. I breathe in deep, fighting the urge to grovel.

I reach for the handle of the drawer to my metal desk and pull out my old notepads from my journalism class. I slowly stack them on top of my desk, pretending I'm bugging out for sure. Clare's still on the phone. I walk over to the copy room, grab an empty cardboard box sitting next to a Xerox machine. I throw my notepads in. Soon, I feel the producers from behind their luxury cubicles look over to us. But just as quickly, they look back at their video monitors or their copy rolled tight onto their typewriter carriages. I pull out the next drawer filled with my AP Style handbook, pocket US Constitution courtesy of the ACLU and solar-powered calculator. As I pull my wool jacket from behind my chair, Carol, the bureau chief walks over to us. Clare finally looks up.

"Are you leaving?" Carol asks me.

"Yup," I say trying not to let my vision tunnel. I sit back down and pretend to reach down to tie my shoes, all the while breathing deeply.

"Get off the phone, Clare."

We both stand up, look at each other and follow Carol to her glass office.

❀❀❀

Clare still tries to boss me around by telling me which questions she wants me to ask my grandmother: How do you feel about amnesty? Are you scared you'll get deported? What does America mean to you? This is the same crap the other reporters ask at news conferences, on TV and radio. *Chingado.* They never seem to change because really, unless you're listening to Radio Kali, or watching KMEX Canal 34, nobody really wants to hear the everyday details of their gardener, nanny or cook. I know the other news stations have asked these same questions. If I change them, I'll be back working the temp agencies before I know it. If the New York CBS doesn't like the Los Angeles CBS way of doing things, they can blame Clare aka Joey Ramone.

That's what I'm thinking when I call Grandma Merced.

"Do I get paid?" she wants to know.

"That's not the way it works."

"So, then, *por qué chingados* am I giving you an interview?"

I'm about to hang up until I hear my mom start yelling at Grandma. It's the first time I hear my own mother take on her mother.

"Because this will help your granddaughter at her job," she says.

Grandma says nothing.

"And she can pay you more rent money so you can save it for that house near Mariachi Plaza."

They struggle over the phone receiver until finally it's unmuffled.

"Okay," Grandma finally says into the phone. "*Pero*, I need to get my hair done."

I tell her to go to Caesar's Palace on Whittier, and I'll pay for the dye job. So, right after I visit with the *pinche* immigration attorney, who looks straight into the camera instead of at me, I head back down on the I-10, then the 60. Lucky for me there's no traffic or accidents to slow our van down. Once we get to East LA, the cameraman has the nerve to ask me if the TV equipment will be safe.

"Yes. Jesus Christ!"

I have to start producing my own *pinche* news segments that tell a true East LA story. And I've got to do it fast, because God knows everyone at CBS thinks I'm just a two-bit *chola* who will one day crack and shoot up the station.

❀❀❀

"How do you tell a true East LA story?" I say into the tape.

Very slowly, I think, because these fuckers will twist it up to make money or make themselves look good or both. I stop the news van in front of the worn-down yellow house with its cracked paint and overgrown yard. For some reason, it bothers me that the cameraman doesn't say anything while he follows me. I know his jowly face is criticizing my life, and even though I couldn't care less, I want to pop him. I avoid looking at his face until I get inside the house.

Grandma Merced sits up on the beat-up brown couch, her hair shiny black with bobby pins holding stray hairs in place. A little black curly ponytail hangs behind her head, making her face larger, browner. With her bright pink lips and eyes rimmed with liquid eyeliner, she reminds me of Madonna, especially since she wears the big gold *coquetas* dangling from her ears.

She smiles and giggles when the cameraman walks in. Like one of those sorority girls, she smooths the top of her head, then her cheek.

"Ready?" she asks, smiling.

Yes, ready, but first I have to hang the black-out drapes over the windows so it's nice and dark. Grandma's sleek head jerks around like she's an owl, right and left, asking about the darkness. I tell her that even though she has her green card, she can still be targeted by the government. Even through the darkness, I can see that she doesn't understand. She's stubborn about this. She paid good money to have her hair done and she wants her enemies, especially Gertrudis, to see her, to show her she was always the better one, the one who deserved Leandro more than she did.

So, I videorecord her. I remember to take nice long shots of that little ponytail bobbing around as she answers questions because that's mostly what they'll be showing on the clip.

Back at the station, I rush past Clare and go to the editing bay, where I'll be cutting, splicing and dubbing until noon. On the screen, Grandma's black ponytail bobs up and down, right and left.

"I worked for this country for thirty years," I interpret for her, dubbing in the English. "And I never even got minimum wage, never went on the welfare or even got free medicine. This country owes me."

In the background, I hear the slap of her fist on the open palm of her hand.

"She's good," Carol says, nodding at me.

"She sounds crazy," Clare says. "Couldn't you find someone softer?"

"No time." And it's true.

I'm coming up on one p.m., and the engineers have to feed the video to New York by one-thirty.

"Jesus, you guys won't get any sympathy."

Us "guys" don't need your sympathy, Joey. I focus on Grandma Merced's little dried-up ponytail glowing black and blue. She rages big, even though she's only a little piece of the news hour.

"I deserve my money," she declares. "I deserve to be here, too. I deserve my house."

She sounds crazy, but I can't help nodding my head in time with her ponytail. It's good. Even the producer assigned to my segment nods her head.

When Dan Rather announces the California Highway Patrol segment on the New York feed, my exhaustion disappears. The best part happens when Carol gives me the thumbs up in front of Clare. By the time I get home, I'm so tired, I nap until the six p.m. feed airs. I watch it with Tía Norma and Grandma Merced. I'm afraid to look at them while my grandmother's black form speaks with a distorted voice, a white-lettered English translation popping up below her. Tía Norma misses class just to watch it live, even though I told her I have a tape of it. After it's done, Grandma smiles a bright red lipsticked smile.

❀❀❀

Lily comes the next day, my day off. I see her through the sheer white curtains on the living room window, and she sure doesn't look like any of the women we're used to. She walks like she knows where she's going and what she's doing, like she's going to kick not only my ass, but Grandma Merced's and anybody who gets in her way. When she reaches the dusty screen door, she looks like shimmering smoke.

Listen and pay attention to *chisme* in the newsroom, that's what I have to do, especially if I want to start working on my own news stories. And Lily looks like she's a story, with her braided hair twisted around her head, red silk rose behind her left ear and thin eyebrows. She looks like a combination *chola*, María Félix and Frida Kahlo. Did she see the news story?

"Lucha!" she says. "Sorry to bother you on your day off."

Her floral perfume clears out the smell of cigarettes mixed with sweat and Jean Naté body splash. Even Grandma says so when she comes into the living room dressed up in her bar uniform, tight skirt, red velvet pumps and bright red lipstick.

"It smells like flowers," she says, reaching for the cigarettes from her big black purse. "Where's Suki? Did you see me on TV?"

Lily nods, congratulates Grandma, then walks to the kitchen and waves us over to the kitchen table. Outside, a single car with a radio plays "Earth Angel."

"Suki's closing the store before she gets here."

Suddenly, the floral air overwhelms the kitchen, killing the smell of beans, *chiles* and tortillas. Grandma Merced stands still, like a rabbit watching a wolf.

"What's wrong?" I ask.

For the first time, I see Lily ask my grandmother for a cigarette.

"Gertrudis is marrying Moti," she says before she flicks the Bic lighter and inhales deeply.

Grandma drops like a sack onto a chair. Lily holds her upright and tells her that Tía Suki got the word from one of her customers. Just then, Tía Suki shows up.

"She never loved Leandro," Grandma says, looking straight at Suki. "I loved him and he loved me."

"He tried to take your house," I want to scream, but instead roll my lips in between my teeth.

Tía Suki shakes her head while Lily keeps smoking. Next door, Moti plays "*Al Fin*" by Los Bukis.

For the first time in a long time, my grandmother can't say anything.

"How?" I ask.

Tía Suki breathes in deep before saying that the *chisme* is that Moti's marrying her to get amnesty.

"He doesn't need to do that," Lily says. "There must be another reason."

Grandma finally opens her eyes. "Moti's a *desgraciado*. He can't love Gertrudis."

I jerk my head at my grandmother. Since when did she care about Leandro's wife?

Instinctively, I pull out the bottle of Presidente brandy from under the sink and pour some into her favorite shot glass, purple with the words "Route 66" printed in black letters. I know we're in trouble when my grandmother doesn't toss it down the way she usually does. Instead, she just sips it, a tear sliding down her laugh line. Then, she just drops her head on her arms and hunches herself over the kitchen table, her back heaving and falling. We hear her mumbling, but the moment Lily touches her back, Grandma begins wailing. Her head rolls around in her arms until it lays on its side, her mouth open and gasping. She reminds me of those goldfish I see at the pet shop, gasping for life just before they die.

I don't know what to say to this woman who's crying for a man who not only dumped her for another woman but who threatened to report her to immigration just to steal her house.

Grandma says nothing, just sucks on her brandy, leaving blood red lip marks around the rim of the shot glass.

"It's been twenty years," she finally says, struggling not to sob. "Twenty years since Leandro left me for her."

Tía Suki raises an eyebrow, but Lily raises her finger cutting her off. I close my eyes so neither one can see me rolling them hard into my head.

"¿Y por qué?" Grandma says, rearing her head up like a black-haired lion. "Because I wouldn't have his baby."

Lily stops rubbing her back. It's Tía Suki's turn to put her head in her hands.

"You already had three daughters to take care of," Tía Suki says through her fingers. "You couldn't."

I finally get up and get a shot glass for myself.

"The wedding is tomorrow," Lily says. "At El Santuario de Nuestra Señora de Guadalupe."

Merced nods. "I want to go," she says. "I want to let these sinvergüenzas know they're insulting Leandro's memory."

"Are you crazy?" Tía Suki asks, her mouth frozen open.

Lily tries to soothe her.

She pulls away and says, "You'll be insulting Leandro's memory!"

This time, Grandma stands up and shouts, "I'm his real love. I always will be."

"This is not a pinche novela," I tell her. "This is a wedding."

"Cabrona," Grandma curses me as she heads for the bedroom door.

"Gertrudis still wants the house," Lily tells us.

"Fuck," I say. "We still have to go to El Paso and Chihuahua."

Lily and Tía Suki laugh softly.

"Let's leave tomorrow," Tía Suki says. "We have to keep her away from the church."

Part of me wants to see Grandma at the wedding, giving the María Félix eyebrow to everyone, especially Moti. Another part of me knows that she'll lose it with Gertrudis. There's no way we'd be able to keep her from attacking the bride.

When I call Clare, I tell her I'm doing a follow-up story with my grandmother, her amnesty journey. She snorts.

"Let me talk to Carol," I say.

The moment I mention our bureau chief, Clare backpedals and agrees.

I don't even bother to ask her about a camera. There's no way they'll let me take it across the border. I'll just take the little one from work, the one they call the lipstick camera, and film what I can. Lily hugs me and says she'll see me bright and early. I'm glad Lily's coming with us. She's the main reason my *tías*, not to mention Merced, can cross the border without any problems from Migra. No Lily, *no papeles*. Not just Lily but the *botánica* has made enough money to pay for processing.

After Lily leaves, I walk back into my room, light candles to the Virgin of Guadalupe and pray that this will be my big break.

CHAPTER 30
El ritmo de la vida

It was Christmas Eve and for the first time since Alma started working at El Yuma twenty years ago, she would be going home to an empty house. Lucha had just moved closer to her job in Hollywood, and Norma was spending the night at her *gringo* employer's house in Pasadena. A song by Marisela on the jukebox soothed her, kept the image of her mother lying in her hospital bed from haunting her.

Alma bent down for a damp rag floating in the wash bucket and furiously wiped down the bar. When a tear fell on the shiny wood, she rubbed harder. As she focused on cleaning the sticky remnants of beer and liquor, Don Pedro emerged from the men's room, adjusting his black newsboy cap. He paused before walking behind the bar and grabbing a bottle of Budweiser from the mini-fridge.

Alma blinked, bent down to dip the rag into the bucket of soapy water. She dunked the now-gray cloth, swirled it in the warm foam. Slowly, she rose, clutching the damp rag, squeezing until her knuckles turned white. She moved closer to him.

"*¡Es mi mamá!*" she shouted.

Don Pedro jerked back. Alma had never shouted back at anyone, least of all at her ex-husband. His eyes opened wide. And when he took off his cap and threw it at her, instead of fear, Alma's anger swelled. Don Pedro choked the bottle as he drank the last of the beer. He wiped his mouth with his fingers and set the bottle on the bar.

"*Es una cabrona*," Don Pedro finally said.

Alma flinched. For a moment, he looked like her father Donaciano, with his dark burning eyes and his balding head. Don Pedro turned away to the mirror behind the bar, his face half hidden by the green and brown liquor bottles. Between the blinking red lights she had hung around the mirror and the neon Budweiser sign, his face pulsed red then blue then red.

"I'm sorry," Don Pedro choked out. "It's just that, I can't forgive her."

When he reached for her, Alma pulled away. She should've gone to Pasadena with Norma. She should've taken the factory job Moti had offered her. But she didn't want her mother to lose her job, didn't want Lucha to lose her father, but she had lost him anyway.

"She's in the hospital," Alma said, hoping Don Pedro would stop.

"She tore us apart," Don Pedro said, grabbing her hand.

"*You* tore us apart," Alma roared, surprising herself as well as her ex.

"After what she did to you, why do you still protect that *hija de la chingada*?" Don Pedro countered.

Alma sat still, staring deep into her glass as if the emptiness would reveal something. Alma picked up his worn, wool cap, folded it into a tight little square and spit on it.

"How dare . . ."

Before he could finish, Alma threw the cap in Don Pedro's face, smiled and walked past the empty pool tables.

"Don't expect a check next month," Don Pedro called out as she walked out through the heavy velveteen curtains. The thick cloth muffled the beginning notes of "*Tarde o Temprano*" as she strode into the chilly night, her anger warming her under the winking, cold stars. She crossed First Avenue without looking back.

❀❀❀

On Christmas day, Alma woke up late, but refreshed. For a moment, she forgot that her sister would be spending the holiday with the *gringo* family.

"Alma!" a man's voice called through her window.

Alma pushed back the curtain. Don Pedro's rain spattered wool cap floated outside the window alongside his open palm.

"Alma, open the window."

She hesitated but then she realized it was Christmas. She needed to see her mother.

"*Feliz* . . . !" Don Pedro started waving.

"You have to take me to White Memorial," she told him, then shut and locked the window.

Alma quickly shimmied into her dress from the previous evening. It still smelled of smoke, but between her house cleaning job and covering for her mother at the bar, there was no time for laundry. The hospital would be closed to visitors in a couple of hours. Out on the porch, Don Pedro waited for her, cap in hand.

"I just want to . . ." he started, but Alma yelped, then jumped down the steps toward the front gate.

She ran so fast, she nearly tripped over the *huizache*'s thick roots.

"Merry Christmas," Norma said as she jumped out of a cab and ran up the cement walk to the tree.

"The *gringa* let you go?"

"She's not a *gringa*. She's from Mexico City," Norma corrected her.

Alma let it go and hugged her. "Don Pedro is taking us to see Amá."

Both turned to the old man sitting on the porch of the bungalow. He looked older than his seventy-five years, but their mother had looked much older that day she collapsed in El Yuma.

"Amá?" Norma asked.

Alma took Norma's hand and led her inside the house while Don Pedro stayed outside, waiting. As Alma grabbed her coat and hat, she told Norma about Merced's heart attack. Merced had been sitting in the corner of the bar, chain-smoking with a bottle of brandy and a shot glass. Now and then she'd sing along with a song on the jukebox. Alma, busy wiping shelves behind the bar, heard a thump when the song finished. Moti ran over from the pool table and yelled for Alma. By the time she reached her mother, Alma knew Merced wouldn't survive this latest round of memories.

"Don't tell me," Norma said. "She was listening to '*Amor Eterno*.'"

Alma nodded. Norma twisted her mouth and shook her head.

"After all that *cabrón* did to her," Norma said, then let a little giggle escape. The giggle scraped against Alma's anger, and tears sprung suddenly.

"It's not funny, Norma," Alma said. "I think, this time, she's going to die."

"Are you crying?"

Alma pressed her palms into her eyes as her sister came near her.

"I don't know why," Alma said, "I just hate the thought that she's going to die."

Norma stiffly hugged her sister, who began weeping against her neck. Alma clung to her, almost bringing them both down, but Norma stood firm.

"She sold you," Norma said quietly. "Just like a pimp. Don't you remember?"

"She's still my mother," Alma cried.

At that moment, Alma could see why Merced still loved Leandro more than other men, more than her daughters.

By this time, Don Pedro had made his way inside the house. The trio waited as the rain tapped rhythmically against the windows.

❀❀❀

Don Pedro backed his Ford Granada down the steep driveway, careful to avoid the *huizache* tree swaying with the rain. Alma and Norma scrambled into the back seat.

"I'm no chauffer," Don Pedro started to complain, but as soon as Norma gripped his shoulder, he stopped.

When they reached White Memorial Hospital, Christmas lights blinked through the rain. In the lobby, a giant tree glittered with silver garlands and matching glass balls. Next to it, a nativity scene sat on a small credenza. Alma stood in front of it until Norma pulled her away. They had an hour before the nuns would chase them out, so they hurried. Alma wondered what she would tell her mother when she saw her. Norma pressed the elevator button.

Nurse Nalgas, who was in charge, had convinced them that since it was Christmas, Merced's family needed to be close to her.

"But just two at a time, okay?" Nurse Nalgas warned.

It didn't feel like Christmas, Alma thought.

"It's Christmas," she said before Norma took her by the arm and pulled her toward the room.

Don Pedro settled himself into a vinyl chair in the hallway.

Above Alma and Norma, the fluorescent tubes hummed with white light that revealed a glossy, white-walled room. Merced lay in the bed closest to the dark picture window.

Merced was reclined against two pillows, tubes inserted in her nostrils, eyes closed.

"*Cómo chingan*," she whispered.

Alma and Norma laughed. Alma wanted to believe Merced was talking about the nuns, not her daughters, but even Alma knew better. Norma was right. Alma nearly turned and left. But she rooted herself to the linoleum floor and reached for Merced's limp, rough hand. Merced breathed in deeply through the clear tubes.

"You smell like El Yuma," Merced said.

"How do you feel?" Alma asked.

Merced barely moved her head. "Well, how do I look?" she mumbled.

Alma squeezed Norma's hand, hoping to stop the quip she knew her sister could not help but say.

"Suki?" Merced whispered.

"She's at work," Norma told her. "She's opening another *botánica*."

This time, Merced's eyes cracked open. Alma waited for Merced to spring from the bed and rage at them. But their mother just leaned deeper into her pillows.

"*Ingrata*," Merced mumbled, but she squeezed Alma's thumb. "Give her my recipes."

"What?" Norma gasped.

Merced squeaked, insisting, "*Dale mis recetas, ¡mensa!*"

Don Pedro popped his head into the door.

"So, there's the little sick one," he said before Nurse Nalgas appeared in the hallway. She jerked her head toward the sisters.

"How's the *señora* doing?"

"Bratty," Norma quipped before Alma could stop her. "As always"

"You owe me," Merced mumbled before pulling her hand from Alma.

You owe me, Alma thought, then pressed her hands to her face. Her anger bubbled. She sighed, then grasped Merced's curled icy fingers and screamed. Nurse Nalgas rushed from around the curtain divider, where she had been checking in on Merced's roommate. Don Pedro rushed through the door to find Norma pulling Alma off of her mother's body.

"Mamá," Alma wailed.

Norma sat down at the end of the bed, allowing her sister's sorrow to unfold. Alma gripped the blankets, her head turned aside to gulp down the air.

"No, please," Alma gasped.

"Do you want a priest?" Nurse Nalgas asked Norma.

"What for?"

Alma stood up, nodding. "Yes, please."

Norma stood up, spread her legs, crossed her arms and said, "That woman never went to church!"

"She prayed every night," Alma shouted. "Even when she was drunk."

When Don Pedro whispered that she should get the priest, Norma threw her hands in the air and walked out.

CHAPTER 31
Unabombers

The duties include running around the newsroom, dropping copies from the teletype off at various desks, including those of the assignment editor and bureau chief. That is actually the best part of the job, because by the time I spend about a month in the newsroom, I also have to take calls from the crazy men who dial up CBS News to share their conspiracy theories, ranging from Keyser Söze's supposed infiltration of the FBI to the Unabomber's appearance at Disneyland's Club 33.

The morning desk at CBS's LA bureau is a complete circus when I first start there, right after graduating from UCLA. At first, I can't wait to walk through the black double doors with my CBS name tag and my new herringbone-patterned jacket bought with the last of my school loan money. One hundred percent wool, the jacket is the most expensive piece of clothing I have ever owned. It reassures me that I belong in that newsroom, even after Clare Schaefer, the assignment editor, mistakes me for the delivery woman from the Farmer's Market.

My desk is next to hers, and the inbox is already overflowing with receipts, news copy and newspaper clippings. My first duty is to file and distribute all this paperwork before noon, Clare instructs me. Just as I'm about to finish, one of the news producers grabs my arm and pulls me out of the chair.

"You can't sit there," he says. "We need you to translate for the on-site reporter."

"She just got here," Clare says, but then the phone rings, and Clare gets distracted.

I'm led to a parked van filled with camera equipment and video tape. Suddenly, I'm in the back seat behind a smoking reporter and a camera man, speeding into downtown for a news conference about the two Mexican immigrants who've been beaten down by California Highway Patrol officers on the shoulder of the Santa Monica freeway.

"*Me golpearon como un animal,*" the woman says through puffy lips, her swollen eye covered by thick gauze and white medical tape.

I translate for the reporter who tells me which questions to ask her. I push the baton of a microphone up closer to the woman, who is sitting close to her lawyer, but it's not close enough.

"Get closer," the cameraman hisses.

The moment I do, the lawyer glares at me. I have to ignore him and go forward with my question.

"*¿Y por cuánto tiempo te golpearon?*" I ask about how long she was being beaten.

"*Veinte minutos.*"

"Ask her if she's here in this country legally."

I freeze. What kind of a dumb-ass question is that? I want to say but don't.

❦❦❦

I've always been a heavy sleeper. Sometimes I miss my alarm, and I'm late to my news assistant job at CBS. Not too late, but late enough for Clare to make her little remarks.

"Are you on CP time today?" she'll ask as I slam my coffee mug on the desk and look through my schedule. She must've learned that from Nacho, the security babe at the gate. I know she's been after him for a while.

"I'm always on CP time," I tell her after one big swig.

Usually, a mugful will do me but sometimes, when I'm working twelve hours, I'll swallow a NoDoz. Better than Jolt, but not as good as speed. In a half hour, I'm feeling like the Energizer Bunny.

I discovered this little trick when I was only fifteen years old and had to share a room with my mom and Tía Norma. I also had to share my bed with my mother. My grandmother refused to give up her bedroom, especially since she was the only one allowed to have her boyfriends spend the night with her. Between both Tía Norma and my mom snoring, I barely slept. Eventually, I learned to sleep through the snoring, the farting, the loud moaning that came through the thin walls of the small bungalow. After Tía Suki moved out to live with Lily, my mother and Tía Norma's snoring barely bugged me.

Waking up became a problem, though. Mom would have to practically dump me out of the bed, and even then I could barely wake myself up. To keep me from rolling over and just falling back asleep, Mom would gently slap me with hands she'd run under cold water.

"You're going to be late for school," she'd tell me.

Then, she'd just give up and let me sleep. I'd wake up refreshed well over an hour after school had started, but of course that wasn't working with my teachers or the principal who called the house one time when Grandma was sleeping. That's when she stepped in and started just yanking me out of the bed and throwing me into a cold shower. Then, she'd sit me down at the table and pour me a mug of coffee.

"You're not leaving until you drink all of this," she'd say, pointing at the hot coffee. "I don't need your teachers or principal *chingando* because you're too lazy to get up on time."

At first, the coffee worked. But then when I got to class, I'd just fall asleep again. I don't know how the principal knew to call our house when my grandmother was still there, but she did.

"*Desgraciada*," Grandma Merced yelled at me when I came home one afternoon. She should have been asleep, getting rested before her shift at El Yuma bar, but any kind of authority figure threw my grandmother for a loop. Maybe it was that she had to deal with the *Migra* every time she crossed the bridge from Juárez to El Paso. Or maybe it was the truant officers she had to bribe in El Paso, when she made my mother and aunts work the hotel and cabarets. Whatever it was, she told me to figure out a way to stay awake in school or else she'd put me to work.

I got so desperate, I asked George for help. He told me about NoDoz.

"It is legal?" I asked. I didn't want Grandma Merced breaking my ass over *drogas*, like she had threatened so many times.

"Of course," he said. "You can buy it at Thrifty's."

"How much?"

"Maybe two bucks."

I pulled out a couple of dollars from my mother's purse, hopped on my purple bike and rode over to the drugstore. I was so nervous about taking the NoDoz, I didn't sleep much that night. When the sun rose, I was the first one in the kitchen. I brewed my coffee and took a couple of the white pills before my mom walked in to make breakfast. As I walked to school, my head started to buzz. The paint on the houses suddenly brightened, and cars stormed down the road louder than before. As I walked, bacon mixed with *rancheras* and news reports blasted around me. The houses shook with music and food. In class, I actually learned things. My teachers were not boring, just quiet. My only mistake was that I hadn't brought more pills with me, because by the time lunch rolled around, I was starting to doze off again.

❀❀❀

"The fractured family never survives as a whole. It must split up to survive," the psychiatrist says as she eyes me. I'd finally landed the interview with Ted Kaczynski's shrink, and I need juicy sound bites for tonight's news.

"This is your last chance," the assignment editor had told me before I left with the camera man. "If you don't get this, you better start checking the *LA Weekly* for a job."

Ugh. Clare stresses me out with her threats, but I know it's because she's the one who wants to be on camera. But this time, I got the interview. This time, Dan Rather is gonna ask for me, because I scored the only Latina psychiatrist who happens to be working with the most infamous terrorist in the United States.

"Why was his family so fractured?" I ask Dr. García.

"Once he was isolated in the hospital for months because of hives," she says, looking down at her notes. "Months-long isolation splintered him off his family unit. From then on, he was splintered off, not only from his family but also his social peers, except for those in his cohort."

"Who was in the cohort?"

"It was a very small, restrictive cohort," Dr. García says as she looks up. "He was still very isolated and less inclined to emotionally connect with anyone around him."

I almost laugh. That sounds like my grandmother, except she didn't isolate herself at all.

"How sad," I say without thinking.

Dr. García smiles.

"He does not have a sense of family," she says. "Maybe if he had a grandmother to give him some discipline . . ." She laughs but then stops.

"Please don't use that," Dr. García frowns. "It's not very professional."

I look at the camera man, who's smiling, and slash the air with my flattened hand. Gerardo nods, and then we pause for a second before continuing.

"People like him are always searching for absolute truth," Dr. García says.

When I ask her what she means, she picks up a picture of herself with a baby.

"This is truth for me," she says. "I'm a mother with a baby. I'll always have my daughter in my life, no matter what happens to me or her."

Dr. García explains that for Kaczynski, the truth lies in numbers, and the numbers can say whatever they want to him. In his case, his truth was that he deserved freedom from social accountability because he was living a righteous life in the wilderness.

As I rewatch the interview in the editing bay, Grandma Merced's face keeps popping up. She and Kaczynski are similar in the way they both feel like they know the truth, the only truth. At that moment, I know the truth about them. They both want and need love, but they can't show it. So, they destroy.

CHAPTER 32
¿Cómo fue?

When Grandma Merced dies, I pay for the funeral. The Gutiérrez brothers do a nice job with her corpse. Her once iron-grey hair is dyed a deep, Crayola black, fluffed and wavy set around her face and shoulders. The liquid foundation smooths over some of the wrinkles around her eyes, has lightened the dark hollows of her sockets. One of the brothers even stuck on the fake lashes I provided.

"I want to look like María Felix when I die," she had told me just before I started my freshman year at UCLA.

I remember the conversation well. We had just finished watching *Enamorada*, María Félix's luscious ode to selfless love. After many years passed, Grandma was still stunned by the discovery that Leandro was set to marry another woman within a month.

"Such a ridiculous man," Grandma had huffed after she found out the woman was Gertrudis.

"Gertrudis," she whispered tightly just before pouring her shot of brandy into the Dodgers shot glass that I had bought for her at the stadium.

"Can you believe it?" Grandma yelled. "How could this woman with fried blonde hair and a skeletal body take Leandro from me?"

By this time, Grandma was so wound up, she had flung the shot glass onto the linoleum floor. Instead of smashing into bits, the glass bounced and landed upright. I rescued it as Merced prepared to kick it. But her drunken legs betrayed her, buckled her straight down onto the floor.

"How did it happen?" Grandma kept murmuring as she cried and lay on the floor until I pulled her up a little.

"Let's go to bed," I said, all the while wishing that Tía Suki was still living with us instead of mom and Tía Norma, who just aggravated Grandma.

"*M'ija, m'ija*" Grandma implored me. "When I die, make sure I look good. Make sure that when that *everybody* comes to my funeral, they see what Leandro loved."

❀❀❀

Grandma Merced had never wanted a priest for her funeral. After Leandro, her only love—or obsession as Tía Suki called him—had married Gertrudis, Grandma gave up on the Church.

"No priests," she had whispered from her hospital bed. "I don't want those *cabrones* to take me to my grave."

I never even thought of getting a priest for Grandma Merced's funeral. Even if my mother had insisted on one what good would he do? In all of the years I'd known her, she never attended a single Mass. The only time I ever saw her pray was at the Virgin of Guadalupe shrine she had sitting on top of her bureau. El Yuma bar was my grandmother's true church. And the only supernatural being she believed in was the Devil. She didn't believe in the power of the priest, who told her she would be hell-bound for loving a married man.

"I still love him. Even after he married that *puta güera*," Grandma Merced told me from her dingy bed.

Why, I wondered.

As if Merced had read my mind, she grabbed my hand and said, "He saved me."

The fluorescent lights hummed, drowning out her shallow breathing. I squeezed her hand as the monitor beeped and blinked like that Pong game. Grandma Merced looked like an old baby with her balding head and full lips pursed into a stubborn pout. The cirrhosis had eaten away her liver but had left her bloated with fifty-years' worth of drinking, smoking and longing.

"He saved me from El Sauz," she continued. "He saved you, too."

I continued to hold her hand, knowing that my grandmother had saved herself.

❀❀❀

At the funeral, there are no flowers, just a giant rosary made with half-blooming rose buds draped over the shiny brown coffin Tía Suki paid for. Mom blubbers, wondering why her own daughter won't pay for a priest, now that she worked for CBS Evening News.

"*Qué vergüenza*," Mom sobs to me. It's hard not to roll my eyes.

"It was a passionate love," I tell the small crowd gathered at the Gutiérrez Funeral Home. Most of them are friends or coworkers from El Yuma bar. Some are former lovers. An old Mexican man, wearing a fedora and a collared shirt, looks like those old men that hung around at Martin's barber shop. He jerks his head when my mom's sobbing grows louder.

"*Ay, Amá*," my mom cries, beside herself.

"Leandro saved her," I continue, reading from my news reporter pad. "He saved her, not only from a loveless marriage, but a soulless life."

Some of my grandmother's fellow bartenders nod their heads. The old man in the fedora looks straight ahead, unblinking. Tía Suki has this skeptical look on her face but grips Lily's hand. Lily shakes her head and whispers into Tía Suki's ear.

"Merced loved her Presidente brandy, Winston cigarettes and men, especially, Leandro. He was probably the only person she loved more than herself."

Suki laughs with Grandma's co-workers and lovers, but Mom's cries grow quiet. The man in the fedora rubs his eyes and takes out a handkerchief from his back pocket, wipes his face. My mom stands up and staggers over to the coffin. She rubs the length of the unpolished pine and lays her head as if she hears something. Her body heat warms the coffin, triggering its fresh woody scent.

"God knows she treated her daughters like crap," someone in the audience says.

"I'm sorry, Amá," my mother mumbles, then pushes open the lid.

Grandma Merced's bright red lipstick makes her mouth glow, and the long-sleeved velvet dress shimmers under the track lighting of the chapel. Her arms cradle a full bottle of Presidente while a pack of Winston cigarettes lies in the cold grip of her thin hands. Her nails, like her lips, glow blood-red.

Suddenly, my mom screams, pulls the bottle out and throws it against the wall. Before she can grab the cigarettes, Lily and Tía Suki grab Mom, they wrestle her down the aisle.

"I'm sorry, Mamá," she calls over her shoulder.

There is laughing, whispering, craned necks in the crowd.

After another deep breath, I go on. "At least she saved herself."

Some in the crowd nod but the rest stare, waiting for more. I close the notepad and step down. I pick up the rosary and put it in my grandmother's hands and wave over the crowd to view her one last time. Most of the Yuma crowd crosses themselves after touching Grandma's hands. Others kiss their fingers and lay them on her cheek. One or two whisper a prayer. The man in the fedora hums a song as he looks down on my grandmother.

"How did this happen?" the old man says, as he palms his face.

Just as the man in the fedora walks back down the aisle, Lily and Tía Suki walk through the open door leading to the lobby. The man turns around, tips his hat to them and walks out. Tía Suki looks long and hard at his face. "Apá?" she calls out.

The man does not turn around, but walks faster until he reaches a maroon Cordoba parked in front of the mortuary.

"Goodbye," Tía Suki calls after him.

That is strange. But my grandmother's life was never normal.

I walk over to coffin and shut the lid.

❀❀❀

After eight hours of driving down the I-10, only stopping to gas up, I know I have to sleep. It's been a year but I finally have the time and strength to return Merced's ashes to El Sauz.

"Sorry, Grandma," I whisper back to the urn filled with her ashes.

As soon as I drive into Tucson, I pull into a Holiday Inn and pay for a night's rest. Heat rolls over me. Jesus, was it this hot when Grandma hitchhiked all the way from El Paso? Probably.

The cool hotel lobby almost soothes me. As soon as I hit the bed, I dream about El Paso. When I wake up, all I remember are chocolate mountains looming into a clear sky.

Downstairs, I ask the woman at the front desk for directions to Mi Nidito, the only Tucson Mexican restaurant I'd heard about. The *huevos rancheros* I order are nothing like my grandmother's.

"Flavorless," Grandma would have pronounced, pushing the plate away.

After breakfast, I head down to Congress Street. Except for some homeless men, downtown seems almost abandoned. After a few minutes, I end up on Fourth Avenue. I park the car across the street from the Antigone bookstore the hotel staff recommended. What a funny name. I remember the myth of Oedipus' daughter from my Greek Heroes class at UCLA. She's the one who sticks by her father as he wanders around blind after finding out he had slept with his mother. Antigone is also the one who buries her brother Polynices, after her other brother kills him in a war over the kingdom of Thebes. In the end, Antigone and her brothers die, never reconciling, and their uncle Creon takes over Thebes. At least Antigone stood by her family.

I can't find Jane Austen, one of the few female writers I read in my Brit Lit courses. But I do find a book titled *Like Water for Chocolate,* a novel by Laura Esquivel about a passionate love that destroys and saves three generations of women. This has to be a sign from Grandma Merced. It's love that drove her from her little town in El Sauz to El Paso and finally to East LA. Now she's going back.

The next morning, I get back on the I-10, the book and urn sitting on my passenger seat.

❀❀❀

As I leave Tucson, sheets of water blanket the windshield of my little Japanese sedan, hiding the car and trucks on the I-10. I never saw rain like this in LA or anywhere else in California. Later, I would find out it was a monsoon. I trust my new all-weather radial tires. I have to. And I trust the safety belt holding the urn with my grandmother's ashes. The blue pewter urn reminds me of the giant pot she used to steam the batches of tamales she'd sell on the sly at El Yuma.

"I'm gonna get you to El Sauz if it kills me," I say, trying to convince myself that my dead grandmother, who used and abused her own family, is worth a wreck.

I promised I would take her back. She trusted that I would return her, one way or another, to her beloved *huizache* tree in El Sauz. When she first told me about that tree, I thought she meant the one planted in her front yard in East Los, a scraggly tree that bloomed twice a year. Its fragrant catkins reminded me it was spring in a city whose weather is an eternal spring-summer.

"It's where I first kissed a boy," Grandma told me while she lay on the pull-out bed that I had bought for the living room of her yellow bungalow. After Gertrudis' marriage to Moti, she took to sleeping there instead of her bedroom. I knew she was depressed but I didn't know that her heart was giving out. Tía Suki and I had taken to checking on her every Saturday morning while Mom and Tía Norma slept in. I would raise her up by putting extra pillows between her and the back of the couch until she said she was comfortable. Tía Suki would brush Grandma's iron-gray strands and plait them into a giant rope of a braid. I powdered her face from a Prescriptive's compact I had bought especially in her shade and then I would line her eyes. She never complained or struggled. Her measured breathing calmed me. We knew she was dying, but it was time. Once I finished rolling the bright red lipstick on her mouth, Grandma would utter, "*Estoy lista.*"

Tía Suki and I would pull the green polyester curtains back, and the *huizache*, like a performer, would dance with the Santa Ana winds or, if we were lucky, shake its nearly bare limbs with the winter rains.

"You like the rain?" I ask Grandma. I check the seatbelt to make sure the buckle doesn't scratch its blue dotted surface.

CHAPTER 33
El Huizache

The Mercado Cuauhtémoc bustles with Sunday shoppers, including Mennonite families with their muted dresses, bonnets and wide-brimmed hats. The air bristles with roasting *chiles*, cut fruit and drying cheeses.

"*Queso menonita*," Grandma Merced whispers.

"Your grandmother loved that Mennonite cheese," Rufina says as she leads us past Rarámuri women vendors amid their *chiles*, avocados and woven baskets.

We cross an alley filled with vendors, farmers mostly manning stalls fronted with boxes of sweet potatoes, corn, pecans, onions and tomatoes. Before we enter the market, the urn burns in my arms. Grandma gently grips Rufina's bony shoulder.

"I think something important happened here," I say. "Something hot."

Rufina faces the alley and closes her eyes. I hold the urn with my fingertips and start walking down the alley until we stop in front of a stall selling sweet potatoes and bloody red *chile ancho*.

"Yes, here," I say, nearly dropping the urn onto the cold black asphalt. "She's burning up."

"From love," Rufina says, her eyes still closed.

I want to close my eyes, too, but I'm afraid the vendors will think we're just a couple of crazy women. The last thing I want is a run-in with the police. Rufina opens her eyes and tells me that the stall stands on the same spot Grandma sold the harvest from her father's farm. Against this wall was where she and Grandma would watch the other vendors, including the other women from El Sauz who competed for customers and sometimes for men. Of course, this is the same place where she met Leandro.

The moment Rufina finishes, the urn cools down, turns ice-cold, nearly freezing my fingertips.

"We should move on," I say. "Let's get some *queso* for Grandma."

At one of the indoor restaurants, Rufina sips on her *agua de jamaica* while I set a piece of Mennonite cheese in front of the urn. I close my eyes and see Grandma sink her teeth into the soft, salty cheese.

"I want a slice of asadero cheese," Grandma tells me. "And sweet potato candy."

"Grandma's very hungry today," I announce.

"Love makes you ravenous," Rufina says as she scans the market. "Merced wanted everything."

"Except Donaciano," I can't help saying.

The sting of Rufina's swat opens my eyes. Grandma giggles.

"Look," Rufina says, "Merced had already met Leandro by the time Donaciano and I had relations."

She tells me that she took care of my mother and aunts until Merced took them away to El Paso. That Donaciano was like a zombie with no heart, no will to live when Merced left him. The girls were suffering, the town was suffering, because he closed up the store, and all the townspeople from El Sauz had to either go to Juárez or Chihuahua City for their supplies.

"It was terrible," Rufina says. "Pardon me, *Comadre* Merced, but you almost destroyed the town."

Grandma holds up the last little bit of cheese and pops it into her mouth. From the folds of her *rebozo*, she takes out a bright red lipstick, her Maybelline favorite.

I knew it wasn't Grandma Merced or Donaciano who devastated El Sauz. It was a fire that burned there before she was even born and continues. The *machismo*, *marianismo*, the misogyny . . . I learned these things in college, and they help me see Merced as the girl and the woman she was and could've been.

"El Sauz almost destroyed Merced," I say.

With a deep sigh, Rufina stands up and walks over to the urn. She stares, almost expecting Merced to answer her.

"What do you want?" Rufina asks her dead *comadre*.

"Everything," Merced whispers.

"*Terca*," Rufina says. "She'll always be stubborn, even in death."

I can't deny that.

We have to move on to El Sauz before the sun goes down. Grandma is silent on the drive, a straight shot on the 45D highway past Villa Ahumada and El Sueco. As the Chihuahuan Desert spreads out like a golden blanket before us, the asphalt road cuts through neatly, its edges feathered by barbed wire and shaggy yucca.

"Turn left here," Grandma tells me at an intersection that seems to come out of nowhere. El Sauz's plaza gleams under the afternoon sun. A few children play on the swings and slides in the middle of the plaza. Little legs dangle from the branches of trees. Children's screams fill the air.

How much has it changed? Grandma is quiet.

The swoosh of ashes sways with each turn of the car around the plaza. When we stop in front of a little store catty-corner to the plaza, the ashes swirl against the metal. In spite of the chilled air outside, the urn heats up the closer we get to the storefront. I get out of the car and go up to the store's Dutch doors and knock on the upper frame. A curtain is pushed aside in the door window and a little girl's face peers up at me. I smile and wave, but the girl disappears only to have an old man appear in her place.

"Excuse me," I say in Spanish, and I ask if they are open.

"In an hour," he says, rubbing his eyes. "It's coffee break time. You should go over to the café."

I follow his jutting chin toward the other side of the street, where there are metal tables and chairs out on the sidewalk.

"Okay," I say, "I'll be back in an hour."

So, I cross the street and sit at one of the tables with a view of the store. I carefully place Grandma's urn on the table and ask a waiter to serve coffees for me and Grandma. Merced's young face seems even younger now, almost childish. She's no more than fifteen but is wearing her blue velvet wedding dress and purple *rebozo*.

"How does it feel to be back?" I ask her with my eyes closed.

I knew Merced would not answer any questions. She looks around and suddenly jumps up from her chair.

"*Mira*," she says, pointing to the little store, its door now a vibrant *chile* red instead of the calm navy blue of a few minutes ago. A tall man wearing a fedora is walking toward the store entrance. His white pressed shirt is tucked neatly into his ironed wool slacks. Across the street in the park, a *conjunto* plays lively *norteño* music in the park's gazebo. A crowd slowly gathers, ignoring the man walking toward us. Somehow, I know it is my late grandfather, Donaciano.

"You finally returned," Donaciano says, reaching out for Grandma's arm. She pulls away but her eyes grow wide, exhibiting a fear that I had never seen before in my grandmother. Donaciano approaches her again, but I cut him off. Grandma Merced turns to look at me, and the fear seems to fly out into the blue sky. With that, she throws her *rebozo* over her shoulders like she had seen María Félix do so many times at the Colón theater in El Paso.

"I'm not staying here," Grandma Merced warns him, her eyes slanted, her mouth straight.

Donaciano steps back as if she has struck him. He looks at me and for some reason winks as I get closer to him. And now, Grandpa Donaciano turns to walk back to the store, now open to customers who are leaving the impromptu *conjunto* concert. The navy-blue door opens wide, and the little girl who greeted me is there bouncing a rubber ball.

I pick up Merced and cross the wide street to the shaded corner.

"*Hola, chiquita*," I greet the little girl. "*¿Cómo te llamas?*"

"Isolde," she squeaks, catching the ball and holding it under her arm.

"What a pretty name," I say. "Can we come in?"

"*Sí*," Isolde says and leads us into the brightly lit store, which smells of clay and cloth. Rows and rows of clay pots painted with flowers and birds stand neatly in rows on the east side of the store. On the west, there are neatly folded aprons, tablecloths, potholders, runners and *rebozos*. Isolde runs to the back, calling, "*¡Mamá!*"

A woman with short black hair and black jeans approaches us.

"What can I do for you?" she asks.

I quickly explain that my grandmother used to be married to the former store owner. I ask if she can tell me what the store used to look like back in the 1950s.

"I'm not that old," she says, smiling. "I have some old pictures that my mother kept from the old days, though. Isolde, bring the big book."

Isolde staggers under the weight of a vinyl photo album. When Isolde's mother lays it on top of a glass counter, Merced starts warming up. I place the urn close to the album, its metallic surface reflecting the book's deep maroon cover.

"I'll leave this for you," the mother tells me. "But be gentle with it. The photos and newspapers are really old. Watch her, Isolde."

The little girl nods and pushes a stool to the other side of the counter. At first, she watches intently as I peel the front cover from the cellophaned page, under which there are black and white photos and newspaper clippings of people and words frozen in time. Soon, Isolde grows bored and pulls a coloring book from below the counter and begins coloring. I look closely at the first photo, which shows a young man with a well-dressed older woman in a long skirt, fashionable at the turn of the century.

"Doña Margarita," Merced whispers, "Donaciano's mother."

Isolde looks at the urn, waiting for Grandma Merced to speak again, but no sound emerges until I turn to a newspaper clipping announcing the marriage of Grandma to Donaciano. There is a photo of Grandma and Donaciano in a black suit, fedora and tie at the bottom of the article. Grandma is wearing her velvet dress and *rebozo*. Both look at the camera unsmiling.

I pause, close my eyes and see Merced coloring with Isolde.

"You know how to color very good," Isolde says to Merced.

The article states that Donaciano was born to a distinguished Chihuahua family, including Doña María Briseño Lorca de la Garza, the widow of Patricio Zamora Briseño. They were married on January 14, 1935. The article confirms what I already knew: Grandma was a child bride. Donaciano was 37. Obviously, it was Doña María's money that had funded Donaciano's store in El Sauz, the only store for miles around.

As I flip through more pages, I find a photo of a girl watching a movie on the exterior wall of a building. Next to that picture is a broadside for the Mexican movie *Santa*, starring Lupita Tovar. I peel back the thin film protecting the yellowing clipping. Was that girl Merced?

Isolde turns her head and reaches over to pat the film back onto the photo. "No."

"Let her be," Merced growls like the old Merced I know.

Isolde's eyes grow wide, then turn to her mother, who is busy folding up a new shipment of *rebozos*. She jumps down from the stool and scrambles to her mother's arms. I hurriedly take out my digital camera, snap the photo and slip the news clipping back under the sticky film.

"*Gracias, señora,*" I call out and lift Merced back into my arms.

The woman strokes the top of Isolde's head and stares hard as I leave the store.

"You scared her," I admonish my grandmother, who clinks a bit of bone in response.

Back on the main street, we circle the plaza once more before heading down one of the streets toward La Colonia. The car kicks up dust on the dirt road behind us as we drive around the fenced houses. As soon as I hear Grandma's voice, I stop in front of an abandoned adobe house. My grandmother's teen self-hops out of the car. She is now wearing a cotton dress, freshly pressed and clean. On her feet, instead of the low-heeled leather shoes, she's wearing the soft, braided *huaraches* that were so popular when she was growing up in this small dusty town.

Before I can open my car door, Merced has disappeared behind the rotting wooden door of the house. I scramble around the barbed wire protecting the yard and squeeze myself between two lines of wire held tight by wooden posts. A barb snags my jeans, tearing a hole and cutting into my skin.

"Shit."

"What a foul mouth!" yells an old woman coming out the door.

"Tía Pina!" Merced yells and appears by her side with a large woven basket.

The woman looks down at Merced, frowns and goes back inside. Merced shrugs and walks through the rusted barbs and rotting wood and sits in the passenger seat of the car.

I sigh and try squeezing again through the opening between the stiff wires, only to tear another hole in my jeans. I hope my tetanus shots are up to date since I haven't updated my health insurance yet.

It's not until I re-start the car that I notice Grandma's eyes are wide open, but she is still her teenage self in the passenger seat. Grandma silently points the way ahead. When I get in, the car seems to have grown colder. As I drive ahead, the houses gradually disappear and the road grows bumpier. When teenage Grandma raises her hand, I brake and stop the car. I get out and notice the air is chilly but still. Merced jumps out and heads for a field filled with green, low bushes with glossy leaves and green *chiles*. Rows and rows of peppers appear as my grandmother walks into the field, occasionally leaning over and picking a few, holding them up to her nose and then placing them in a basket.

The young Merced wiggles her way between the endless rows, then turns and waves to me. The urn I'm still carrying turns from pewter color to silver, burning hot and bright as I follow my grandmother through rows of plants. As soon as I reach her, she points down to a shallow hole. I understand what I'm supposed to do, and slowly lower the urn into the pit and cover it with the sandy, dry soil. My grandmother now crouches beside me and kisses my cheek with her cold, damp lips. Suddenly, like a rabbit, she shoots up and starts running toward the horizon. For a moment, she stops and turns to look at me.

"Lucha!" Grandma calls.

I stand up and yell, "¡Grandma!"

"*¡Gracias, nieta!*"

I close my eyes and fall back among the glossy leaves, like those that have swallowed my grandmother. After a while, I get to my feet to survey the plants, but they have disappeared, revealing dried golden grass. The golden field stretches to the horizon, endless, waiting for the green to return.

EPILOGUE

Dear Merced,

Your ghost will probably never read this. You never really bothered to learn to read, except maybe to recognize your own name. Maybe my mother can read this to you, because she, for some reason, has always been loyal to you, even after you pimped her out. Yes, she told me this and many other things that you would never say. But I understand now. You led a hard life, and so you made it harder for everyone else, including me.

Because of you, my mom and I can never be close. Because of you, my *tías* will never come together to celebrate you. I learned to understand pain. This, I learned from Tía Suki who understood more about your abuse at the hands of your father, her grandfather, Plutarco, and your first husband, Donaciano.

But, because of you, I learned to fight back. I learned to stand up for myself, even if it was against you. I never told you this, but I used a move I learned when you told us about some guy at the bar who tried to grab you from behind. *"Le di el codo,"* you said. I used that elbow in college when I washed dishes in the cafeteria. The perv backed off after that. You never took shit from any guy, except Leandro. After Jorge, I also learned not to put up with jerks.

I learned about your thwarted love for Leandro. I understood that pain because of my own disillusionment with Jorge. You couldn't move on, especially after his marriage to Gertrudis, and especially after she came after our house. If anything, you fought like a witch for that crummy house on Indiana. You took us along with you.

Now that you're gone, you're still here. You're in the pot of beans we have on the stove. You're in the *queso menonita* you craved and in the brandy you drank. Of course, whenever I drink coffee, I can still taste your strength and bitterness. I could never smoke your favorite Winston cigarettes. The smoke burned too hard, just like you.

I hope you find some rest in the *chile* fields of El Sauz, where you used to play with your sister Cleófilas, my *tía abuela*. I know this is the only place you can rest, breathe and find peace. Well, this and the movie theater, where you would watch María Félix take out her frustration on the men around her. She was powerful in her beauty, just like you. She was also cruel. But there were reasons, too many, that built up through the years. Luckily, your bitterness faded with the years. Maybe it's even become bittersweet.

Rest in peace,
Lucha